Jude Golby and Another
Delivery Artefacts

[bc18b]

First published in limited, numbered hardback in 2022
Paperback edition published in 2022

www.broodcomb.co.uk

ISBN 978-1-7397339-3-3

Cover image *The Minds* [bc19a]

Printed in Great Britain by TJ Books Limited, Padstow, Cornwall

Jude Golby and Another
Delivery Artefacts

for Robert

She answer'd him: O Guest, these dreames exceede
The Art of man t'interpret, and appere
Without all choise, or forme, nor ever were
Perform'd to all at all parts. But there are
To these light Dreames, that like thin vapors fare,
Two two-leav'd gates, the one of Ivory,
The other, Horne. Those dreames that Fantasie
Takes from the polisht Ivory Port delude
The Dreamer ever, and no truth include:
Those that the glittering Horn-gate lets abrode
Do evermore some certaine truth abode.
But this my dreame I hold of no such sort
To flye from thence; yet, which soever Port
It had accesse from, it did highly please
My Son, and me […]

The Odyssey, Book XIX, ll. 767-781

Letter

Dear Jane,

You are angry. You are upset. I know.

I offer no apology, but I do regret some things I said when last we met, particularly about Janis. Suggesting that 'listening to a six-year-old gibber would not be the best use of my time' was said when both our bloods were up. To see her grow would be an honour and a pleasure, but the truth I was trying to get you to understand was that there is a distinct chance I *wouldn't* see her grow, regardless of how much care I took, and to insist Uncle Jude sit still and tight where I can be *wuvved* and *stwoked* and *wuvved* again is about as unappetising a fate as I can imagine.

The news from the hospital was not good, true, yet it was also not final. You need to accept that as I need to accept it. The nature of the illness is there's no timeframe that can be attached, and although sooner rather than later is a safe wager given the inability to insert the ICD, *later* is always possible. I am not going to sit and wait to drop down dead. I've spent a lifetime in college rooms and lecture theatres. To live *now* is all. I regret so much already—

The likely truth is I'll finish this consultation opportunity without incident and be back with you in a few months. It's brain stuff, Jane, the life of the mind. They won't be running me up stairs or bouncing me down cliff faces. In all probability, the greatest risk I'll face at the facility is a racy biscuit. Chances are – given the eternally tantrumatic nature of Fate itself – I'll live twenty more years. In a philosophical sense (hate away, Jane), we none of us know when the blade falls. I might outlive you all—

As I said, I can't control the communication limitations. If I can write a letter to you while I'm there, I will. The lead at the facility is a woman called Hoskin and I've given her your details as my emergency contact. I will not 'just disappear'.

You are angry. You are upset. I know—

I'm not responsible for your emotions, however. Sorry to be harsh, but a person who is not responsible for their own emotions is a pretty workable definition of a child. You have to find some acceptance this is the choice I've made, no matter how reckless you think it.

I also understand there is an outside chance this could be the last communication we will ever have. If so, I love you, little sister. I always have, even when *you* were a gibbering six-year-old. I love Janis. Hell, I even love Nicolás, and I wish you'd consider a reconciliation. I know you think he's changed, but really he hasn't. He was a cock when you met him—

Love, Jude

PS: Forgive the letter. I've chosen to write so that days will have passed before you get it and thus make your objections/interventions moot. By the time you get this, I'll be at the facility.

PPS: Follow up with the doctor and get yourself both tested for the gene. I know it's improbable as you're female, but still. Acquiring greater knowledge can never be a bad thing.

Testament

1.1 On the wall in his college study, John Moonfeld had a picture taken when he was rescued from the children's home. There had been cruelty – almost all physical – and when the police finally began to take notice, the panicked carers locked the children on the top floor. It was assumed from the amount of flammable liquids found that the intention was to burn the building with everyone in it, but the children had fought and the police arrived before the fire could be lit.

The original photograph is from after the arrests took place. The boy Moonfeld is being led out by a policewoman. He's about twelve, cut, dirty, covered in blood. His face is unusual as a cheekbone was broken in the fight. The policewoman is leaning over as if to shelter him with her body. Moonfeld's right hand is flung out to the side, fingers wide.

"It's a reminder," he said of the picture, "it'll be ditched when I no longer need it."

By the time he said this, the original photograph was nine deep in the frame. In his twenties, on an unimportant day, he put tracing paper over the picture and – fast – traced the outline of himself as a boy. He couldn't draw so it came out blocky, square-fingered. His bust face in particular came out like a melting mask. He liked it though, and put it in the frame on top of the photograph.

Over years, at odd intervals, he'd do another, always using the last made as a template, *Telephone* in pictorial form. As might be expected, these updated pictures grew more abstract, but his outflung right hand remained identifiable as a hand. In the original the palm faced backward, fingers splayed, as if boy-Moonfeld was trying to stop a child to his right running forwards into danger, yet no one's there, and he could never answer why he was in that pose, or even *if* he was, as it might have been a chance moment that got caught on film. Yet he kept that hand, and every part of the original to the right of it – the body, the face, the supporting policewoman, the stumbling legs – turned into thick bars of rough black ink. It wasn't pretty. It wasn't art, and at whatever stage the drawing was at – when he was thirty, forty, fifty – the image never seemed to have any meaning, apart from what meaning was given by his constant renewing of it. However, when he was dead, existing only as consciousness at the facility, the thick black lines no longer seemed the remnants of a forearm, a leg, a dragged bone. They were standing stones, tomb markers, fallen lintels.

1.2 Others knew Moonfeld better, but when approached I was told there was an issue with having a close friend or family member involved. I knew there'd been familial upset over the fact Moonfeld had left his body to science and assumed this was the reason. All I was told was that Hoskin, the project leader, wanted someone who knew the man well, and in an academic context, but not so close that rivalry or *intellectual looting* would be a temptation. She insisted the person chosen not be in the same field (Mathematics) as Moonfeld. *A consultation*, she told me then answered no other questions until after I'd agreed—

Despite the level of subterfuge in setting up the arrangement, there was no secret to the facility itself. The site was a gang of converted farm buildings up a hill in rough grassland, salt in the air from the sea nearby. I'd expected guards, a wire gate with something tame stencilled on a steel plate – *Works Only*, perhaps – but nothing was visible.

"No one knows about us. It's security enough," Hoskin explained.

She told me the place had been developed for a holiday home with B+B apartments in the outbuildings, but the previous owners had lost their cash. Ockmarsh was to the east, Petersdock to the west.

As we walked up the slight incline, I looked the place over. The main building was huge, formed from the old farmhouse with the barn and hayloft on the left. On the right of the house a wing projected towards us. The hayloft still had the old door and winch on the third storey. Those doors, opening onto nothing but empty space like an inverted lift shaft, had always made me ill with vertigo.

Hoskin waved at the barn on the left. "Barn," she said, then led us to the converted stables opposite. She showed the rooms there, then led me through the kitchen in the wing of the farmhouse and through to the main building. I felt as if I was tagging along after a quartermaster, trying to pick up the details she was firing at me over her shoulder. The kitchen, the storage rooms, the loos and the bathrooms. The only rooms we did not go in were the dining and living rooms, which couldn't be navigated for the machines within.

"There's a swimming pool beneath the house," she said. "Directly below here. No water in it. One of the many tits-up factors. They didn't think through how to get enough water here to fill a pool."

I nodded, but inside I was lost. The IT and other equipment in the main rooms was so extensive and unfamiliar I might have been looking at an old super-computer from the seventies. Every available space was filled with *stuff*, spilling out into the halls and up the stairs. The windows were blocked, and all round was the hum of cooling fans.

Inside, the farmhouse had been converted. The living room looked to be a medical facility. The dining room had dozens of ceiling-high displays of graduated lights, each bubbling in neon towards the bottom of its scale. Next to them stood a monitor with the wave patterns from voice recognition software. On a shelf by the door were discs the size of side-plates. The shelf was labelled, *Tongues*.

Hoskin told me I wasn't to enter as these rooms held sensitive and dangerous machines. What she meant by dangerous were the magnetic scoops and blades to hold/guide magnetic material in a rigid liquid suspension. An adapted fMRI machine sat in the room beyond. The force it wielded could tear the earrings through a person's ears—

"In fact, it's best to lose all the metal from your life while you're here," she told me. "Use Bics if you're writing." She pointed up the staircase. "My room and study is up there."

"This is a little breathless," I said.

"You'll have time to orientate yourself later." She pointed to a door that separated the hayloft from the main farmhouse. "That leads down to the empty pool and the room of minds."

The door was open, darkness beyond. From below came a scraping sound like a box dragged on concrete. I wanted to ask why she was showing the whereabouts of a waterless pool, and what was meant by *the room of minds*, but I was pulled toward the kitchen.

She introduced me briefly to the team as we passed them. Only the Welsh woman, Anwen, registered. Hoskin then took me back to my room in the stables. I put down my case.

"You should have left that here before," she said.

"Yes." I smiled. "You're fast-paced here."

I looked around the room. It was small, decorated with flowered wallpaper, an industrial-looking can of chemical spray prominent on the bedside table. She saw me notice it.

"Fleas," she said. "This block is a converted stables, and they could never get rid of them. Weather like this—."

The room was dreadful. "It's nice."

Hoskin said, "You understand the agreements that you signed? It's written in legal, but it means your arse."

I nodded. "It's kind of you to clarify the terms. The documents were dramatic enough."

"It's important to make it clear. This is mine. This project belongs to me. I'll protect it. It's *mine*. You understand that."

It wasn't a question, but I nodded my understanding. I couldn't make her out – whether her bully front hid humour or not – but I'd made the decision to proceed as if it did. It seemed safer. I held her eye, and at last she smiled.

"Okay," she said. She pulled her shirt from her chest and shook it to get air moving. She opened the windows to allow some wind through the room. "This heat," she muttered as she did so, "both personally and professionally, is giving me the most colossal pain in the arse."

Arse, I thought. *Twice now*. She liked the word. I could tell by the way she tasted the *r* in it.

"What do you know?" she asked.

"I'm to help with something John was working on when he died." I looked her in the eye. "I explained right from the start I teach literature, but they said it was a personal matter. I'm not a mathematician. I did explain that."

"No, that's right. It is personal."

After a pause I said, "I don't see how though."

"No." She looked out of the window, at a loss now the moment was here. "How do you want to do this?" she asked. "Tear it off fast or peel it off an ickle bit at a time?"

"Perhaps somewhere between the two."

She shook her head. "I hope you're going to be robust about this. I only have time for gladiators on my team, Jude."

1.3 Hoskin tore the plaster off fast. She'd developed a way to preserve a mind beyond the death of the body.

In the kitchen, she put a glass cylinder on the table. It was about thirty-two inches in circumference and two and a half feet high. At the midway point, there was a slight twist to the surface. Next to this she put a small pot.

"I don't do lay people," she said, "so try to keep up with me. I've asked Anwen to look after you so ask her any questions for stuff you don't understand." She tapped the cylinder. "This is a jar. It looks like glass but it's what we call *communicant glass*, designed to give after it's been created. It's also porous from the outside-in but not the inside-out."

"I understand."

"No, you don't. Not even slightly do you understand."

Over the course of an hour in the kitchen, she explained the process by which a human mind could be preserved. I liked her less in the telling. It was clear other people, other discoveries, existed in the shadows behind the process, but she eased past their achievements with the care she'd use to avoid people in a crowded lift. Her tale was heady stuff, too fast for me, but I listened to everything I was told, aware a significant part of my ability to deal with the information was my total disbelief in what I was being told.

What I understood (and this testament is being written after considerable digestion of the information given that first day) was that there was a problem with how to get the information in a human mind out, which then met another problem: how and where to store the data when it had been removed as the organising structures of a brain would not be there to accommodate the mind's gubbins in its new state. Names and dates and trials and chemical terms flew by my ears, and in truth I was tired of science-speak, having recently lived through my fill of it as regards my own health—

Hoskin had been a part of the early experiments with the process, she told me, where the *mind-out-of-the-body* was only expected to live for hours if not minutes. These trials had only had arguable success, consciousness assumed from the whipping fire-hose of almost coherence appearing on the interface.

When this initial team was disbanded, Hoskin returned from the Netherlands and began to work on a chemical called [   ] – here I thought she said *Oomingmak*, but knew that was the title of an old song that sounded similar to the word she'd used – but everyone called it *Baba*, after Ali Baba, because it effectively unsealed every meat part of the brain in a global, door-jamb rattling bang, splitting all the hinges when each synapse and connection slammed open, enabling the contents of a mind to be delivered entire. The problem was that, while Baba wasn't fatal, what it left behind wasn't human anymore. The process was a life-ending event and so could only be explored with care and informed consent. Hoskin said the word *consent* as a child tastes an olive.

For the trials, there was no problem with finding willing volunteers. Although the conditions needed for a good specimen were hard to find, there were still dozens of volunteers leaving their bodies to science who met the requirements, and there was no competition with doctors for the organs – if anything they preferred a mind-fried living corpse to plunder at will – and it only took a tweak in the consent form to allow the process to take place. They waited for the doomed volunteers to slip into their terminal unconsciousness – or the lethal injection if Hoskin was in Switzerland – and then flooded the brain with Baba to facilitate delivery.

By this time, I was sitting with elbows on knees, fingers circling the skin at my temples, drowning in terminology: *hippocampus*, *Ranvier-node disintegration, Schwann cell conversion, myelin leaching.* Hoskin was entertained visibly by my intellectual distress—

She told me the information was stored in a substance she called *chain-fluid.* A sample of this fluid was in the pot she'd brought to the table. She let me touch it, roll it on my fingers. "It's like transparent gravy," I said.

It was, and it was not unpleasant until she told me it was the exact consistency of the glue inside an eye.

Chain-fluid was a liquid, she explained. Where a normal liquid could mix, chain-fluid could not – or rather it could, but it could not – because the milliard links of it always retained an order. It was part metal, she said, and according to its nature it turned constantly, too slow for the human eye to discern, all links touching all other links, with communication between them that was ordered, obeyed physical laws. I pictured a lasso dancer twirling his rope inside a bucket.

The links of the chain-fluid were seeded with charged organic matter that fused with the links over time. During delivery, this chain-fluid was pumped through the chemically-prepared brain, over and again, the matter-seeded links absorbing each time, thousands of cycles through the now-fried mind, until there was nothing left, the chain-fluid scouring everything out like steel wool from a burnt-black pan.

In the final delivery, magnets were used to aid the pulling out and settlement of the brain's information. They acted on the chain-fluid directly, two accelerative magnets pulling the substance slowly forward.

"They look like forceps," she said.

A complex series of blades and scoops concentrated magnetic force on the chain-fluid, keeping it in a shape where it would be best able to coalesce again. I pictured cracking open an egg and trying to lift the albumen and yolk out keeping both intact and in the same relationship with each other. *The delicacy required must be incredible*, I thought and said so. Hoskin agreed, and I felt like a very good pupil indeed.

"The best we can hope for is optimum placement," she said.

Once the fluid had settled into this suspension, via an interface the size of a cottage, everything in a human brain, the mind, the knowledge, the personality, the memories and the essence – *But never the* s *word* – was decanted into a jar entire. She flicked the empty jar again—

"Could you tell me less?" I said. I rubbed my head for a long minute while she waited me out. "And then?"

"And then—. Silence," she said. "Months of silence. Those first ones—. I can't tell you how hard it was to wait. Because the mind was delivered whole in one vast dump. Baba opens everything, and it doesn't structure the dump. It just comes in one hellish excretion of information." She saw my dismay, took another road. "You've used Excel? If you take the data in a spreadsheet and dump it in another, the formulae don't come with. You get the panic symbol." I understood her to mean the *#DIV/0!* symbol. "The same happens here, except it's not in the slightest same. The decanted mind is a box of old toys in an attic, everything mixed together, dolls and soldiers among the Lego and cars, but in this case it's memories, facts, stories, complexes, fairy tales, fetishes, morals and laws, personality traits, general human mooeyness, elemental origins, all that what-the-hell with no order to it. Imagine a teddy bear whose right leg is *gravity*, whose head is *the molecular weight of tin*, whose left arm is *your first memory of thunder*, and each of its button eyes is *the concept of green* and *the capital of Mali*. All that needs sorting."

"Who does the sorting?"

"The mind itself." She hesitated. "My original assumption was if the chain-fluid had an order, the mind would have a pattern of completion in the final delivery, and it could *use* that order. Like a sponge whizzed in a blender slowly comes back together again. It was a reach, but I thought it was worth it."

"Hence the months."

"Yes. Hence. And more. One of the successful deliveries, Elephant Baby, took twenty-two months to fully return. That's why we call her Elephant Baby."

She explained in those months of waiting she almost abandoned the project but for the noises coming from the machines and the recordings – *The howls in the feed*, she said – and the coherence gradually visible on the interface.

There were other signs. As the decanted consciousness took hold, so the chain-fluid clenched in different ways, but only in some of the containers. It wasn't a leap to assume the contorted jars were the ones where something was happening. Even more persuasively, the jars warped into distinct shapes. Each jar's inhabitant could be identified by the shape the communicant glass was forced into as the consciousness within it bit. At the start they'd been simple squat cylinders; now they were loose and fat about the base, sitting baggy on their monitor posts as if a fair sold goldfish in sacks the size of human torsos.

She ran a finger round the twist in the jar she'd brought. "This is an example. See where the glass has been pulled?"

"Yes." I was silent for a time. The only thing I could think to ask was, "They?"

Hoskin nodded. "The minds. All who came through are here, in this facility. There are four whose completeness is something we're confident about. There are others who were part of the first trials down there in the pool who've not returned, or not yet returned, or returned unable to join, or in pieces." She paused, spinning her pot of chain-fluid. "I think you understand that one of the four is John Moonfeld."

"I understand that, yes. Yes." I took two steps into a laugh before it died on me. "How did you pick me?"

"You wrote an obituary. You knew him, and in a context that was professional as well as personal."

"I think I meant, *Why me?*"

Hoskin leaned forward. "He's the first of the legacy minds. Minds that are, or were, at the forefront of their fields, and whose death puts a brake on human progress. Minds that can contribute beyond their death. The other minds in the pool are trials, and our interaction with them is restricted to gauging whether or not they're entities that are whole and can communicate. *Who* they are and *what* they communicate is immaterial. No one cares. They're nobody. But with John Moonfeld, we need to know what has been delivered is – in his thinking essences – the same man that you knew."

"You want me to test him?"

She frowned. "Not as such. The question we need to ask——. The question we need answering is, *Is he the same?* And ultimately, *Is he sane?* That's your job, Jude."

1.4 I ate with the team but found it difficult to talk for the mauling my brain had received. In turn they gave me the space to absorb the information I'd been given. I apologised for my quietness, and when I rose to leave Hoskin suggested Anwen show me the pool the next day.

"Just in case you're touchy and/or feely about all this," she said. I was in bed before sunset.

Sleep came in short packets. It was more submission to the weariness of the lumbering heat than rest. Each time I woke I got caught in loops of thought. Foremost was the meaning implicit in Hoskin's words because it seemed to suggest I'd be talking to Moonfeld, and that thought inside my mind was like an egg failing to attach to the lining of an inhospitable womb. To talk to my friend was not a real possibility, which surely contradicted everything she'd said. I couldn't be here for that, I kept telling myself. I was there only to interpret dry data. I'd be a palaeontologist with the teeth from a cave bear's skull, not in the hot wind of a living animal's bellow.

I slept. I woke. I lay staring at the ceiling taking apart Hoskin's language. What was strange to me was familiar to her, which was clear from the ease with which she talked of the process. *Deliver, decant.* She'd made it sound like the minds were cards flicked into a hat. I wondered if she'd chosen the words with care, or if they'd been unconsciously adopted. They fitted, and I admired the distinction between *deliver* and *decant.*

At other times, I had only one word in my head as I lay there clad and shod in sweat. *Torso* was one, the word she'd used to describe the size of the communicant jars. *Torso* sat in my mind for what felt like hours, and I had to walk it out of the way of my other thoughts like a wardrobe. *Torso.*

Another time of waking was run through with her term *the howls in the feed* on a loop. *The howls in the feed. The howls in the feed.* It wouldn't budge. *The howls in the feed.*

At four, I woke up and sat for a time at the end of the bed, feeling smeared out by weariness and confusion. I'd misunderstood something along the way, I decided. John was dead and they wanted me to verify a document or testimony. I was here to authenticate something and had misunderstood everything told to me.

But then why the machines?

I wondered why I'd come. Even back then, right at the start, I understood the decision had been a reaction – perhaps an infantile one – to the news lately received that my body would not support the insertion of an *implantable cardioverter-defibrillator* and so I might drop dead any moment. All *tomorrows* to which things might be put off vanished, and I snatched at the first chance for novelty and distraction, but now I felt old, fifty-three and nothing more than an accretion of skeletal creaks housing a low-level despair and a salt-knackered heart.

"What am I doing here?" I whispered.

I realised I was grinding the hard skin of one heel on the shin of my other leg. I clicked on the light to examine myself. I'd been bitten by a flea, and all possibility of sleep fled in disgust.

2.1 The next morning at breakfast, I made an effort with the others. Lenford, Tom. Because of the heat, they all wore light clothes, the men in shorts. Tom had the look of a boy sitting primly upright in class: the stiff-backed performed alertness of the teacher's pet. Lenford was older, something to do with the computer set-up. Anwen was small with hair that needed to be moved behind her ear. She wore friendship bracelets on her wrist.

"So. Literature," she said.

I didn't have a response so simply nodded. She smiled.

After breakfast, Anwen took me down to the empty pool. The pool ran the length of the facility, and like all domestic pools it had the smell of rot and damp's mischief-in-the-walls. The air was cool down there, almost pleasant, and unlike the furious whirr of fans upstairs, the kit down here was cooled by calmly purring air conditioners. The pool was empty of water, and in the middle was placed a hut that came up to the level of the pool sides and took up over half of the volume. On the edge stood a small crane and a truss. I'd seen similar at my local baths for swimmers with mobility issues. At the bottom of the ladder, in the deep end, was a mattress.

"Heat is an issue," she said, "so we keep the lights low. It means it's a bit dangerous. It's not funny, but Len fell in."

"He's clearly okay so—. A bit funny."

On the floor of the pool, matting had been put down to offset the slip in the tiles, but also to deaden the footsteps that would echo around the space.

"The minds have no visual fields," she explained, "but they claim to experience vibration as bands of light, so we sound-proof what we can. That's why we talk quietly too."

The minds, I thought.

At the deep end opposite the ladder, I saw a horseshoe arrangement of tables, and on them a number of shapes. Around, under and through there were wires into machines and discs, running up the tile walls to the great ducts in the corner of the room with a stop-off at a wall-mounted tablet. My ankles felt cold. I got closer to the array. Most of the jars were still squat cylinders, but as I got closer I saw a few of them were mis-shapen. From a distance they all looked filled with water, but up close the fluid in these altered jars looked different. It adhered to the surface as if the chain-fluid peeled onto and off the jar like a tank tread. Each fluid had a different pattern.

"Len calls them *the bellies*." I reached out to touch a jar with a twist to it. She stopped my hand. "Don't touch," she said. "The surface con-ducts touch as sound. The jar is a global eardrum feeding input into the mind."

"Not *these* jars?" I said.

Anwen hesitated. "No," she replied.

I asked why they hadn't developed. The word *develop* was wrong, but it was all my mind supplied me with.

"They were the first of the trials. Nothing happened. I mean there's literally nothing inside these jars apart from the gunk. I know it's strange we keep talking about a substance, an object, a concrete noun kind of thing, but nothing came through in delivery."

"But you keep them. You're not certain they're empty."

Anwen paused. "There are protocols for chain-fluid disposal," she said. I got my nose close to the jar with the faintest of twists. "The ones where the jar has been altered are partial minds. *Silent minds*, we call them. The process was started but never took. Nothing connects in them. I don't know—. Maybe two or three thoughts, ideas, memories chase each other along the chain like fish in a shoal, unable to cohere. That's only my interpretation. Something's connected to bite the jar that way, but it's not a mind. Hoskin says it gives a new meaning to the phrase, *He's not all there*."

I didn't laugh, and when I met her eye she was staring at me with a nervous look. I felt it too, a breed of the shrieking willies that sent my skin flickering like a silent film. It was the enforced quiet, the gloom and the hum, but it was also the intuition that there were other presences around us in the jars. I wished she hadn't told me the eardrum detail.

"It must be something to be in here alone," I said.

She grinned. "I'll take you. Lights off, at night. Seriously."

Anwen was happier in the hut. To offset the slope of the pool a raised wooden platform had been constructed, and up a few soft steps we entered a room far smaller than the outside of the hut itself. The hut was mounted on a complex hydraulic system designed to dampen vibration. The floor was soft and rubbery to cut the effect of footsteps, and beneath and around the inner room was a thick layer of soundproofing.

She asked me not to speak once we were inside. "Not yet. Not 'til you've decided for sure."

"Decided what?"

"To stay. To talk to Moonfeld."

I felt it again. Heartbeat falling into a sprint – with all the attendant worries about how that elevation of pulse might affect my fused heart – as belief's thin end of the wedge pushed into my mind.

The interior of the hut was as bewildering as an aeroplane cockpit. Three computer stations, banks of machines up the walls, wire everywhere, a monitor that took up the side of the hut. Each machine was covered with a black cotton material, thin enough to see lights flicker through it, but thick enough to make me feel as if I was in a tiny theatre space. Even the one computer lit had a little cotton hood. On cat feet we crept past them to the jars.

Instinctively, I grabbed Anwen's sleeve. I wanted to share my delight and momentarily forgot this was mundane to her. The jars were wonderful. They were like sections from the boles of old, canker-gnarled trees, albeit translucent and without texture. One had the same twist I'd seen in the silent mind, but the twist had been carried through until the whole jar was a misshapen screw shape, fatter at the base than the top.

The next retained much of the cylinder shape but with a bulb the size of a baby's head at the side. An obscene finger grew from the side of it. The jar beside it seemed melted about the base, but on inspection I saw the surface of the glass had been sucked in at the midpoint to create a wormhole that led inwards and down. The last was the shape of a sack stuffed with apples propped slovenly on its plinth.

They were ugly; they were beautiful. I loved them, wanted to touch them, and marvelled at the pressures the connecting consciousness within must have brought to bear in order to warp the glass in such individual ways. Above all, I understood – I could *see* – they were human. The structures weren't random but formed with intent behind them.

I recalled an art historian colleague explaining an Anselm Kiefer painting to me. I'd criticised it for being essentially random, but the friend talked me through the evidence of decision and intent, and how the knowing eye views the piece to see the worth in the artwork. In the same way a good personal trainer can tell who has the strength in two similarly-muscled people, so she could see which of two abstract paintings had the guide of the human hand in it. I had seen it then, and I knew it now in the jars. An identifiable will had put the gnarl to the shapes. There was evidence of a guiding hand behind each one, evidence of a – and I felt foolish as soon as the word came to me – *mind*.

I gestured in request to get nearer. Anwen nodded. The jars had to remain open for the insertion of tubes. Three ran in from the top, with another entering at the bottom of each jar through a valve sunk into the glass. The plinth had dials and a speaker with earphones on a hook, and behind each was a wall-mounted tablet showing bewildering data displays. The jars looked to be filled with light, but that was an illusion from the lights on the plinth. In fact, the chain-fluid was almost transparent, with little to distinguish it from carbonated water that had been allowed to get flat.

I got closer still and saw each jar was surrounded by metal blades screwed to the hut wall and formed around the jar, almost invisible in the gloom. The effect was of a dinner jacket or cloak exploded with the constituent parts held in space around the jar, the lapels at the top, pockets cupping from below, vents behind, sleeves vertical at the sides. Under the influence of these magnets, I felt my fountain pen wander in my pocket.

I wanted so badly to speak. Anwen understood this, and when I turned to her she already had her finger across her lips to silence me. I nodded. With the same finger, she pointed out areas of the jar where the gathering mind had gripped the glass and warped it, gradually, over months. The texture was integral and complex, here granular and there like the skin of a chestnut pod. My fingers itched to touch.

She tapped me then pointed to the left of centre.

I peered in, not seeing anything. She moved her finger in a circle twice. It was like trying to see the foetus in an early ultrasound, but then I saw it.

As transparent as the fluid surrounding, there was a structure in the jar. It looked closed, a sack with a tendril in. The more I looked, the more I saw thicknesses amongst the chain-fluid. What seemed a discrete part of the liquid looked like a transparent scrotum with two transparent ring doughnuts where the testes would be, a *vas deferens*-like structure running like a thread of light from the inner surface of the lower torus, but because of the light, the sack was just translucent enough to be seen.

I looked down into the jar from above. Underneath was a black disc like those I'd seen on the shelf in the dining room. It slotted into a hole in the base, and the jar had clearly formed a space to accommodate it.

Through the chain-fluid, the disc looked like a black bowl with a pool of silver within. All four minds had them.

On the front of the plinth was a name. *Ichika.* I crept to the next. *Pike.* The next, *Elephant Baby.*

The last read, *Moonfeld.*

Flat, loud and distinct, a voice said, "Who's there?"

2.2 I was shaking by the time the sound-proofed door was closed behind me. Lenford was working on a junction box at the pool side.

"Loosening, isn't it?" he said. "When you hear them speak."

I nodded. It was the perfect word.

I took a few minutes to get my heart back, and it irked me that the others gave me the space, but I needed it. The shock of the voice was as jarring as a bad fall.

"Who was that?" I asked at last.

"Elephant Baby."

"I didn't realise there would be a voice."

"Oh." She glanced at Len. "I thought Hoskin told you."

I rubbed my face. "Where did the voice come from?"

Anwen picked up a disc from the pool side. "Speakers in the plinth pick up the vibrations in one of these. We call it the tongue."

They needed the minds to communicate, she explained, but there was no link between chain-fluid and interface, nothing to move to make sound—

"This is where they brought me in. I think Hoskin thought she'd push a mic into the jar and that would be that." She showed the interior of the disc. "In there goes *oobleck*, a non-Newtonian fluid. That means it's a liquid, but it becomes solid under the percussive action of a speaker. It's simple to make. You can make your own out of corn starch and water. But my idea was it'd give the illusion of movement to speech, and if it was held against the glass, the vibrations could be interpreted by the mind."

She explained how it first worked. A speaker linked to a jar via a suction cup. When Hoskin first tried speaking to the mind, her voice was run through the speaker at dangerous volumes in order to get the vibrations going. The mind on the other end – Ichika – had the vibrations fed directly onto the surface of her jar. At that time, they'd no clear conception of how interaction might take place, but they needed to know if the twist in the jars meant there was consciousness in there. Slowly, the surface of Ichika's jar started to bulb under the suction cup towards the sound.

"Remember that a mind is chain-fluid seeded with organic brain matter. My idea was to have discs made that fitted into the jars so that when we spoke, speech vibrations were fed to the mind. My hope was that the minds might learn this and use the turning action of the chain-fluid to rub against the outside of the disc, creating vibrations in return that we might interpret. You wouldn't believe how much amplification we need. If you listened to the raw feed, you'd be deaf at once. And they learned. It was mind-blowing. The minds actually learned—."

She explained how the minds gradually tuned to words the interface could distinguish, instinctively using the fluid's action to communicate. The minds learned how to use the only part of themselves with movement to create a rasp, literally, around the base to set the non-Newtonian fluid vibrating.

"Like a chain turns the gear wheel on a bicycle," she said.

"Like a snake throttling its prey," Len muttered.

"That's why we have so many of these tongues. Look."

She turned the disc side on so I could see the dimpled wear on the groove. "But you can't see anything in the jar."

"No, but here's your evidence. This is where the chain got hold to set up the vibrations. Here."

She gave me the used tongue. It was plastic, but it felt organic, dirty, as if she'd passed me a used hearing aid. With distaste, I put it on the side of the pool.

"You think *you* got a shock?" she said. "Imagine how we felt when it first worked. It was terror. Literally like hearing a ghost."

"Loosening," said Lenford.

I said, "It was a human voice?"

"It wasn't at first. The computer interprets everything, and part of that interpretation is the voice. The computers learn the vibrations, and the voice gets clearer over time." She looked at me. "That's what I do."

I looked nervously towards the hut. "Moonfeld?"

"No. God, no. He learned to speak fast, but he still sounds roboty." This wasn't what I'd meant.

"How did the voice hear?" I asked, hearing a frail note in my voice.

"Elephant Baby. She's so attuned anyway, but the outside of the jar acts as a huge eardrum. They hear everything."

"I like Elephant Baby," said Len.

"I like Elephant Baby."

Their casualness was starting to grate, and I was getting uneasy. It was too many strangenesses at once, and I felt shortness in my disordered breathing. The gloom of the pool acted on me, and I was aware of the weight of the equipment and building above. The wedge of belief had been forced under the door and the thought I could actually speak to my dead friend started me shaking. I felt faint and sick and weak.

Anwen saw this and took me up to the kitchen. Tom was there, making tea. He offered me a cup, and I just stared at the mug mutely, unable to talk for the strain-whine I knew I'd find in my voice.

"Something stronger?" Tom asked.

I nodded. I'd promised my sister Jane I would knock alcohol on the head for the damage it might do my heart, but that thought was not accessible that day. It was not yet noon, but wine held me together for an hour before I was ready to re-engage.

2.3 I spent the afternoon learning what happened in the upstairs rooms: the method for the original delivery of the data, the controls the machines operated on the mind's 'life', the room where the voices were made from the tongues' raw data. All the myriad parts of the process were made known to me, and I made no more sense of them than if they'd told me it happened *as if by magic*.

The young man, Tom, followed me around for much of the day. He was absurdly handsome, and handsome always put me in an attitude of profound distrust. At first I thought he was eavesdropping on what I was being told. Tom was a mathematician and as ignorant, or only slightly less ignorant, as I was about the technical aspects of the minds' delivery and maintenance. Yet I soon realised Tom was watching me, my reactions.

Over a late lunch, I asked him his role at the farmhouse, trying to bounce a little of the scrutiny back onto him. Tom's role, it appeared, was to interact with Moonfeld, to follow his reasoning as Moonfeld continued to think. They needed an expert to track and check the quality of my old friend's work, and that was Tom.

Tom told me Moonfeld's most famous book, *The Yamanata-Moonfeld Cruciate Ridge*, had hooked him as a student. I remembered the book. John had signed a copy of it for me for a giggle, knowing I'd understand nothing. As he spoke, Tom kept his eyes unblinking on me, but turned his head so he was gradually looking at me from the corner of his eye. It was a distinctive habit, and a strangely familiar one—

"I know you, don't I?"

Tom nodded, relief on his face. "I had my hair cut."

It came to me then. He'd been one of Moonfeld's graduate students, one of the brighter ones, and he'd been in the dead man's train for much of his study at the university. He'd been at the funeral, and once I remembered this, Tom came to mind vividly: long hair, in a tuxedo – presumably the only black suit he had – a smitten young woman in an inappropriate LBD gripping his arm. I'd never spoken to him, but he'd been around.

I circled my finger to indicate the farmhouse and said, "Wow."

Tom laughed. "I know. If you'd told me I'd be here a year after leaving, I'd have rung the nuthouse."

"So you—. What? Help?"

"I follow him."

Him, I thought, *He's talking about John.*

"I need to follow his reasoning and work it into publishable shape, if it comes to that. He's the first of the legacy minds. Did she tell you that?"

"The term is so awful, I don't think I'll ever forget it."

"So I need to follow him. So I need to know – we need to know – if he's right in the head." He grinned. *Dear god*, I thought, *women don't stand a chance*. "Even saying things like *right in the head* sounds wrong."

"Surely you can make that judgement for yourself?"

"No. Yes." Tom swallowed. "He's a brilliant mathematician, and I'm not sure if I am. In maths, you're supposed to know by this age. So—. It's hard for me to make the decision whether he's working in an area where I can't understand, or whether he's talking nonsense. If it was just a question of the field, I'd have a chance of making the call, but what he's working on now is—. I don't know. The maths looks unnatural."

"If you know him," I asked, "why can't you be the one to say if he's the same person? Why am I even here?"

"I didn't know him like you knew him. For years, I mean." He paused. "Truth is, when his mind returned, he didn't recognise me at first. I think Hoskin thought I'd oversold my relationship with him. Maybe I did, I don't know." He looked out to the desolate countryside that led, somewhere, to the sea. "He doesn't remember my name," he said, and I felt in my lungs the pain this caused the lad. "He was always a bit like that so that could be evidence of him being himself, or of *not* being himself. I don't know. Whatever it is, they trust you and not me."

I heard the word *himself*, and for a giddying moment wondered who that was, and when after a second I realised – again – it was Moonfeld who was meant, fourteen months dead, friend and confidant, buttress of the pub and reputed genius, the disorientation hit me again.

I excused myself, went to find Hoskin, but she wasn't anywhere above ground and I couldn't face the pool again. Anwen was in the room of the voices—

"I need a day," I said. "Can you tell Hoskin? Tell her I'm both touchy and feely about all this."

The larder was well stocked with wine. I got hammered, and I didn't care if they thought they'd hired a drunk. *It's medicinal*, I told myself. *I'm taking it for my heart.*

3.1 My dreams were specific, vivid. I didn't know if it was a human trait, or a peculiarity of *me*, but I always have clear, stiff dreams when in a strange bed or I've travelled. They have a thickness to them and cling to my waking mind as it lifts from sleep.

My last dream was too mundane for deeper meaning. I'd dreamt I was on the plain of jars in Laos, playing hide and seek with the red-cloaked dwarf from *Don't Look Now*.

I told the dream to Anwen over breakfast the next day. She'd never heard of the place, so I told her of my trip there, describing the stone jars that littered the plains around Luang Prabang. They looked like torso-sized match-heads pulled free from their sticks, fire untethered from that which burns. I told her how no one knew their use or history. Cold rooms or cauldrons; hearths for signal fires; kilns, or keeps for the rain. The best guess was that they were burial jars whose lids had been levered off and lost over centuries of ransack. In the open mouth, human remains were unlocked for the birds. I imagined for her the scene of it. Blood-stewed teeth, a grubby skull, the runes in the skeleton of the hand, and, first to rot, the last words of the living thrown in before the mouth was closed, a herb to sweeten the jar.

I told her my dream's ending, the jars gradually began to hum, the choked pockets of their unformed throats opening into the earth to form a choir of stones, apart from one that hacked because of the red-cloaked child in the sump.

"You've colourful dreams," she said. "You wanted to take a day?"

As soon as she'd spoken, I was embarrassed. I knew I'd been talking too fast, and I'd spent too long in lyrical description while Anwen had waited, quiet and awkward. I wanted to apologise, but an apology would just turn the volume up on the awkwardness, so I simply nodded and said I'd be back for dinner.

Lenford lent me a backpack and I headed out on the Ockmarsh road up into the hills behind the facility. It was blazing sunshine, which cleared my head of some of the weight I'd been feeling in the farmhouse. Somehow the gloom of the empty pool pervaded the entire house. With the blue of the day, and a proper night's rest, it was easy to ignore what was in that long underground room, and I felt better than I had in a long time. The action of walking spurred my thoughts and my mood, and I recalled my last soused memory of the previous night: the realisation that leaving the facility, without going down to the empty pool and the room of minds ever again, remained an option. I could go and think nothing more of my time here.

I'd no map, but at every intersection fingerposts showed the way back to the village. I headed down the narrowest lanes, walking where seemed safe upwards over the farmland. The fact of the hot weather was a wonder, as always – the green too green and the blue too blue – and everywhere there were the particular sounds and smells of summer, as if even the insects and birds and the scent of the wildflowers displayed a peninsular reserve and discretion. It was a primary colours sort of day, straight out of a children's book. *Lashings*, I thought, *Ginger*, *honeycomb*, *cockles*, *hay*, *buttons* and *smugglers*.

I took care to get good and lost, cutting through woods where I could, taking field routes, following brooks and the concertina line of the shallow hill terraces. In an hour, I could smell myself.

Moonfeld occupied my thoughts. The past fourteen months had eroded more than I would have expected, so the man returned as slowly as a photograph in a chemical bath.

His physical presence returned first. Whiskers, and whisky, long-worn shoes and brown corduroy trousers. A stiff Orvis shirt, the blade of the collar peeled like old sunburn. He was – he'd been – a hearty man with fussy speech, semi-coherent sentences bubbling out of a froth of consonants. *Jovial* was the word, I decided, laughter under everything he said, sentences often petering out into the word *terrible*. The amount of noise that was not speech the man could generate was astounding. *A jovial introvert*. On tiptoe when he offered an opinion, never angry, hands in pockets, sucking Guinness sweat from his top lip, shy with women. If awkward, or thinking, he'd stand on his heels and peer down at his feet in surprise as if all of his toes had grown dicks.

I rarely saw him teach, but when he did, Moonfeld had none of that loose air. The teaching man was precise, slow, and if in everyday life and relationships he'd the fuss and mess of so much static, in mathematics he was tuned to a clear signal. He confused students, I recalled, who took the man who drank in town pubs for the same man of the lecture hall, and many found themselves deliberately and methodically dismantled in front of their peers for poor logic, or for one of Moonfeld's most shameful transgressions: *Idiocy by Default*, *Idiocy in Extremis* or *Culpable Idiocy*. I wondered whether Tom had been one of those dismantled.

I'd known the man well. I recalled the moment we'd reached a new room in our relationship. I'd asked about the picture Moonfeld had on his wall, a frame which held a number of sheets of paper one on top of the other. The last was thick lines only, like an exploded diagram of a Chinese ideogram, apart from an abstract hand to the right. Moonfeld had told me then of the children's home he'd been in when a boy. I'd not felt embarrassed by the revelation but honoured by the confidence. The mistreatment had been physical, beatings for the least sin, and it had left Moonfeld with what he called *a freight of fear*. He'd admitted that even now, even recently, that fear might pave over him, leaving him immured in panic. *Everyone has factors*, Moonfeld had told me, having drunk himself into verborrhoea—

"Not one of us is *prime*. Every one of us has numbers that divide, diminish us, and that's one of mine," he'd said. "Fear. And specifically fear of pain. Now, Jude, I'm not in any way saying I've loads of factors. I'm not a thirty-six or a forty-eight, for Gauss' sake. Think of me more as a thirty-four. Few factors, but one of them a big fatty—."

I laughed, getting stares from other walkers on the road, but it was a sorry laugh, because I realised everything I'd recalled was physical. It was all externals, and nothing that would have come through in whatever was in that gnarled jar back at the facility. Nothing of my memory would remain.

This was what concerned me the most. Not that I'd fail in the task, or that what I'd find would be distressing – it was hard enough to believe there was anything there at all – but that I'd be reduced to asking questions only John would know the answer to. If I couldn't recognise him in any ordinary sense, the reality of the man – if this wasn't some monstrous, cruel joke – had to be tested by other means, and that would demean us both.

Later, I allowed that the fact I was considering the offence to a dead man's feelings told me a lot about what I already believed.

After noon, no relief from the sun, I noticed a brown heritage sign pointing upwards to the brow of a hill. Nothing but grassland seemed to be up there, but I climbed up a stone path cut with wooden steps and stiles. It was cruel in the heat, and what looked a steady rise from the bottom required my fists to work my knees by midway. A woman took my money for entrance and a pamphlet in a hut at the top.

Where the grass grew rough, there were courtyard houses from circa 500 BCE. There was little left but the circular walls that described the courtyards, markers on the ground to show where the houses had been. Between the different courtyard ruins were connections of stones that were clearly lanes. I'd always been drawn to nooks and hiding places, and here were tiny, narrow-entranced rooms, once covered with thatch and now open to the elements. The rooms might have held a larder, cots, a family. As a child, I'd have gone wild over them. The central ground each house opened onto was hard-packed earth. I spent an hour there, looking at each house, taking time to stand in each of the open rooms and imagine myself living there thousands of years ago.

Some of the houses had a *fogou*, a hidden tunnel covered over by stones. I bent to look in one and felt the creeping panic of being caught in an enclosed space. I read the guide on the structure. In curious synchronicity with the dream of the night before, the *fogou*'s use was unknown: cellar, refuge, prison, church. To be imprisoned there, beneath the floor—

On the hillside, a sweet breeze blowing, I read the guide through. I spoke words from it aloud. *Corbel, capstone, jamb stones, rab*. It made me happy to say them. *Querns, spindlewhorls, gabbroic*.

I'd walked miles. It was evening when I got back to the farmhouse.

3.2 Anwen was waiting for me, bouncing her bottom on the kitchen door. "Hoskin started yelling," she said.

"How long did she last?"

"Breakfast. Are you hungry?"

I was. We ate, and when finished she replenished our wine. A little of the heat had finally lifted so as the sky darkened we went onto the patio outside the kitchen door. Anwen lit a candle, then a cigarette. "I only smoke a couple a day," she said. I asked where the others were, and she told me they'd gone to the pub in the village—

"Hoskin in a pub?"

"No, she's gone for a dip," she said. I grinned when I realised Hoskin was down in the pool. "What?"

"Nothing. I like that. *She's gone for a dip.*"

"Metaphor," she said. "I'm sure it's the only reason the silent minds were put in the deep end of the pool. *They're off the deep end* is too good to pass up." She paused. "How did you know him?"

I explained it was often easier to have friends in other disciplines in a university. No competition, no rivalry to add a note of distrust. "He could sound off about his subject freely and know I'd never divulge anything."

"So you know a lot of maths?"

"I know a lot of the words he used."

"Like what?"

I made a show of thinking hard. "*Cruciate ridge. Primes. Yamanata. Topology. Sums.* He said *sums* a lot."

She laughed. She'd a wayward tooth high in her gum that tacked outwards, thick as a bean. As she laughed, her upper lip became conscious of it, and her smile slid down again to hide the tooth. It made me think of a woman smoothing down her skirt in the wind.

"I know it must be difficult," she said, quiet. "Tom's the closest we have to someone who knew a mind before delivery, but even then a few lectures and a few tutorials doesn't give you knowledge. It doesn't give you feelings. He'd like to think it does, but— For emotions to be engaged is—." She paused for a long moment. "Difficult," she decided at last. "At least that's how I imagine it. I mean, I've feelings for Baby. Not strong—."

"Enough to keep the mind turning at night."

She leapt at this. "Yes. *Yes*. But I didn't know her before. So I've no idea whether the mind in the pool is the same person who died. Or what—."

She stopped.

I put my head back against the wall of the farmhouse. It still retained heat from the day. All that remained of the sun was a line of peach-hair on the horizon.

"I'm the only one who's come here? To—." I thirsted for the word. "Verify."

"Yes."

"You didn't consider the wife, Helen?"

She gaped at me. "The wife?" I flushed, aware I'd not thought that through. "Can you imagine? *Come and see if your jugged husband is the same as when he was alive.*"

I smiled. "I like that. *Jugged hubby.*" I took a drink. "You must have chosen me carefully. Knowledge of the man, but no deep, irrational emotion."

Anwen's eyes lowered to the stone between her knees, a finger nudging sand into a circle. "That wasn't quite what I meant. That sounds callous. I didn't mean—."

"No, I know. I know what you meant." I paused. "And it is hard. Walking today—. What I knew of him, so much of it is gesture, tone, action. It's body stuff. It's the senses. With mind alone, what's left to identify him as *him*? It's not like I'll recognise him in any sensible sense of the word."

"Memories. Things only he could know. If he's not whole, or not right, then there'll be gaps and errors."

"I don't want to test him."

We were both silent for a long time, long enough for the sun to vanish and the sound of insects to increase in volume.

"What was it you were showing me in there? The sac in the jar. It looked like—."

Silence.

"You can say it," she said. "It looked like bollocks." I nodded. "The remarkable thing is none of the unwarped minds have anything even approaching that structure. And the wonder is that it just appears. Whatever the sac is, it forms on its own as part of the returning process. There's no magnet protocol for that part of the mind. It just forms. Len draws them in his book constantly. Hoskin doesn't have the first idea. Well, she has the first idea, but nothing like a workable theory."

"What shocks me most is that they do it themselves. The minds. They come back themselves."

"Yes."

"Did Hoskin just trust that would happen?"

She considered this. "I think there were indications from the work she did in the Netherlands that it might. But yes, it was trust. She wound up the toy and waited to see what it would do." She paused. "What did Moonfeld sound like? In life?"

"God, I don't know. He'd one of those voices. Deep. Educated, not just in mathematics. Baritone. Do you know who Scott Walker is? A rumble to it. You heard him when he spoke, even if he was just mooing away like a drunk fart." I smiled. "Women loved his voice. A colleague once said he'd one of those voices that made her tits itch."

She laughed. "Right. Not sure how to programme that."

"What's her first name? Hoskin."

"Claire."

"Oh. Oh dear. She doesn't look like a Claire at all." Anwen laughed again. "She comes across as driven."

"Yes." She seemed to want to say more but didn't.

"Tell me about the others," I said.

"Ichika was the first. I mean the first to return. When she chose subjects, Hoskin picked those with mental trauma in their past. Those who'd lost limb function and had learned to forge new neural pathways. Or a stroke. She thought it'd give them an advantage when delivered, speed them up. Pike had had a stroke. But then Baby took nearly two years to return. That's why we call her Elephant Baby, by the way."

"Why didn't you put her in with the silent minds?"

"The twist in the jar, for one. That's the first indication that something is coming together in the jar. And because eventually there was a voice. Once I was in there alone and a nursery rhyme came through. I swear, the first time you hear it, it's like an ice lolly's been run up your spine. She started singing. And we've had no time to grow her voice by this point so it's just a mechanical robot sound. Can you imagine? On your tod and then a robot starts singing? And then nothing for another seven, eight months." She leaned on her side and took out a wallet, pulling a piece of paper from inside it. "Strange thing. I couldn't find the nursery rhyme anywhere. She must have made it up herself, or learned it from another child who did. I remember making one up at school about a teacher called Mr Herbert who filled his pants with sherbet." She caught my look and turned very red. "Here it is. She only sang it a couple of times, and she doesn't remember it now. I'd to race to write it down and I missed bits."

I took the paper from her. It was well-used as if she'd opened and read it often. I read the rhyme through. "Do you mind if I copy this?"

She shook her head. I transcribed it to my notebook. When I'd finished, she said, "So. Tomorrow."

"No. I'll go now. Another night and I'll leave it undone." I grinned at her. "I'm going for a dip."

"Do you want me to come?"

"No. No, I'll go alone."

I stood. "They don't remember how they died," she said. "They remember their illnesses, but the days before, the injections of Baba, they don't recall at all. Like is said about childbirth or accidents. It's best not to mention it. Don't tell them how they died. It's like the newest *faux pas* in the world."

3.3 The lights in the room were kept low. It took time for my eyes to adjust to the gloom in the hut. Anwen had said to announce whom I was talking to as Elephant Baby would natter if given an opening. I wanted to remain nameless at the start and asked if Moonfeld would recognise my voice, but Anwen told me simply to avoid introducing myself—

"The acoustics of how they hear sound is another order of complexity from the inner ears they once had. We have to introduce ourselves every time. You can't imagine. I mean that literally. We've no way of knowing how they hear. He won't recognise your voice."

"I'm here to talk to John Moonfeld alone," I said.

At once, I was stuck. I didn't know whether I should stand, sit, pull a chair from one of the computer stations, or sit lotus position on the wooden floor of the hut, gazing up at the jar in mute worship. But for my apprehension, I'd have laughed at myself for my need for social protocol, as intrinsic to my being as a tic. I pulled a chair up and sat in front of the jar that looked like a sack full of tree cankers.

Moonfeld.

"It's not Tom," said the mind.

Loosening, Lenford had called it. The word was so fitting.

"It's not Tom. I'm new."

"A new operator. What is your function?"

I had nothing. "Quality control," I said at last.

"Button man."

The speaker made three identical sounds. *Like an alarm clock clearing its throat*, I thought. To my ears, it was *hoar* repeated with one of those spooky Scandinavian vowels forming the sound. *Hå hå hå.* I began to shake, because I realised it was the computer's interpretation of laughter, of how the tongue had been manipulated in its bowl: no words but a sound so completely without mirth I heard it as aural violence. *A translated noise*, I thought. The computers had tried to translate emotion and failed. It was cruelty even to have tried.

My bowels were water. I'd been in the room of minds less than two minutes and lost my grip entirely. I stood—

"Excuse me," I muttered. "I've got to go."

"Have you left a hob on?"

I made my way up the ladder and into the toilet by the disused steam room. Sitting there, I tried to calm myself, to bring my breathing under a measure of control. I breathed, and slowly the humour in the situation grew, especially when I realised my meditative circled fingers were ridiculous considering where I was. This laughter centred me, but then the obscene three-note guess-laugh returned to mind and my balance failed again.

It wasn't Moonfeld, I thought. *It couldn't be.*

From nowhere, I began to feel anger, blood-red and leashless. Although Anwen had told me there'd be no resemblance to the voice I knew, what was in the hut was not human. It wasn't robotic exactly, but it was bland and without colour. Each word was finished with the tiniest pause, which gave the voice a mechanic regularity, which I'd been told would develop with time, but even so the tone and rhythms were wholly off. Where was the man's fuss and mess, his noise and the bubbling descent into the word *terrible*?

It wasn't him. It couldn't be him.

There was a knock on the door. "Everything all right?"

Lenford. "I'm fine. Going to the toilet."

There was a pause before Len said, "I'm just checking everything's okay in there."

The anger found a focus. "It's going fine, thanks," I said, "although I'm sad Samuel Beckett's dead as he'd have loved it. Seriously, the turd went into the water like a cormorant, Lenford. Is that enough detail for how things are going in here? Fuck off."

"Just trying to help. Everyone has that freak at the start."

At once I was weary, cowed. "Sorry," I said. "I'm sorry. Just give me a minute to sort my head."

I breathed, breathed, breathed, and soon found grip I could trust. In the hut in the pool, I retook my place. "I'm back," I announced.

"Quality control. Quantum chemistry. Queen's Counsel. Québec City. QC."

I had no idea how to progress. "Quality control, yes."

"Is it my quality you control, or the quality of others? If so, Hoskin is brusque and I would like to make a complaint."

"Tell me about yourself," I said.

Again the three-part laugh sounded, as jarring as the first time. "John Moonfeld, mathematician, somewhat diminished. Birth dates and death dates. Height, weight, eye colour and hair colour. Distinguishing marks. No previous. You are the test, aren't you?"

"I am."

"Don't tell me. Let me guess. I will assume that you are at least a maths poop, otherwise what would be the point? I am currently working on an area of topology called the *cruciate ridge*, specifically a uniformity of texture I call *gooseflesh*, or *ostrich skin boots*, layman's terms. It is not a texture. The path has taken a turn, an unexpected turn, and Tom and I are now in a place we never thought to look, much to Tom's confusion. I assume that you know Tom. I describe the *gooseflesh* as a wall. It is not a wall—."

There was nothing in the voice that I could get a purchase on. It was too flat, mechanical, a card in the spokes of a bike being walked home. It was curious the mind talked without breaks – not that I expected it to separate its thoughts into pithy bits for me to understand – but there was an aspect of speech that was missing, and it was a while before I realised what it was. *The need for breath.* A human would pause for breath, pause for half a second before the start of a new thought, halt and re-order thoughts and breathe in the thinking space, but even that lack of a gap was noticeable. The mind simply spoke until it was finished.

This lack of a need for breath locked into what the mind had said about hair and eye colour, what I myself had realised earlier in the day: there was nothing left for identification. Humans didn't recognise each other by their thought patterns. They recognised each other by their voice, their stance, their physical presence in the world. Moonfeld had smelt of bad fags, one of those people who seemed to absorb the smell of cigarette smoke as paper does. Later, after he'd given up, he smelt of mints. He'd smelt hot with mints. Where was that now? I'd felt comfortable with him; for almost no other straight man had that been true. Where did that feeling of ease now reside, now that I existed in a state of borderline panic just sitting in front of an illuminated jar speaking to me in the guise of an old friend? At the very least, the voice could have remained, but the clippedness of the speech, uncoloured by accent or quirk stood solidly in the way of acceptance, which threw me so completely I let the mind speak on, for to maths-less me the mind could be selecting words at random according to some algorithm of grammar and I wouldn't know the difference.

As the mind talked on, I realised I'd also no way of ascertaining the truth even of the set-up. Beneath the jar, the *oobleck* of the tongue crawled and bopped according to the grinding of the chain-fluid, but I'd only Hoskin's word for it that the voice came from the thing in the jar. There was nothing beyond the lack of a plausible motive to suggest I wasn't the butt of a joke. And yet the sense remained – the sense I'd had while walking – that what had been achieved was true, and that by unimaginable means this was Moonfeld, a mind whose workings had been continued beyond the death of the body.

"So you are not a mathematician," said the mind. "I told you seven palpable falsehoods. You should have popped."

"I might not have been listening."

"A mathematician would have been listening as hard as a teenager outside a cat-house door."

Moonfeld might have said that, I thought. *That was a thing Moonfeld might have said.*

"It's not Helen. They wouldn't have asked Helen."

"No," I said. A pause. "You can't tell sex?"

"Not unless you talk about lipstick or football. Every voice comes through the same."

"I see." Despite my unease, I was surer of my ground, my task, now. "I'm not a mathematician."

"I am doing better than you now because I know you are a man. I should ask you hot or cold."

"How am I doing?" I asked.

"Terrible. Shameful performance."

"I'm sad."

"You are a man, and logic says you must know me at least well enough to judge me, which means you were probably at my funeral, so tell me about it."

"Yes, where were you?"

The three-note laugh sounded, as happy as three short blasts from an electric sander. "I was nowhere special."

I leaned back in my chair. "Tasteful hymns," I said, "a crucifix in your fist. When the vicar spoke of your ascent into the embrace of Jesus, a lame woman was healed. She rose and danced with her skirts up——."

"You dirty bastard. You dirty little bastard. That is a dirty thing to do. That is very bloody dirty."

I was laughing, laughing despite the shake in my hands and the tightness in my shoulders and neck. Doubt was tough, but acceptance was pushing my emotions into the red. My voice was in and out of static, hoarse, as I told the mind his remains had been buried at his home, near the tree line, no marker but people's memories, soon to fade.

I told him a stranger had been there, so similar in looks to Moonfeld the sight of him blew out the mourners' heartbeats for a second, like a joke candle. This unknown brother or cousin took a stone from the soil by the grave as he paid his respects, pocketed it, and everyone afterwards copied him in perfect unrehearsed mimicry. Voice raw and failing now, I told Moonfeld I'd done the same. I'd searched out a pebble from the soil and pocketed it. Mud on my fingers, mud on my whisky glass, mud on the cake at the wake.

"The cake at the wake." The mind left a pause. "Is that the sound of you breathing? What is that sound? Is that you breathing?" He left a longer pause. "You are Jude. Breathe, Jude."

"Sorry——."

Sorry was all I could manage. The panic had hit, bedding down like a stain into a carpet, seemingly never to come out.

3.4 It was less a blackout than an absence. When I returned to awareness, I'd a glass of whisky in front of me. I'd not drunk whisky since the funeral. I was in the kitchen, Anwen sitting across from me.

She smiled. "You seem more yourself."

For some reason this struck me as hilarious, and I began to laugh, long, waves of it making me hiccup, and when the laughter subsided Anwen's look of concern sent me back into it anew. It lasted minutes.

"This is, without doubt, the strangest thing I've ever done in my life," I said, quietly, "and I don't understand why it's got me so fraught. I'm not usually so—." I waved a hand. "I yelled at Lenford."

"He said."

"I feel like a child. I feel like I did when I was a kid. You know? When you're an adolescent and all your emotions, whatever they are – anger, whatever – are revving to the red. Like you're testing the limits of what they'll do. I feel like I'm back there, on the whip end of them."

Anwen told me she'd written of similar extremes in her journal and described her emotions as *spatchcocked*. "Like the way the bones sit normally in an emotion have been cracked at the knuckles and forced flat?"

"All the better to cook you with," I replied, adding in a whisper, "It was the strangest thing. The strangest thing."

Silence. I drank from the glass, made a face and put the whisky away from me. "I always think whisky tastes of armpit," I said. "Is there a cup of tea? I'll make it."

I fussed about with the cups, saw the time. Midnight.

"I'd a friend in school," I said with my back to Anwen. "I call him my friend now. I didn't know him that well. Odd kid. Away with the fairies a lot of the time. During 'O' Levels, I had an exam with him, and he went up to the English room and took a dive. Three storeys onto his head. He lived, but—

"It turned me. It turned everyone in the school. A few days later I saw a girl deliberately break her fingernails off by dragging her fingers down a brick wall. Kids curled into balls in the corridors. There was another attempt. It was crazy, and looking back on it, that time was like a drug dream, or being deeply, deeply ill with flu.

"And the odd thing is that now I can't tell you the timing for anything in my late teens. Between that time and when I went to university, the shock of that event erased time and memory so I've nothing but bits that, if you stitch them together, you might make up memories enough to account for three months' worth of time. It's gone. Something changed. I cracked and never came right. I don't mean damage necessarily, but the shock of it changed me.

"And it's that level of upset I felt down there in the pool. If I'm honest, it's that level of upset I've been feeling since I got here." I sipped my tea. "I've never told anyone that before. Not the event, but how I felt." I sipped. "I used to wander the streets, crying in doorways for the memory of poor, brain-damaged Alec, who I didn't even know that well. Sounds romantic, doesn't it? But any doorway you can adequately hide in always stinks of piss. God, I'm sorry. This isn't making any sense."

"It is. Your head needs to get over that hurdle. Your friend John is dead but you can still talk to him. Nothing is better suited to screwing up your head than that. We've all had it. We've all been through it. You'll have ambivalent feelings towards him, towards them. Elephant Baby—. I know her. I keep having to disillusion myself of the belief that I knew her when she was alive. Even that I was related to her. A cool aunt I never knew I had. She's not cool, mind."

"What can I expect?"

She shrugged. "I don't know. You're in a hidden camera show?" I laughed. "Okay, been there done that. So, disbelief is your gateway drug. Horror. Horror's bad. Horror takes a long time to shift. I don't mean they're frightening. I mean their state is horrifying. So vulnerable. No way to defend themselves, and a skull like porcelain now. Pike's jar's so thin at the base where it bulges." She shivered, a performed act rather than an involuntary reflex. "That gets me like a needle going into my navel. But by the time you're horrified for them, you've accepted the truth of their reality. They're real people, real minds.

"And then you begin to interact with them, and like them. I *like* Elephant Baby." She stretched. "What else? You'll be resentful they've more life than they were entitled to. That's not bloody rational. You take their side. You want to defend them against you-know-who." She looked at me directly. "You get angry for them. I'm angry for Baby. I'm angry because she's the lucky one. Moonfeld isn't lucky. He's what all this is for, but she's only conscious because she's an expendable step in the experimental trail. When the programme's done and perfected, ordinary people like Baby won't get a look in, because they're not special. They're not *legacy*."

We were silent for a long time. In truth, it was only now coming clear to me that my blackout might have been less the panic of the situation and more a cardiac episode I might never have awoken from. I felt okay in myself but I should have been scared flat.

I watched her hands. When she spoke, she planted them like five-legged spiders, moving them to enforce points as if shuffling the cups in a game of thimblerig, but now she was at rest she was stroking the sides of one hand's fingers with the thumb and forefinger of the other hand.

"Is it him?" she said lightly.

I shook my head. "I don't know."

"Still resistance there."

I nodded. "I'll go in tomorrow morning. This morning. I might make it through a conversation this time."

"Early's best. Tom and Hoskin start with him at nine."

I went to bed. Although weary, the other possible causes of the blackout occupied my thoughts. I knew a loss of consciousness due to abnormal heart rhythms could revert to normal spontaneously, or I could even black out *despite* a normal heart rhythm through *vasovagal syncope*. Whether the shock of my time in the room of minds could have caused that sudden drop in blood pressure, I didn't know.

I had medication, *quinidine*. I also had an *isoprenaline* inhaler for emergencies, together with an *isoprenaline* pen in case I was already out when an emergency hit, the electrical storm of arrhythmias entering a continuous loop, which ends in death. I was supposed to provide the instructions for this to people I was with. I had not. And that evening I knew I never would because a possible consequence was that I'd be sent away—

While waiting for sleep I said *ice lolly* to myself, then again in her accent. *Ice lolly. Lolly. Lolly.*

3.5 I dreamt the chain-fluid was a miles-long transparent snake coiled into the jar, jointed like a tank tread, spine bones sticking out like the ears on a wingnut. Elephant Baby sang her nursery rhyme. Moonfeld's snake swayed up from the jar's mouth, peering about the room, the end of the chain an eye spinning like Kaa's in *The Jungle Book*.

4.1 I was up at six and filled with a wrung bone weariness. The fleas had been at me again. Anwen had given me Tiger Balm for the bites, which was like wearing a virtual menthol sock. I sat at the end of the bed, staring in cow stupidity at my shoes and feeling embarrassed about my panic attack. It was like being the only one seasick on a boat, and I didn't want to face the others.

Lenford was in the kitchen. "How d'you like your coffee?"

"Sinister," I replied.

Len laughed. "Strong and black it is."

"Listen—."

"Shut up," the man said cheerily. "We've all of us been through the same wringer."

Anwen came in. She looked grumpy, hair nested. I told her my snake dream. "You dream very literally," she said. "I dreamt of your schoolfriend. Thanks for that."

I took my coffee down to the pool. Outside the hut, I stood for a while getting my feet, but I was antsy and the constant hum of the machines seemed louder than it had the day before. As I stood there, listening, trying to gauge my level of aplomb, I became aware of another sound almost at the limits of hearing. The sound slid upwards and downwards in pitch. It sounded like whalesong.

Inside, I found the chair was still in front of Moonfeld's jar. I wondered if there'd been any design in the placement of the jars. They were lit objects against a dark background, on plinths like ancient sculptured busts. The symbolism of it was telling. The intention behind the minds was to raise them up and continue to hear them utter their wisdom, like oracles. It reminded me of a thought I'd had the night before. With Moonfeld's rounded jar, the light in it and the chair before it, the scene was of a fair booth waiting for the medium to sit behind her crystal ball. *The wise mind*, I thought. I wondered if in the future every home would have one, an ancestor who became the god of the house. Certainly every school or college would have one. I could think of nothing more stagnant.

"Who's there?"

It was not Moonfeld, I knew. "Jude."

"I don't know a Jude. Boy or girl Jude? I like a boy Jude."

Anwen was right: the voices did settle in. Baby's was still colourless, but it was – it *felt*, it *sounded* – organic. The flatness was like the voice of someone medicated. Anwen had joked the minds sounded like twenty-somethings born pretty, rich and stupid. She was right. I heard it in Baby's voice.

"Boy Jude."

"I like a boy Jude."

Whalesong sounded again, more audible this time but still quiet. I looked behind me at the myriad cones of the soundproofing in the hut. The sound had travelled through it to the outside with only minimal loss in volume, but Anwen had said they'd screamed in here in trials and never heard a thing. I resolved to ask her about it later as I found it curious that Baby – chatty, likes a natter – never spoke again for the hours I was in the room.

I sat down in the chair.

4.2 "Are you dead?"

"Dear me. Am I dead? Yes, I am. I know what you mean. Intellectually I understand I am no more in the physical sense, but I am still clearly thinking. My mind feels as it ever did, but then it would even if it was not because my mind is what I am thinking with. You went berserk yesterday."

I laughed. It surprised me. "Like a tripped switch."

"That reminds me. Do they have a back-up generator?"

"I'm sure they do." I paused. "Does that worry you?"

The mind was silent for a long while. "I do not worry now. After all, the worst has happened. The worst has happened, and I can still work. That has not changed. I even have more freedom now because I do not need to sleep."

"You don't sleep?"

"I have fugue states, but it is not sleep. And there is much to think about. Have you thought about the legal implications? That will keep you in your hamster wheel for days. And then there is the unresolved correlation between gravid numbers and buoyant numbers in the cruciate ridge hypothesis. And the structures. The *******."

There was an audio drop-out that made the last word inaudible. I took the chance to reword the question—

"Do you feel alive?"

"A question of *Culpable Idiocy*. Yes. You are quite focused. I do not feel dead. I feel the same as I ever did."

"Sorry," I said. "I'm rude. I have so many questions."

"They all do. That is all they do. And it gets wearing, but what can I do? If you ask me an original question, I will sing."

"Do you miss having a really deep itch?"

The laugh. "That was not a challenge. I had not considered that loss. The fleas are giving you gyp?"

Gyp. Culpable Idiocy. Berserk. I got comfortable on my chair.

We spoke for hours. Nine a.m. came and went with no sign of the threatened Tom and Hoskin. We talked of the mind's awareness of time, intuiting from the human routine the shape of a day, then narrowing down the cycle rate of the computers' hum until he'd a measure for a second; he'd a clock. "It's maths even you could do, Jude."

We talked of his experience of returning to consciousness. "It is as inexplicable as an anaesthetised cat making for his litter tray mid-coma," Moonfeld said. "Do you remember that cat?"

We talked of the experience of being *jugged* – a term the mind loved, wowing his laugh-drill seven times – and decided *jughood* would be the noun for it.

I quizzed his impressions of the other members of the team. Hoskin the mind had down as a squat figure, nothing like the tall athletic woman she actually was. Anwen he adored so he'd given her his wife Helen's features. Lenford he saw as a giant (he was not), and Tom he had recalled as someone completely different. It took a long while to clarify who Tom was, and again I felt how acidic the young man's distress must have been.

Moonfeld spoke of the awareness he had that he was now *in service*. He'd no other function—

"No one enjoys my company," he said, "and that hurt. Then I got lost in the idea I was hurt. The thought I could be hurt made me want to laugh. Then I focused on the word *thought*. What does that mean? And then *laugh*. What does that mean? Nothing makes sense. Eventually I turned away from it. There is no point thinking about it. It's just an endless loop of questioning meanings."

Moonfeld spoke a lot about power, or rather its absence. It surprised him how much power was in the physical. He'd thought it otherwise. Power was in the will, in the personality. Yet now he could do nothing. Not that he'd the urge to chase a stick, he said, but he was as inactive as it is possible for a person to be. Even those with locked-in syndrome have blood circulation, metabolism, ageing. He was literally nothing but fluid- and matter-stored thought. In terms of personal power, he had none, or almost none—

"I have more power than Pike or Ichika," he said, "but the exercise of that power is withholding information, and that damages me as much as others. It damages my self-worth. Imagine, Jude. I have a sense of self-worth. But the fact is I have to do as they ask, so if I talk about my memories and they ask me not to, I must comply. If they say they want to start at nine a.m., I must comply. If they say they are off to Bedfordshire, I must comply. They do not coerce me, but I am beholden to them."

"They also can't punish you."

"True. The chances of them flicking my switch is small."

He'd mentioned Helen, so I didn't feel tactless asking if he missed her. Moonfeld said he had, and once returned wanted nothing more than to speak to her. It took months of arguing in a circle with himself before he accepted for certain he would never be with her again, even to talk. Her distress would be too great, even supposing her disbelief in his continued existence could be shorn away. For him, the ache never left.

"You've been to see her."

I had, often, but not much in the last six months. I drove past her house almost daily, and now never dropped in.

"The garden looks magnificent," I said.

I meant this as positive but after speaking thought only of how sad it must sound. She'd looked after Moonfeld, been the handmaid of Herr Topology, and ever bemoaned the lack of time she had for her green domain. A garden magnificent told of unlimited time to spend outdoors.

Moonfeld was a peculiarly honest man when it came to his feelings – a relic of the therapy after his time in the children's home, I thought – but where mood was concerned he was as interested in the theoretical, even metaphysical, aspects of his new emotional state. By rights, emotions should not exist in his current incarnation because the physical trains and the tracks they ran on were absent, but although Moonfeld spoke of an evenness of state – *Like the drone of a bagpipe* – his feelings were still present. Impatience, or anger, was vivid for him when Tom failed to grasp some nuance of the mathematics. When he talked of the ********* – again, the audio feed from the speaker dropped out here – he was frustrated when Hoskin shut him down.

"Frustration. Where would that live?"

"Where does it live in a meat brain?"

"This is true." I paused. "You said you don't sleep."

"No. I do not miss it either. Fugue is the wrong word. It is more of a wandering. It's where I first saw the *********. I am not unconscious when I am in that state, but I am aware I have been wandering in my mind because I have no memory of time passing. And I always remember time passing. I have done since the children's home. There was a woman who monitored our housekeeping. *Mrs Hoover*, we called her. We had to wait for her inspection. If the standard was not up to scratch, there would be punishment, but the standard was dictated by how she felt that day. Tick tick tick. I never lost the immediate spasm of dread whenever anyone started up a hoover.

"I think of the home constantly now, Jude. Do you not find that strange?"

"They say old men often lapse into memories of childhood when they're in their dotage."

"God, you are a prick." Moonfeld left a long pause. "I think of the home constantly, but I think of it as a memory of fear. It is echoed in the *********. The fear I remember is the same as the fear I see there. It is perhaps because all buildings are similar. But somehow the place is familiar because of my memory of the home, and my memory of the fear. The darkness at the top of the stairs. The stairwell. The odd-levelled landings. Those particularly because they remind me of the ********* *********. I am—."

I stopped him. "What's that word?" I asked. Silence. "Did you just say something?"

"I did."

"Can you put it in a sentence for context?"

"********* are standing *********, Jude."

It was clear to me now. Certain words were being dropped out of Moonfeld's responses.

"Sorry, go on," I said.

"We were speaking of emotion. As I said, there is nothing inside this jar that can hold it, transmit it, so my emotions must be a construct. But why do they still have an effect? The spiralling mood lift when I come to a new understanding in mathematics. The heart thud. When I asked you about the funeral, I felt desolate afterwards and wished I had not asked. There are times in the evening or night when I feel the melancholy of Sunday afternoons. You understand what I mean? I cannot concentrate on anything. Just sadness, not even especially sad, like a loose fog of it has come off the moor and drifted over me. And it was not a recalled ache, Jude. I felt sorrow, like a squirt of ink in my chain-fluid, and I had to wait while it slowly dispersed." A pause. "I must apologise. My words are woolly. *Sorrow. An ache.* They make no sense."

"You were talking of the home."

"Yes. The senescent noodlings of an old fart, I think you said." The laugh. "With beatings, casual cruelties, servitude, humiliation, there was significant fear. Fear that what was happening to others might also happen to yourself. There was a blond boy who was seldom in the dorm of a night. Yet the one thing that scared me most in all that time in the home was not the physical abuse. It was a story I was told by an older boy. I'll try and tell it as I heard it—."

There was a lighthouse, the mind told me, a rock light out in the sea. There were three men on the light, and the weather was so sour that when it was time for the next crew to replace them, no boat could reach the lighthouse for the seas. Their food was spent. As the days of high seas went on, they began to report strange occurrences in the sealed lighthouse. Footsteps above them on the stairs. A shadow standing in the lamp room, or a hand stain, smaller than any of theirs, left on the lens after it had been cleaned. They conserved their oil, but come evening this thrift only filled the shadows with malevolence. They kept calling for help, but the weather refused to break, and even though hardy sailors made the attempt, because the situation with the food was getting so desperate, the boats from the harbour could not get near the rock light. Soon all radio contact ceased, and no matter when the mainland called, there was nothing.

Eventually the weather bootstrapped itself out of the storm and a boat was sent to the light. They had to break in the doors as the light was completely sealed from the inside. They searched the light from base up. There was no smell to the place, and the living quarters were bare. The domestic rigour of men in service had remained despite their suffering. Everything was locked into its place, ordered, plain and clean. They went upwards. None of the high windows were open. There were no bodies at all. But three men do not vanish in a rock light, or if they do they don't lock the doors from the inside before they go, or shut the window they fell from behind them. The searchers continued upwards, and in the lamp room at the top of the tower, they found three black ravens, silent, huge, two staring out to sea, and the third staring at the rescuers, head cocked to the side.

"I can see how that would spook a kid."

"A boy told me it in the home. I tried to find it years later and could not. I expect it was in one of those horror anthologies from the sixties or seventies. They had lots of them, all with a snake going through a skull on the cover. Were they Corgi?"

"I can't remember. There was one about an earwig that chewed its way through someone's head and came out the opposite ear. That was the whole story. Kept me awake for nights. It would be rubbish if you read it now, as an adult."

"There are times when my mind is wandering when I feel I am back in that home. I remembered the lighthouse story for the first time in years. And the shock of the ********* is the same as the ending with the ravens. I understand that to you the story is just a stock shock ending that makes no sense. *He was dead all along.* Or, *She let her hand fall to pat her faithful panting hound, but her fingers felt the hot wet stump of his severed neck.* Or, *Three black ravens.* But my reaction to the tale was born in childhood, and not a good childhood."

I was smiling. "I know what you mean. A boy comes downstairs late at night. He looks otherworldly, but he's just half asleep. His father asks him what's up, and the boy replies, *A wolf dreamed me.* It gets you in the hair follicles, up the chain of your spine. *A wolf dreamed me.* It's from a poem by Tony Connor."

"Oh. A poem."

There was still that mechanical click between the words, still the need to imagine a little oomph in the phrasing, but I knew this was the moment that shot the bolt on my belief. It was not the knowledge Moonfeld had, not the personal information and detail he knew that would be next to impossible for another to know, not the history and the expertise—. It was the boredom I heard in those three short words. *Oh. A poem.* It didn't matter I had to intuit much of the emotion, colour it as though hand-tinting a frame from a black-and-white film, the boredom was entirely John Moonfeld. No, not boredom, rather a stale perplexity at what possible interest poetry could have to anyone. It irked me. It irked me precisely as it had when the man was alive.

"You said you felt fear."

There was a pause. Moonfeld said, "I do not know. Is it fear?" The laugh. "All my worries have lifted. This is true. Is that the same thing? The things that were weights. The things that divide a man. My factors. The big fatty of seventeen into thirty-four. All those have gone, Jude, and I do not think that is a good thing. I do not think any of this is a good thing.

"Is that fear? I do not know. Sometimes in Hoskin, I get the impression she is expecting me to thank her for my continued life. I think she wants to be thanked, or she feels that she has not been thanked enough. But I do not think she thought any of this through. I work in science, so I know. No one ever thinks these things through. Scientists are optimists otherwise they would not be scientists. But they also tend not to consider the human aspect. I wonder if she realised before she started just how much would come through." A pause. "I am all here, I take it?"

"Yes," I said. It was difficult to say. "I know you."

"Yes. You know me now." The laugh. It was a different sound, and I couldn't have said why I thought so. "It is hard to express how fine it is to have you here for company in my jughood." There was a pause. "I always loved how you loved words, Jude."

"I don't know if they'll let me stay."

"They will let you stay for a time. I can always withhold my services from them."

I waited, unsure what to say next. I needed the loo, and I knew I was over the time allotted, but I'd no idea how to leave. I cleared my throat, said, "I'm going to go now."

"Come again, Quality Control."

It was towards midday. At the end of the pool, dimly lit, Tom, Hoskin, Anwen and Lenford stood leaning on the pool wall. It was incongruous, like a group of seniors at a Saturday swim. Anwen had her laptop on the side with the wave pattern of Moonfeld's feed on the screen. They'd been listening.

"You were a long time," Hoskin said.

"I was talking to a friend," I replied.

4.3 The team followed me up to the kitchen. Hoskin was staring at me with the intensity of someone wanting to land a punch. "You're convinced?" she asked.

The scene was banal – a whistle-kettle on the fuss behind us, a gang of chipped mugs on the table – but the moment felt enormous, like a proposal or news of a pregnancy.

I nodded. "He's the same. And seems sane." I smiled. "Sorry, that sounded odd."

My words parted the group. Hoskin and Tom dug themselves into a conversation about contingencies I didn't understand, but I gathered they'd put a pin in several concepts until they had certainty they were reliable. Tom held his ground, I noted, and Hoskin took it, allowing his greater expertise. I realised they were lovers then.

Before they lost themselves in a discussion about the perceived regularity of gravid numbers on the cruciate ridge, I asked them about the song I'd heard on entering the inner room. It stopped them flat—

"What song?"

"Like whalesong. Before we started talking there was a noise. And then later, after the last thing Baby said." They were blank. Anwen was blank. "You must have tapes."

Anwen still had her laptop. She cued up the parts I'd mentioned. "Say your name before you speak to them, could you?" she said, curt. "It's not just for their benefit but for mine." She played the feed from before Moonfeld and I started talking.

"There," I said.

It was awkward, because I saw they'd never heard what I'd heard, and in truth it was difficult to hear as it was just rhythmic swoops and hoots that would fit neatly into the background hum of the computers.

"It's nothing," said Hoskin.

"Listen. Baby says something." Anwen played it, took it back, played it again. "You said she talks. *A natterer*, you said. So why does she stop talking?"

Anwen played it again, altering a level on her display to bring the background to the fore. A swoop sounded, like a man with an impossibly deep voice saying *wow* whilst burping. The sound was short, almost not there at all, and at the limits of hearing.

"He asked her to be silent," I said. "Don't laugh. They're talking to each other. They can talk to each other."

Len was shaking his head. Hoskin looked faintly exasperated. Only Anwen – the one who knew best – was looking concerned, recognising the possibility of communication that was not recognised by the computers, but she didn't speak.

"No, they don't," said Hoskin, deliberate.

I left it. "Okay, but I think you're wrong." Hoskin turned back to Tom. "Don't go," I said. "There's another thing. Anwen, can you find phrases fast on that thing?" She nodded. "Can you find the words *odd-levelled landings*?"

Anwen found the part of the feed. I saw the moment the realisation hit her what I wanted her to play. She stopped, looked shame-faced, eyes on her thumbs circling one another.

"Hoskin—?" she said, half a question.

"There's no drop-outs on the tape, is there?" I asked. "I got him to go back, say the words again, put them in a sentence for context, but there was a drop-out every time. At first I thought it was a glitch in the speakers, but no glitch drops out on the same word every time." Anwen was bright red. Hoskin cold and focused. "What is it I couldn't be allowed to hear? And how is it he didn't hear it?"

"They don't listen to the speakers," Anwen replied, small. "You ever had a phone call where your voice echoes a step behind? You can't talk. It's out of step with your thoughts, and it doesn't sound like you. It's the same for them, only worse as it's a generated voice. They tune their own voices out."

Silence. "Thanks," I said at last, "but that was the minor question."

No one would speak. I saw each of them was stuck in awkwardness so extreme I could literally see them itch, but I did nothing to lift them out of it. They were waiting on Hoskin, I knew. They were waiting for her to decide.

"Play the feed," she said at last.

John: God, you are a prick. [Pause] I think of the home constantly, but I think of it as a memory of fear. It is echoed in the structures. The fear I remember is the same as the fear I see there. It is perhaps because all buildings are similar. But somehow the place is familiar because of my memory of the home, and my memory of the fear.

The darkness at the top of the stairs. The stairwell. The odd-levelled landings. Those particularly because they remind me of the laby-rinth markers. I am—
Jude: What's that word?
John: Labyrinth markers.
Jude: Did you just say something?"
John: I did.
Jude: Can you put it in a sentence for context?
John: Labyrinth markers are standing stones, Jude.

No one said anything for a long moment.
"Can you stay longer?" Hoskin asked.
"Labyrinth markers."
Hoskin cleared her throat. "Something else comes through when the minds are delivered. Artefacts. They speak of places they never knew in life as existing structures within their visual understanding. But nothing can be in that chain-fluid that wasn't in their original brains. Nothing should be strange or unrecognised to them. But they speak of distant buildings, and when we drilled down into it, they all see the same struc-tures. And they're drawn to them."

4.4 The minds did not see. They had no eyes. Yet within their con-sciousnesses they had visual fields they'd constructed and populated to make an environment for them to 'see'. Hoskin asked me to picture a trip I'd once taken, long before, and then had to trace my way back to in memory—
"Like the tip, or your old school, or your mother's house."
"Or my *mother's* house?"
"Whatever. You picture it not as a direction, or from above as you would if using a map. You remember the houses, the traffic lights, the turns, the colours. If you closed your eyes now and remembered your way to your local rubbish tip, you'd see it in your mind, wouldn't you?" I conceded I would. "A mind does the same, but the landscape they inhabit seems to be unchanged from the moment they returned to con-

sciousness. What they see – and I'm using the word *see* in a loose sense – is something they've known in life. We assume it's part of the process of reassembly, like a memory palace where the features of their minds are stored in order to come together. By definition, the internal landscapes are individual to each mind. For Ichika, her internal field was a moor—."

"A battlefield."

"Yes, some bloody battlefield, but a real space, with real features and real distance. For Moonfeld it's a big building in the countryside outside a town. For Elephant Baby, it's a flat in the city. Pike—. Pike?"

"He was not forthcoming on that score," said Len.

"Yes, he was," said Anwen, quiet.

"Soon after returning, they see structures in the landscapes. Distant ruins. Strange buildings. But there should be nothing strange in their internal fields, because everything they are is in their memory and mind and nothing should exist that wasn't part of their brain when it was alive. Yet each of them sees this unfamiliar structure, but while the places are the same, the minds describe them as different, which means they're interpreting something they think they can 'see'." She made the quote marks with her fingers. "Baba opens everything, all the cupboards, all the meat latches and bolts, and the whole of what's in your head comes out." She leaned forward. "But there's so much in a brain that's not used, or whose use we don't suspect. Banal functions, mechanical functions, internal admin functions.

"Take the laying down of new memories. The minds clearly make new memories, but we don't know how. The mechanics must have come through in delivery for it still to happen. And what we suspect is that a part of the brain that was normally entirely unconscious in all humans has come through in clear, as code breakers say, and the fact this part is now a presence in the conscious mind is an accident of the process. What function it has we don't know, but equally the minds don't know because it wasn't part of their consciousness when alive. And so they make these structures to accommodate the thing that's come through in clear."

"And they're drawn to them," Anwen said.

"Yes. They're intrigued by them, and they want to approach them," added Hoskin, "which is of no concern in Baby or Pike or Ichika, but bad in Moonfeld. The structures are seductive to the minds."

Anwen put in, "Ichika said it was as strange as waking up with a tail. It's not part of you, it's frightening, but you have to play with that tail."

"They all display the same structures?" I asked. "If it's just Moonfeld, it could be part of his work. Maybe he told them about it in his whale-song voice."

"No. The others spoke of the structures before Moonfeld got here."

"Could they be communicating between the jars?"

"What would that mean? Telepathy. For god's sake. No."

I flushed. "I meant contamination between the fluids."

"The jars are separate," said Hoskin. "There's no place they cross. Each feeds into the hub with no connection possible. The structures, whatever they are, are internal to their consciousnesses."

"They fear the structures."

"They don't fear them, Anwen." Hoskin's contempt was clear. "They're drawn to them because they don't recognise them. They are curious about them."

Anwen ignored her, faced me directly. "We went back to Ichika's transcripts and came across a phrase she used. In Japanese. I can't remember what it was. *Hone no haka*, was it? Longer than that. I had it translated. It means, *The circle is the grave of the bone*. Whatever these structures are, the minds speak of them in similar language. It's like the structures came through with a tag to identify them, but the words they use don't sound like modern words. *The well. The labyrinth. The grave of the bone—*."

"*The salt path*," Len put in.

"*The salt path*. The places are different according to the idiom of their internal landscapes, but they're recognisably the same for all the minds. I call it *otherwhere*."

Hoskin looked baleful. "You'll have to forgive Anwen. She's fanciful. Pixy-led, they call it down here."

"Well, that's patronising," Anwen said.

"She thinks the structure could be grammar visible."

I caught Hoskin's eyes and knew she was expecting me to mock, as she was mocking, to say *how foolish*, but as soon as the word was spoken, I was charged with possibility. The idea universal grammar – how humans understood and used language – had come through as a visible structure with distinct forms and parts strewn about an internal plain – like the bones of a corpse dismantled for burial, or pulled apart by animals with here and there a shorn bone or a bald knuckle – was fascinating, seductive.

Hoskin read my face and swore. "I don't know how it's happened," she said, "that I've ended up with a group of—. No, a *gaggle* of such occult—. No, a *coven* of such occult-minded fools. Seriously. It almost makes me think there is some colossal mystical mind-wedgying to turn rational people into such credulous idiots."

Laughter, soon faded. I looked at each face in turn, reading them for a prank, but they were serious. *No*, I thought, *more than serious. They were embarrassed, as if exposed as fools.*

Not Hoskin, however. She looked exasperated.

"I'm not seeing the problem," I said at last. "So what if there's something unexpected? Does it matter?"

Silence.

"The more time passes, the more the minds are drawn to these mysterious structures," she told me. "They gradually lose focus. It's happened every time, in every mind. We can't have that happen." She sat back in her chair. "So can you stay a few more days or not?" she asked. "Another mind on the problem could help."

Laughter again at the word *mind*, and again its sudden damping.

"Why don't you send him there? Into his internal field landscape thing? Send him to explore."

There was a long silence. Anwen sipped from her cup, studiously not saying anything. After she'd taken a sip, she stroked the front of the cup, twice. Len stretched, then put his hands to his head and began to massage his scalp. Tom looked at the table. He seemed bored—

"What?" I said. "What did I say?"

Hoskin took a long moment before replying. "Ichika was sent," she said quietly. "She never came back."

4.5 That night, after another long walk to clear my head, I dreamed of three black ravens in the great white can of a rock light lamp room.

5.1 Early in the morning, I woke with ankles hot with itch, and when I turned the light on an oval pip was hopping on the white sheet. I managed to grab it, squeeze it between fingers until my nails went white, but when I looked, the flea must have been protected by its shell or found refuge in a fingerprint whorl and, alive, it pinged towards me, into my hair. I stayed in the shower until Len started to swear beyond the door.

5.2 I took my coffee out onto the courtyard and stared into the countryside. There was a village down there, in a nest of trees, and to the right a wooded hill.

The morning was cool, but the sky was clear and the threat of heat was in the air. I'd felt it as a burden, the heat sitting on my mood, but today this weight had been removed. My mind was chugging along like an old tractor at the adventure – there was no other word for it – that had opened out in front of me. I could feel the excitement in my skin, in my joints and knuckles. My panic at absorbing the reality of the minds' existence had lifted with my acceptance of them, and what remained was the novelty of the experience, the thought of being among the first to be in the presence of a decanted mind, and the shock and unsettling, wonderful pleasure at being with an old friend again. And now to have a mystery, a function in this unfamiliar machine, turned my blood to gold.

I did not, however, know how to proceed. I'd inferred from Hoskin that my brain – by implication, a different type of mind to theirs – might offer insight, but I lacked the knowledge they had.

When Hoskin came out, coffee in hand, I told her I'd like to spend some time getting to know the history of what the minds claimed to see in their internal landscape. I wanted to feel my way into it until I was ready to feed back. I needed a place to start—

"You know all this," I said. "I don't. If I'm a fresh eye on this, I need to know these structures first hand, not with your prior experiences to colour it. I'd like to know how they're drawn to these places. What they themselves think of the ruins. They might have insights you haven't asked about yet. I want to know how they see. I want to know how these otherwheres are the same and how they're different."

"Don't say *otherwheres*," Hoskin said, "I hate that word in the singular but in the plural—."

"Of course." In my voice, I heard deference that betrayed my need, so newly formed, to be a working cog in this world.

"I need to put a clock on it," she said. "Three days max."

I nodded my acceptance of the terms.

That morning, in a bid to make me happier being around the minds, she put me in the schedule for the rounds. The minds didn't exist without maintenance. Supplements had to be fed into the jar, a balance had to be maintained and the by-products of the chemical process had to be leached out. She told me how the magnets still had a function in the integrity of the minds in the jars. The structure of the chain-fluid itself had to be maintained in part by magnets as there was no way to reduce vibration entirely, despite the hydraulic hut, so considerable care had to be taken when moving around them. She stripped me of all metal, and then showed me how to reach up and through the constituent parts of the exploded metal cloak surrounding each mind to reach the surface of the jars. I had to remind myself again that the jars were not the only place where the minds lived. The computers – Len – kept them alive, interpreted for them, spoke for them; without the weight of kit above and around them they were nothing but – in Hoskin's words – *posh glue*.

Once I could manoeuvre myself around the cloak, Hoskin had me apply the supplement patches to the jars – not Moonfeld's as he was too precious – and get accustomed to the routine of the mind maintenance. Each patch was applied to the area of the communicant glass that was flattest, and they functioned exactly as a nicotine patch (which Moonfeld had asked for). I felt like a tourist trying out a local cuisine or craft, but I went along with it, peeling off patches, writing the date and time, and the expiry time, on the tag. Hoskin stood behind me, approving. The patches came in strips kept in a plastic box, very different from the slick packets I'd expect of mass-produced items.

"Students make them for me," Hoskin explained.

5.3 I wasn't certain what insight I might bring to the question of why the minds were drawn to the structures in their visual fields. Moonfeld was out-of-bounds while Tom was with him so at Anwen's suggestion I decided to start with Elephant Baby. In the kitchen, she told me about the person who had been. Elephant Baby had been twenty-three when she died. I winced. I'd imagined someone middle-aged, not a child. It upset me.

"They do talk to each other," Anwen said. "I was up most of the night. Fleas. I went to the feed room and listened. I was up all night, listening. The songs they sing are too low to be picked up in the normal catch-mic, but a bit of tweaking and I could hear."

"Why doesn't Pike talk?"

She shrugged. "We assume he's gone the same way as Ichika. He didn't tell us he was going is all. He was always quiet. Distressed. I don't know. He went silent soon after Moonfeld returned. Len thinks he went into a sulk." Anwen looked uncertain before saying, "How they're talking—. Whatever they're saying—. It's before Moonfeld. Pike or Ichika must have taught the language to *him*. And when I go back to before Pike fell silent, he's the most vocal. Months ago, he sang all the time."

I could tell Elephant Baby touched Anwen in a part of her self that existed beyond the tinkering of reason or will. As she spoke of the mind, I recognised her care of Baby was protection first of all, but not the protection of a guardian for a ward, but of an older sister for a younger. There was a delicacy to the feeling she had for Baby. I couldn't place what it was, but it felt like recognition on Anwen's part that she and Baby were not equal, that the mind was less capable than she, or more easily damaged. The mind required more-than-ordinary protection. I said this to Anwen, and she nipped at me like a terrier—

"I don't pity her," she said. "Christ."

I showed her my palms in surrender. "That's not what I said. She gets to you. I don't know why, but she gets past your defences."

Anwen looked away, her annoyance vanishing as fast as breath from a window pane. "She does," she said quietly. "She kills me completely. She was twenty-three when she died. She was twenty-three, and the best of life was going to college. And then she was knackered by cancer, and while all her friends are having their puerile dramas—. Self-obsessed dramas about *why he didn't call*, whether they're *respected*, if they're *fat*—. While they're having these puerile dramas—

"God, I don't know. So she's dying, and kind of spacy anyway, and donating her body to science looks like a possibility of some kind of future. A future you can cling to a bit in advance because she might save a child's life or sight with her organs. But the last thing she expected was to be conscious. I'm not sure it was even explained to her. *To be conscious.* That just blows her mind, because however she prepared herself for death at such an age, I don't think she expected in a million years to wake up months later to be *her*. To be herself."

5.4 Tom was already in the hut when we went down. He was wearing the headphones attached to the plinth so that he could talk quietly to the mind. The speakers were turned off and he murmured into a throat mic. To his left he'd set up a flipchart that was filled with arcane symbols. He didn't spare us a look as we sat in front of Baby's jar.

In the kitchen, we'd agreed Anwen would talk to Baby alone while I remained silent. It would distract her, Anwen felt, and we'd get nothing but endless questioning about my past, my boyfriends, my travels. Anwen took a beanbag to get *comfy*. It'd never occurred to me to bring something new to the room of the minds, but the beanbag was perfect. It had a use, dictated a set of rules, behaviour. The ritual in bringing in the tools of a chat, its raiment and ornament, told of a distinct way of being in Anwen. She understood the need humans had to identify the parts of a ritual so that all knew what they were. The chair hissed like a wave retreating from pebbles when she sat on it, and Baby said the sound was loud. "Like a rainstick," she said.

Anwen rubbed her bum into the beanbag for comfort. My wooden chair hardened underneath me.

The women entered a previous conversation. A school-friend Baby had when alive – with a body – had had children early, twins. Baby had gone round, ill then, head shaved. "A friend, you know. It was hard, but it was good. Okay." The friend had showed pictures of the babies when they'd first been born, hundreds of them, and on each photograph one of the babies had been marked with an x in biro. "So she'd know who was who when they were older."

"Practical."

"Bonkers. Why would you do that?"

"So you'd know who was who when they were older."

Baby tittered. There was no other word. The sound was like an old lady pissing on porcelain. Her voice was smooth, no clips between the words. It was a world away from Moonfeld's mechanic rhythm. This was Anwen's work, I understood. She built the smoothness into the voice, and although it retained an unnatural evenness, and I suspected it would never have the colour of a human larynx, it was a real voice.

I could even intuit emotions in there. As in a conversation between two humans, there were dead spots where both were thinking of something to say. Anwen told a story of a friend who, mindful of a child's overhearing their adult conversation, had told someone to *Fuck oh eff eff*, spelling entirely the wrong word. Baby laughed, but the laughter was sad, and I couldn't for the life of me decide whether this was an aspect of the sound, or a thing my own ears brought to the exchange.

Most disconcerting was closing my eyes. The room was dim, but when I closed my eyes, I got a distinct sense of a body behind the voice. With a sense deeper than sight or touch, I knew there were *three* bodies in the inner room.

"Were you upset?" Anwen asked. "With the twins?"

"I was upset in theory." A pause. The mind seemed to take breaths between sentences. "I didn't want a child then, and not one I'd die on."

They talked on. Baby had been to India and had her head shaved at a temple and thought herself proud and brave. Later, a similar shaving left her cold and ashamed, wanting to apologise for her scalp, nude in front of strangers.

I closed my eyes again. The conversation was a normal one, too normal because I was eavesdropping on her life, her sorrow, her death, and after a time her existence in the mind jar—

"You said I was water now?"

"Yes. A form of water. Smart water."

"Haunted water."

"Yes, haunted water."

"Like a lake. High on a mountain. What are they called?"

"Tarns."

"No, that's not right. Something. It's peaceful though, in my head. Like meditation. I did meditation once. I slept. It was a guided meditation. She asked me after if I remembered this bit of it, or that bit of it, and I didn't. Spark out, I was. I'm not sure if that's a good thing or a bad thing. But I remember dreaming of water and a breeze going over it. Mist. Mist on the surface. Do you sweat when you swim?"

Anwen laughed. "Yes, I expect so."

"Isn't that grim?"

"I'm going to stop swimming now."

Baby laughed. "I know. All the sweat. But then if you do, why doesn't the water level rise? Because it must do. On a busy Saturday. You people must be able to measure it."

"You people?"

"Scientists. Boffins. Loads of people have a cheeky wee as well. Am I covered where I am?"

"Yes," said Anwen.

"You must sweat," said Baby. "You can cry. I remember crying when I was learning to swim in a lido. *Put your head under the water*, they said. It doesn't make sense you'd stop crying when your head went under, does it? No."

It was quiet. Anwen leaned forward. "It bothers you still."

The hut was silent, a looming wood in the darkness. When at last the mind spoke, she sounded distant and alone—

"I still seem to be here. But then I feel paralysed. Except I don't. Or like one of those locked-in people. But I don't."

"Jude's here," Anwen told her.

"Boy Jude." My introduction flicked a switch in tone. "What does he look like then?"

"He's funny looking. Handsome from the side but from the front it's a very low quality face."

"Thanks."

"You shouldn't listen in on girl talk."

"No, you're right—."

I lowered my head, hands loose between my knees. It was foolish, but I felt awkward, outnumbered. The two women rummaged through my life. Baby was by far the more intrusive, and the oddity of answering such questions from a gnarled jar was profound, but I answered them all. I even told her how old I was when I lost my virginity, amazing her that I knew the exact date, shocking her more when she'd worked out how old I'd been.

Gradually, Anwen introduced questions about her internal landscape. The mind described Camden Market, and a flat that looked down on it just down from the lock. It surprised me to realise Elephant Baby wasn't from the peninsula—

The Camden Lock she inhabited was deserted, but all the stalls were open – the head shops, the vintage clothes, the ethnic gear and instruments – and she could feel the rumble of a train, hear the flap of a tarp in the wind. The detail was bewildering considering it was a lived visual reality for a mind that had no eyes.

The train disturbed her. Again, I wondered what colour and tone of her voice left me in no doubt of this, but I knew. The fact of the train scared her.

She'd no idea of temperature, and the day was not wet or sunny. She could tell us no more than that, but it was clear the question was bemusing, as if the thought of the weather in her visual field was not relevant at all. She described walking among the stalls and picking things up from them, feeling their weight and texture, but not being challenged by anyone who might own them, because there was no one there. I heard – or intuited – strain in her voice, gradually increasing. It had come first when she mentioned the train, but it grew the more she faced the lack of people in her internal, self-generated visual world. Her empty landscape, filled as much as she could by memories of a happy place, selected for her by her own unconscious – her gathering mind – was still empty, and it had hardened so the contents of the market stalls never changed, no one came, no birds sang, no sirens called.

Anwen knew where Baby's unknown structure was, and she led her there through questioning. It took some time to get her to the structure, and I began to understand the winding path the team had talked about. The streets she walked down and the route she took regressed and overlapped until I was certain – if there was any logic at all to the minds' internal spaces – she must be walking the same streets she'd described minutes before, but she was not. She described them as different. The streets grew dilapidated, with rubbish on the pavements, or the houses grew tall, curtains drawn in the window and silence within. A deserted landscape.

Periodically, Baby said she could see *the tube station*, then it was gone again. When at last she reached it, the underground was on the corner of Gutter Street and Heron Street. As she described it, I realised the station she was visualising was from another era, tiled, soot-black, unlit, a metal concertina gate across the doorway. *Old.* I leaned in, eager to get every detail.

Baby moved towards the entrance. She described the narrowness of the walls, a ticket office with a window blind drawn to the bottom of the glass. There were words written on it, she said, but she couldn't read them. Anwen pressed her, asked her again and again to talk about them, describe them, but the mind started to repeat what she'd just said. Anwen had told me this denoted strain. Baby denied the words were in the English alphabet—

"It's just pick-up sticks. The writing looks like pick-up sticks."

Other details were familiar. A tube map on the wall, oddly less detailed than a modern one. Fly posters for bands. Litter. Again, I heard the off note, as I had when she'd mentioned the rumble of the underground train. It set my skin on alert. *Where did that sound come from if there was no possibility of a reality that was not entirely known to her?* A popcorn bucket, drink cans, a green tobacco wallet, a biro, the wax handkerchiefs that wrap burgers, the tube lint that forms felt ropes in corners—

Anwen led her to a spiral staircase leading down to the trains. She led her to the lip of the first step, and encouraged her to look down into the well. I heard the fracture now in the mind's voice. Words no longer connected to sense, and her repetition of how dark it was became more mechanic.

"I don't want to go on the steps," Baby said. "I don't want to go on the steps. Not those steps."

She began repeating a word or words I couldn't understand.

Anwen called a halt. "Come back home," she told her.

At once, Baby was back in her imagined flat, as if she'd been at the station at the very limits of an elastic band, and the release had snapped her back in a moment, but she was still disoriented, still lost from the trip to the top of the steps.

"Sorry to do that to you," I said. "I wanted to know."

"Jude," said the mind. "Boy Jude or girl Jude?"

5.5 "What was that?" I asked. "That's what you meant when you said a structure? That's a tube station."

"We've taken her farther," Anwen said, defensive.

"Into what? I heard she was upset but—." I stopped. "I don't understand. That was nothing."

"It becomes clearer when you hear how the structures are the same according to different minds. We said from the start they're interpretations of a feature that shouldn't be there in the mind. And she's a kid. That's how she interpreted it. For Moonfeld—. Our guess is the less experience a person has, the more altered the appearance of the structure, so she's tried to fill the void with anything. Moonfeld's starker."

"What was she saying at the end?"

"*It's an old dark.*"

The words intrigued me. We were outside, in the sun of an unusually hot summer, but I felt the words as a change in the air, in the heat of the day. *It's an old dark.* I laughed despite myself, as if I'd been tickled.

"She didn't know me at the end," I said.

"It really fries her. And Moonfeld. Hoskin's terrified that that's what happens. That that's what happened to Ichika. A final frying and the mind's lost. If this is a feature of them all, that's her project down the loo."

"Is Elephant Baby always frightened?"

Anwen thought for a second. "She seems more frightened when I question her. If she is drawn there and she tells me about it later—. No, I don't think so."

I was beginning to sweat. It was unpleasant, but to waste the sunshine was criminal. I shook my shirt.

"I don't know what I'm supposed to do," I said at last.

"Just think and tell us your thoughts."

I nodded, looked off to the bleak countryside that led away up the hill. I'd forsworn shoes for a day now. One heel was absently scratching my ankle. It was pretty country, I thought. The thought of spending longer here – walking, reading, engaging in the insanity of talking to the long-dead – was attractive. *It's an old dark.* To stay here in the sun, getting my mind into a problem like a spade into spring soil, made me alive with possibility. Anwen saw this.

"Stop itching your bites," she told me. "You'll infect."

5.6 As he'd often joked, Moonfeld wasn't in his first pressing as a mathematician, but he'd held his faculties long, and his work on the cruciate ridge was minor but important. My endorsement of the mind put a tick by a number of concepts Tom had had doubts about because the mathematics did not align with what had been previously understood about the ridge. This unlocked such a storm of progress I had little time with Moonfeld on the first day. I had to wait while Tom nailed the maths into his understanding. Strangely, I missed my friend. It was hard to say out loud, even though I knew Anwen would understand what I meant.

It was late afternoon when Tom finally surfaced from the hut. I was anxious to go down to talk to Moonfeld alone, but the lad cornered me at the bottom of the steps. I'd noticed at mealtimes that he felt I should be kept in the mathematical loop, even when I'd told him I didn't understand a word. Now he went into it again, the flipchart under one of his arms knocking on the banister—

There was an anchorage to the ridge, Tom told me, and a hypothesis that a set of numbers termed *gravid* numbers underpinned the ridge. Tom had a habit of using a term, like *underpinned*, then disavowing it as accurate. I remembered Moonfeld being just as irritating. The problem was that no one knew how or if the cruciate ridge, which was in textbooks now, was tied to this unseen, unplotted, possibly imaginary lower anchorage—

"—but it's not a lower anchorage, you understand. It's just the term we use. Think of it as the bones of a tent. We feel our way down the guy ropes to where the pegs enter the ground. It's not a tent. They're not pegs. But the material of the guys is unknown and they don't head in one direction. *Direction* doesn't mean what you think it means. Think of a tent anchored in a human kidney subject to inverted torsion about—."

"No. I refuse. Tom, for god's sake."

Tom looked at me as if I were joking. "Okay?"

"I don't understand what you're saying. It means less than nothing to me." I smiled to cut the sting. "You don't have to tell me."

Tom raised his free hand to ward me off. "Okay," he said.

5.7 The minds' internal landscapes were without comparison for an ordinary human, and the more I thought about the way they saw, the more alien it seemed. I couldn't picture an internal space; it had no corollary with how I saw objects, concepts. In the night, I tried to imagine what this might look like by closing my eyes but got nothing. No space, no landscape, only the harissa paste of closed-eyed-ness.

Moonfeld helped me understand that the place the minds inhabited came from memories. The place had the characteristics of terrain, but the minds couldn't move around this landscape in a physical way because they had no corporeal presence with which to move. What moved was the landscape around the central hub of the mind itself.

These landscapes came most clear to me when Moonfeld spoke of how he came to return. The mechanics of a mind rebuilding itself was fascinating. Moonfeld remembered – they all remembered – a physical process that stood in front of whatever process had occurred in the matter-seeded chain-fluid. For Moonfeld, his earliest memory after delivery was going over and over the formula for non-convex polyhedra. He said it was like taking LSD, that same endlessly iterative thought process. He built Euler's gem in his mind and when the model was complete, his mind was complete—

"My second primal scream was refusing to accept a minus two value for the cubohemioctahedron."

"Well, it would be—."

Yet he said he'd no memory of constructing this internal landscape. It happened without him, beyond him, before him. Nothing was unknown about it – his internal landscape was clearly the children's home he'd been in as a boy – but it was situated in the Fallen Woods, a favourite haunt of Helen's and miles away in actuality. The places the minds inhabited internally were real, but plucked and gathered elsewhere, a collage of true places, exactly like a dream, with a dream's structure and reality.

Perhaps, I thought, *in the wandering of the delivered mind, in the laying down of memories, the same logic and order of sleep was being replicated, and the gathering of the mind was a months-long dream culminating in waking.*

The process was the same for all, Moonfeld told me. Elephant Baby came back to awareness because she 'remembered' moving house. *All those boxes needing to be unpacked.* The symbolism was so transparent as to be almost inexistent. When she'd unpacked, she was herself entire in her Camden Town flat. The historian Ichika returned through replaying old war campaigns to inhabit a battlefield. Pike had returned to the council offices where he used to work.

"God, that's sad."

"Describe this place for me," Moonfeld said.

I did so, talking Moonfeld through the layout of the farmhouse from the pool at the bottom to the hayloft at the top. It was hard to describe a path, and even harder to visualise what was being narrated. Hoskin had said something similar. *The way to the tip or your mother's house.*

"There is no substitute for sight."

"An economy that infects the modern world," I said.

"Meaning?"

"Well, in computing. There's an economy people assume from file sizes now. Value is assigned to information's weight. A picture takes megabytes of data to transmit but a novel you can send in an e-mail. People assign worth in the same way, and it leads to a devaluation of the complexities of the written word in favour of the simplicity of pictures. Everything gets thumbed down into the stupid."

"Hasn't a picture always been worth a thousand words?"

"Well—."

"Since antiquity?"

"Fuck off, John." I laughed. "*That* felt familiar."

"I would like to hear more about this place, Jude."

"Like what?"

"Anything. I have never seen it, after all."

I didn't know where to start, but decided to go with the aspect of the house that was nearest to my memory. The fleas. I told him of the cat so stoned from the flea medication she was usually found sunk in mog sloth in the sun outside, no use as a poisoned well to anyone. I told him of the misery of it, the athletic little bastards at my ankles, behind my knees, occasionally on my upper arms. When first I'd caught one, moaning *Oh, no, no, no* like a child, I'd let it wander out of my grip. For some reason I'd thought the flea would have honour, and once caught accept its fate, but it didn't. It nipped off and left me blind with fury. This flea I hated individually, I told Moonfeld, because it was the first chitinous criminal I'd found. The only other evidence had been the bites, each centred on a wick of itch that started to burn before dawn until I was raking hard-skin heels against the soft skin of my shins.

"I meant the equipment. The stuff. The air of the place."

It made me think. "Like the arts annexe at the college," I said. "That air of artsy teachers with their rivets a little loose. A sense of makeshift, make-do."

"In a town? A university?"

I was surprised. "God, no. This is a converted farmhouse. We're in the middle of nowhere."

"What are you sitting on?"

"A wooden chair. Do you want to know what I'm wearing as well?"

"Black jeans and a collarless shirt." A pause. "I'm right, aren't I?"

"No one here likes you, John."

Moonfeld was interested in everything, the chairs, the tables, the hut, where the team lived, the contents of the rooms. The team had never told the mind where he was, and when he'd asked, they'd dodged the question. The most they had ever allowed him was that he was *in a safe environment.*

Now he had an eager snitch and I described the strange machines in the medical room upstairs and the feed room. I described, described, described, aware of the fact the tables had been turned and it was the mind who should be talking to me, but it didn't bother me. I imagined it was the first time Moonfeld had ever been allowed to talk in the same way Elephant Baby talked to Anwen. Hoskin and Tom clearly drew him back to task over and again, refusing to be deflected. I had an image of a working dog's nose being forced back to the entrance of a warren.

Learn your place, your role.

"No substitute for eyes," I said.

"No," Moonfeld said. "But it is good to have your voice. To hear your voice. I feel there is someone here with my interests first. If there is a divorce, you must ask for custody."

I didn't laugh. There was an odd note in what the mind had said, and I felt embarrassed. I took another road—

"Why did you ask about my chair?"

The mind didn't speak for a moment. "The machines are new and the chairs are old."

"Thank you. That's very clear."

"There is no money here, Jude. I asked about the place to assess the level of money that had been thrown at this. The truth is that I am not important. I have an interest to them, but I am only a step on the way to the minds they want to preserve. Chairs dragged from elsewhere in the house suggest it is an early step." He paused. "It is a daunting thought, really. Have you thought about all the implications? You should think about the legal implications. And the academic implications. The minds they are working towards preserving. Have they been approached? You know who they are. You know some of their names. I am a small fish, Jude."

The image of the goldfish won at a giant's fair came to mind again. I looked around the hut. Moonfeld was right. I was sitting on a chair from the kitchen. The computer desk looked like an old school desk, and one of the wall tablets had a cartoon sticker in the corner of the screen. Now it had been mentioned, I saw cheapness everywhere. A folded piece of paper under a table-leg, mismatched mouses, stencilled property marks from different institutions on the kit, a sure sign of a *beg, borrow, or steal* ethos. I recalled Anwen tinkering away with the tongue units, making them work by collating bits from units in different states of disrepair to make a good one. The patches were not made in a factory but by students. The equipment that was most expensive was also the equipment that could be picked up and reassigned wholesale. Nothing extra had been budgeted for, nothing for the humans, certainly. The facility looked the part, but just under the surface it was makeshift and make-do.

The rooms had fleas.

"Hmm."

"My thoughts exactly," said Moonfeld.

The moment grew long. I knew I should leave as it was getting late, but I didn't want to go. Only slight gains in my understanding had been won, and I'd asked barely a question about *the structure*. Framing that question was hard, for it felt as if I was working up to a request for a favour or money, a question that would make Moonfeld a resource more than a support.

I wanted a concrete thing from my friend, something of substance, of meaning, a question to keep the conversation going or to give me an exit. The only thing I could think of was to ask if he'd any regrets—

"I suppose I do," the mind replied. "A few. In retrospect, not many. And not worth the mention. What I had to do, I did, and I saw it through without exemption. If there was a course to chart—."

"Are you narrating *My Way*? Like William Shatner? You monumental idiot. How did your capacity for acting the tit come through intact?"

5.8 Anwen had suggested asking to look at Lenford's sketch-books. "He's an artist," she explained. Len had spent a lot of time with the structures, sketching the descriptions teased out of the minds. "He was trying to give them form, give us ideas. Most are from Moonfeld's feeds, but he also listened to Elephant Baby. There's even a few of Mr Charisma himself."

I found Len in his lair, the machine room above the swimming pool. It was an open room with a wide doorway, clearly once a pantry of sorts as it had an enormous sink for laundry, yet they'd contrived to make the entrance as narrow as possible with a three-stack of monitors against the jamb, obviously obsolete from the giant monitors on the walls. Loops of wires hung from nails hammered into the lintel beams, plugs low so I'd to duck to get into the room. Even within the room the work stations were behind stacks of unopened boxes. I'd seen it in tech. rooms everywhere. *Block the entrance to the cave, bewilder and deceive.* Inside, there were almost no places to put feet safely; the masters of the cleanest symbols in language – the 0, the 1 – lived in landfill.

When I peered round the boxes, I had a shock. There was a man there, young. "Oh," I said.

He gave me the barest look, the barest vocalisation.

Len picked it up. "Samuel," he explained. "He monitors the stream-feed and the life signs."

"Samuel does," said Samuel.

I'd never seen the man, not at meals, outside the bathroom or on his way to bed. He looked to be physically part of his seat, wedged in with the permanence of one placed there when young and malleable then grown into place.

"Life signs?" I said with a grandpa eagerness to learn that I hated as soon as I'd spoken. Samuel was sighing before I'd finished, exasperation coming off him like heat.

"The organic parts of the mind," Len told me. "The matter in the chain-fluid. It has cycles, rhythms. We're trying to calibrate so we've a data bank to build on. The brain waves they generate aren't like normal so we're starting from scratch. We don't know if we're measuring engines at rest, or racing so hard they're about to spunk their spark plugs." Samuel gave him a slow, strong look. "Sorry, Sam. Poor phrasing."

"He barely sleeps," Len explained outside. He shrugged. "I interpret for him. I'm the conduit so he can stay hidden. Truth is, without him and Anwen there's no communication with the bellies at all."

"Right."

"What did you want?"

"Anwen said you'd made sketches of the structures. I wondered if I might see them."

Len nodded, took me to his room. He was upstairs in the farmhouse so presumably free from fleas. His books were on his dresser. He waved a hand in their direction.

I flipped through the books looking at Len's images of the structures the minds described. There were pages of false starts and increasingly savage erasures, one with coffee. Yet within, I saw a shape or two that was repeated, like a motif, or a doodler's go-to scrawl. On page after page there were *c* shapes, one mirrored, almost touching at the arm ends, like the barest representation of hands, or horseshoes forming an oval.

There were spirals, thick blocks of ink, and a structure that looked like the game of Jenga, which Len had drawn grain lines into to look like wood. Fan blades. *No, not fan blades*, I realised, for as they went round the hub, they got smaller. I was looking at a screw from the end on. *No, a screw made out of bristles*. I turned the page, and it was there again. The screw, this time bigger, with more meat to the blades and a definite closing to a *v* the nearer the blade got to the hub.

It was a spiral staircase seen from above.

"How do you do these?"

"Don't. It's impossible. I draw what they say like a police artist, but I can't show it back to them to see if it's right, so I *describe* it back to see if it's right, but of course they can't tell me if it's right because they can't see it. It's like, *The bear went over the mountain to see what he could see.* And you know what? *The only thing that he could see was the other side of the mountain. So the bear went over the mountain to see what he could see—.* Madness."

I smiled. "This is all real to them."

Len nodded. "You get a sense of their belief. It's what's so disturbing. When people are describing something that they're seeing rather than imagining, you *know*, right? It's fascinating, but in practice, hour after hour, it got pretty tedious." He rolled off the bed, took the book from my hand. "Mostly it's a repeated image. Or I think it's a repeated image. There's enclosures. One shape seemed to be one shape made up of tiny other shapes." He flipped through the book and pulled out a thick sheet of printing paper. "I did this with a paperclip dipped in Camp Coffee. I bent it into the shape I saw, then dropped it onto a zinc plate in the pattern of the bigger shape. I etched the line with copper sulphate and then—."

"There's more than one structure that they're seeing."

Len grunted. "It's odd but I dream these shapes now." He picked up another book. "Look at Elephant Baby's. This is hers. This is what she thinks is in Mornington Crescent, or wherever the hell she is. It's a spiral, and to me it looks like this—." He picked up the book where he'd drawn Moonfeld's descriptions. In it was another, similar shape. "He said to go right, go left, curve, et cetera. I tried to do it aerially. There's even one of Pike's. Again, similar. Significant or not, I've no idea. Say you took the post-it pads from ten people's work desks, chances are you'd see similarities among the shapes they doodle."

"That's the muscles in a human hand, surely? The limits of the pad. Letters, symbols curve inwards because that's the way the hand is."

Len didn't look convinced. "Anyway," he said. "They don't have hands. If they did, this would go a lot quicker."

He opened one of the books that had an aerial view of the terrain of Moonfeld's visual field, what he saw. There was the fan structure, paths that meandered, and towards the edge, at the limits of the page, a circle made up of fat blobs of ink. All over the picture, Len had made notes.

"These are the paths. He speaks of them as always leading away from the structures, but they don't. They approach and then go away. Look at it. It's higgledy-piggledy. But beyond that there's a pattern I can't quite see but I know is there."

I said, "Did you ever see that footage of the cats with GPS collars? The map of where they travelled looks just like this. A labyrinth."

"Talk about Theseus's thread." Len paused. "Moonfeld is outdoors when he travels, in woodland, but there are points on the path where he sees giant stones."

"Stones."

"He says. That's his interpretation. I mapped out the stone paths on the next page." He turned the page. It showed only the paths. "What does that look like?"

"A brain," said I.

Len traced the whorls of the path with a finger. "It's what I see too. The stem, an internal structure, curves in an endless loop. Spirals."

"Mazes have always resembled brains though."

"I guess." He paused. "Don't let Hoskin hear this. It drives her up the wall. She thinks we're seeing the fleas in a flea circus." Len got out another pad. "This is Ichika—."

He explained when Ichika first began to stray toward the ruins in her mind, only Anwen cared. The assumption of everyone else was that there was a glitch in the mind, and the track she was walking with a doped persistence was like a record whose needle jumped the groove. She never reached the centre, but never recalled this the next time she found herself drawn to the ruins on her battlefield, and no one took her seriously as she was the first to come back, the first to cohere into a functioning mind. There was no pattern.

Len flipped through the book pointing out sketches he'd made from when Anwen was questioning Ichika about what she saw—

"Ichika's a very *present* person," he said. "She sees the world clearly. She's a woman of nature. So she talks of these paths she'd walk again and again as *salt paths* she's trodden into the earth. In her internal mind-world, she's trying to reach a circular stone structure, a *ruin*, as she calls it, and the loops and crescents never quite reach this ruin. They circle it and get near it, but never get there.

"Anyway, these lines I made blacker the more she said she walked them, and you get the brain image again. Thick lines towards the outside, thinner the more they reach the centre, because those are the paths she was on the least. At least as far as I could tell from the feed recording."

Feed recording, I thought. "This looks familiar."

It did. There was a kinship among the images. I wasn't convinced it wasn't something that came about from four blind people describing the one elephant, but I saw something between the pictures that transcended the differences. I also no longer thought it looked like a brain – a brain looks like a tree looks like a fingerprint looks like a rose – but more architectural. Ichika's word *ruins* rang with special resonance. To me, the images looked like aerial views of ruins. In the corner was an image that looked like a cluster of cells. I put a finger by a word in the corner of the page. *Meiro*, scrawled.

"This looks familiar," I said again.

"Yes," Len replied. He ran his finger down from the forward *v* of the cell cluster. "I see an edge here. Like it's a three-d cuboid. A tower. In the top is a hole." He circled with his little finger, his hand open. "A well? I don't know. These shapes—." He rounded the *c* shapes with that same delicate finger, not touching the page. "I don't know."

The suggestion of an edge made the sketch grow from the page, and in doing so nudged a memory loose.

"*Meiro*. What is that word?"

"Ichika kept saying it. It came through as English. *May he row.* Once Anwen nailed down what she was saying, it was *meiro*. It means *labyrinth*." Len paused. "That's what I mean by patterns. To me, looking at the phenomenon from a distance, it's clear four different people are describing the same thing. Moonfeld even uses the same word. *Labyrinth*.

"Have you heard of the image control and recognition task? I'll do it with you." He gave me a pen and turned the sketchbook over. "Draw a rectangle. On top of the rectangle, draw a semicircle. Draw a line cutting the semicircle in half. From the top of the semicircle, draw a wiggly line upwards. What have you drawn?"

"I don't know. A tampon?"

"No. *What?* It's a computer mouse." He checked I'd drawn the right thing. "See, you got it wrong. Often people draw things contrary to what they hear. The image control and recognition test is all about how you interpret words into images, but also how the mind recognises images when it can't see them. The point is that the image remains the same, but how we *process* the image in language is different according to the person." He turned the book over. "These are described as paths leading nowhere, or doubling back. The bellies talk of central places in their mind they've never seen before, and these places all have similar features. One, they're hard to reach. Two, they're built on spirals. Three, there are markers. And four, they lead inwards and down."

I stared at Len for a long moment, the intellectual tickle starting up again.

"That's where Ichika went."

"That's where she went. Closer and closer. And one day, silence. That's what Hoskin fears. Not for Pike or Baby or Ichika. She doesn't care about them. But for Moonfeld? That scares her."

5.9 Len made me some copies of pages from his books. The nudge I'd received from one of them came good, and I spent the early evening researching, pairing images, taking notes.

When I was finished, I spent a long time looking at one particular picture of Len's. It excited me. Although I kept telling myself it was illusory – all abstract pictures look the same to some extent – I believed I was looking at an ancient piece of art, a design painted on cave rock, chipped from stone, scratched into sand with a stick.

There were spirals, suggestions of hands, blades and figures. They could have been doodles, but they weren't doodles. There was intent behind them, and more than that, meaning. It was the same feeling I'd had when first seeing the four minds in the hut. Not random shapes but shapes whose appearance was informed by a consciousness. The page was taken from a sketch-book, but I saw it as an image from a cave wall.

One part of the drawing – the tower – was particularly attractive. It looked like the solid square-dimpled block known as a *cong*. The design was found all over Chinese architecture, ceramics and art, stretching back into prehistory, but its meaning was not fully known. The more I looked at it, the more that flat image rose from the page to make the rectangular block fatten and adhere to the classic shape of the *cong*. The shape drew me in.

I kept it to myself. It was Len's turn to cook, and Tom explained he typically used his night as a stick to beat the taste buds of the team into submission. This night it was chicken served with coleslaw made with red cabbage, mangoes and apple, coriander chopped in by the fistful. The chicken came with a black crust so hot it was like biting into a piece of coal that had just lost its colour from the fire, and the meat beneath was stained deep by the marinade. It left every one of us a weeping, snot-drooled horror.

The meal had been served late, and it was dark by the time we finished. The last few nights had been heavy with wine, so I stuck to tea. I waited for the culinary wounds to heal outside, feeling a breeze at last, when Anwen found me. "It's the witching hour," she said. "I promised you a spooking."

The pool was normally kept dim for the minds. At night, it was close to pitch black, and the lack of light seemed to affect the acoustics. I heard Anwen's breathing up close, animal, as if a cat was investigating my sleeping ear. She insisted we use the deep-end ladder, which was giddying. I might have been descending into a bottomless pit. My foot hitting the mattress at the bottom was a shock, but my shock was subject to the enforced whispers darkness dictates so came out as a strangled yelp that sent Anwen into laughter above me. In the deep end, the acoustics were even more unworldly, creating the briefest echo before the sound fell dead.

As my eyes adjusted, I made out the shapes of the glass jars. It was the part of the pool where the silent minds sat so most were uniform cylinders, the faint phosphorescence of the chain-fluid making them distinct in the blackness of the deep end. As my sight adjusted to the dark, my eyes were drawn to those jars subject to the twist of a gathering-but-failed consciousness and the chill came again, beading the sweat on my skin. Just then, behind one of these odd jars, a core of light flashed, illuminating the tiles beyond but also the chain-fluid within, which shone with a powerful diamond glow. As the glow faded to a flicker, Anwen moved into view. She was lighting tea-lights and putting them behind the jars. Her smile looked wicked in the candlelight. She lit another, nudging its tin cup behind the jar.

"Come on," I whispered. She giggled, low. There was no one to hear us, but still we whispered. "Was it you who put the jars in a circle?"

Anwen shook her head, came from the back of the minds. The candles erased the light from elsewhere, so all I could see were the candles through the fluid. For the first time the fluid in the glass looked other than water. A part of me had always doubted its special properties, but now the flame was visibly fat, fatter than light refracted through water would usually have been, and there were moments when the flame seemed to pixellate in its flicker.

Anwen pulled me to the floor of the pool – *the bottom of the pool* wasn't the right term for an empty pool, I thought – and settled me on one of her beloved beanbags. She nudged me round until I was facing two normal jars – *Nothing, no one*, she'd said – and to their right, a jar that had buckled like the skin of an arm subjected to a twist.

"Can you say Chinese Burn nowadays?" I whispered.

"Probably not," she replied. "I know what you mean though. Look at the jars."

My eye was drawn more to the jar with the twist in it than the others. I told myself it was because it was a more interesting shape, and the flame bit the contours in a more hypnotic way, almost licking up the inner surfaces of the glass, but I knew this wasn't the reason. It was because there was nothing in the untwisted jars, and my mind somehow knew this. Yet she'd assured me there was nothing in the twisted jar either. Connections, a kink, a tightening in the chain-fluid as mechanic as a spanner, but nothing approaching the first seed of the first thought of consciousness.

"It never returned," she whispered. "It's not going to sing *Daisy Bell* to you. Yet you can sense it, can't you? The *something there*."

I could. I thought of the first image I'd had when told of chain-fluid, a transparent metal snake coiled so tight there was no air in the jar. The twist-jar was filled with clear *snake*, and somewhere within, equally transparent and therefore invisible, were metal snake eyes watching, and the conviction I'd had as a child – that snakes had eight eyes like a spider, spread in the same pattern – returned and cooled me to zero all over.

In the jar with the shallow twist, I thought the lack of coherent mind didn't remove the image of a snake but instead made the snake simpler, shorter, two turns round the glass. The ones in the warm hut were composed of infinitely long chains and links, thin as whips but coiled equally as tight. *Slime eels*, I thought, recalling a grim scene from a book where an eel erupted from a corpse pulled from Arctic waters. The thought broke a dream, Elephant Baby charming the snake from a jar with her nursery rhyme.

I told Anwen. She said, "You told me. You've the weirdest but most literal dreams. Is it you who's eating all the cheese?"

She smiled, kind, and I tried to return it but I was too disturbed by the twist. *A spanner needs a hand to wield it*, I thought. *The spanner doesn't move without the hand.*

I trusted there was no mind in the jar – it was in the team's interest to be certain of this, after all – but the *something there* affected me on a profound level. It took a long while for me to place how it disturbed me, and eventually it came. I felt squeamish, as if I were watching an eye operation, or a nail were being torn upwards from its finger like the bonnet of a car.

And the light——.

The light in the untouched jars was unusual, but was as inert as in lava lamps; the light in the other jar was animate, falling down into the twist, rolling over some transparent gravel that lined the crook of the twist. The sight sickened me, but what sickened more was the knowledge there were others behind, the unformed ones, the ones whose returning consciousness had exerted a little grip but not enough to form themselves. It touched me at the base, the core, of the injustice I felt strongest about – unfairly as the analogy was so different – that these silent minds were a crowd of silent dunces outside the lecture hall. They pushed into my mind namesake-Jude gazing at the distant spires of Christminster, or the mushrooms gasping for light in the disused County Wexford shed.

These images were fanciful, false, but I couldn't then shake the thought I was sat in a field of tubular mushrooms, mute but alive. *And they would hear our noise*, I thought. The minds might have had the tongues tugged out from the base units, but they were not insulated from sound as the minds in the hut were. Every sound made in the cavern of an old pool was conducted into the glass. If there was anything in the jars, it would have been driven mad.

I wondered about the structure of a mind. Whether completeness imparted consciousness, or if the threads of mind that had put the twist to the jar had had their own small moment of mind. *Perhaps*, I thought, *a memory had come through entire*. The muscle memory for an exquisite passage from Satie, the notes, sequence and restraint built in. Or a less pretentious, mundane muscle memory. Tossing a coin or flipping a pancake. I didn't know why I thought of a memory as having a completeness to itself, as if *the ability to ride a bike* was floating whole in a jar in a remote peninsular farmhouse, like a chunk of meat remaining torn in the water after a shark attack, but I kept returning to the knowledge something had put the jar to the twist. *There'd been strain in there, the drawing tight of some elemental drawstring—*

"I need to get out of here."

I left her to it. As I climbed the ladder out, the lights behind me winked out one by one as Anwen extinguished the tea-lights. I waited for her near the stairs up to the farmhouse, and explained to her how creepy I'd found it to be there. I was angry with her, strangely, and later thought this anger was because I imagined she'd gained a thrill from the place – like a visit to the reptile house – which was how I'd understood her original offer of *a spooking*, yet she didn't defend herself, or look guilty. As I told her how disturbed I'd been, my mind worked on what I'd seen in the pool. Her grin might not have been wicked but shame-faced, her laughter nerves not frolic. She stared at me levelly until I understood this—

"I'm preaching to the choir," I said at last.

"I wanted someone else to know. But I couldn't just tell you. For Hoskin, for Tom—. For all of them, those minds are like revision copies of a document kept until someone makes the decision to destroy them. But you know what? They may never do that. They're just as likely to end up sold to some rich weirdo in America. *A mind's in that jar, don't you know?*"

"I'm sure that's not how Americans speak."

She didn't laugh, but her mood relented. "They might end up on a shelf in a study, or as part of some wanky artist's latest tug session." She hesitated. "They've relatives. Every one of them. There are people who loved them. Somewhere there are people alive who loved them."

5.10 In my bedroom, I was desolate. Anwen's *spooking* had shaken me hard. I felt as if my mood had been kicked down the cellar stairs, too broken to climb back up. I couldn't bear the thought of being bitten again so sprayed the room with *R.I.Flea* and put my head out of the window while the fumes cleared.

On the desk by the window, I saw the picture of the *cong* and Len's image side by side. The shapes were beginning to work on my mind, pulling together disparate strands from books and literature I'd read years before, almost back to my teens.

God, I was tired, and the sheen of sweat from the heat of the night felt as if I'd been run through a laminator. When at last I slept, I dreamt I was swimming in the sea with a whale singing Arvo Pärt's setting of *My Heart Is in the Highlands*.

6.1 I was still out-of-sorts the next morning. Anwen was working – I'd risen late – and the only person in the kitchen was Hoskin. "Aren't you with Tom?" I asked, a stupid question.

"Left him to it. I'm not a mathematician. There are times I'm in the way. You have to know your limits." She paused, waving a spoon. "This thing with the minds. It can't diminish our time with Moonfeld. It's not why we're here."

"I understand that."

"The vital thing is to neutralise whatever draws the minds from the here and now. To take it away. But above all, don't tar it with some allure. For the minds or for the team. Some of them are—." She waggled her fingers, which I took to denote *touchy-feely*. She might as well have said, *Some of them are Anwen*. "We don't want to lose them as we lost Ichika, but also we don't want to alienate them. You may have noticed, but we don't have much of a lever with them."

"You can't torture them. You have no ways of making them talk."

"You're funny. And beware of speculation. Some theories—. Speed is important, but so is respecting the work Tom has to do with Moonfeld. I know we need to fix this drift-to-the-weird for future deliveries, but it's secondary. We've only a finite time with them."

This last sentence I failed to hear the significance at the time. *Finite* implied a clock ticking, and I'd assumed a form of immortality—

Later in the morning, I asked oracle Anwen about the question of longevity, and she explained chain-fluid was *a worked fluid*, and it would fail. The fluid would gum up, or lock. The minds wouldn't know anything was happening, and it would take time, but they'd gradually age.

She grinned. "Did you think they were immortal?" I lied and said I hadn't thought about it. She was not fooled. "Cariad," she said.

I felt foolish, and it stung deep, and I still wore my waking mood so was in no state to see the humour. I took my tea outside, deaf to her apologies, partly as she could barely articulate them for her laughter.

6.2 Len's drawings, and particularly the linocuts, had stayed in my mind. There was no doubting the kinship between the different minds' descriptions of the structures. Yet I suspected there was also a common ancestry with the markings in ancient myths and artefacts. I didn't know how much weight to give to the way these thoughts had fed off each other.

Neither did it escape me that the notion of common ancestry was at the heart of the problem. The strange ruins in the mental landscape, constructed in all particulars by the minds themselves, had the same features: spirals, closed spaces, winding paths and the suggestion (the suggestiveness) of the word *labyrinth*.

As a young man, I'd been fascinated with theories that the roots of religion could be traced back to the earliest human minds, where symbols and structures recognisable in religions today had forebears in the lives of cave people. The truth of the theories was the least important part: simply thinking about them again fired my thoughts, and my imagination burned with an anthracite intensity.

I sat in the garden and thought, a notebook beside me to scribble down ideas. The first nudge of the images Len showed me reminded me of that long-lost reading, and when I concentrated on simply allowing my thoughts to wander, up from the deep came details of those old books, slowly coming together. Phrases I recalled lit me with possibility. I believed in my core that there were concepts that were set to resonate in the human mind, and if this were universal, why would this not be true of symbols, of belief?

Those phrases and words lifted out of my deep memory like squid from the deep dark. *Markers. Stones. Labyrinth.* Other words from specific reading. *The milk-yielding tree.* They upped the tick on my heartbeat.

Science's damping of that tick had always dismayed me. I knew intellectually an idea or phrase was unlikely to denote or describe a true and measurable *thing*, but that the concept of *labyrinth* had a meaning and depth visible to two different humans at all seemed to be of sufficient wonder to be pursued.

I've no doubt I was being fanciful, but I was pleasurably seduced by my scribbled idea that symbols and shapes were like musical notes, and a few lay on harmonics that resonated perfectly with the human mind.

Seduced was the right word. There was seduction in the words used by the minds. *The grave of the bone. The well. The salt path.* They put me into a state of profound excitement; the terms alone delighted me, as if a funny bone of the imagination had been knocked on the jamb of a door. I became locked into a conviction an idea was at least persuasive enough to consider. This idea was that what had come through as an artefact in the minds was an understanding of the ancient human brain.

6.3 Late morning, I went to talk to Moonfeld. It was precautionary, I thought, as I expected the mind to mock me.

I told him the idea the structures could be symbols in the deep brain, not so much visual reconstructions of physical functions – *Meat processes*, I called them, an unfortunate phrasing – but tied to the essential parts of human perception, interpretation and imagination. The structures – whether part of the collective unconscious or not – were a buried element of human mind that existed somewhere hidden in the modern brain and came through in clear on delivery.

I expected derision. It didn't come. Instead, Moonfeld said it was interesting. "*Interesting,*" I said.

"It is not the best word."

"Is it also *nice*? Is it also—?"

"You have kept your sarcasm, Jude."

I paused. "What do you mean *kept*? I'm not the one who's dead."

Three laughs. They were less abrasive, evidence of Anwen at the tinker. A human-ness was present now, overlaying the mechanic bark.

"I keep thinking of your picture of the home. The photo. You drew on it, over and over."

"I do not know why I did that. It was not a conscious act. The later changes were boredom. Not passive boredom. Active. Boredom with the picture itself so I altered it. I assumed I would one day see it and know it was no longer needed. That never happened."

"Why did you change it the first time?"

A long pause. "My experience in the home was part of me. But the picture got old. I think it needed to be updated to reflect how I still was in the home. That sounds dramatic. I recall being told that I had put it behind me. Helen said that. *You have put it behind you.* Is that not a strange statement? *You have put it behind you.* When I thought about it I realised why it sounded off. The fear cannot *not* be part of me. It would be like putting the kitchen in a house behind the house. *I put the staircase behind me.* Nonsense. That time of fear happened when I was too young, and I grew around it. You can't make a bonsai grow tall and straight after it's been bent into shape."

"You said you no longer fear."

I wanted more than anything to hear that this was true. To fear without the possibility of fleeing was the worst thing I could imagine. It was cruelty, torment; it was burial alive.

Moonfeld didn't answer. "I do not sleep, but I have fugue states. When I come out of them, I do not know where I am. It was the same when I awoke in life after a dream. My first belief was that I was back in the home. The dread clutch. It is entrapment. That is not the right word, but it will do for now. But because I am here, locked into a confined space, I reach for the last time that was true, which is the terror of the home, but there is no fear now. What would that be? Panting? Increased heart rate? Adrenalin? None of those things are possible. I am not frightened," he said, "but still I fear. It's the old fear of the home that never went away. A dark place of shadows."

The speech then broke up into a whining screech, nails on a blackboard filtered through a voice disguiser, so loud it was painful. I swore and covered my ears.

"Sorry," said Moonfeld. "I was singing the *Twilight Zone* music. Did that not come through?"

I swore ornately. "That godawful noise—." I asked Moonfeld what he thought the structures were. "*Labyrinth markers. The grave of the bone.* You must have some idea."

"I do not, Jude. This is why it unsettles. It is as peculiar as finding I have a tail, or I have woken up as a frog. No, more like finding I have another voice in my head."

I considered this before it struck me this could not be true.

"There's no way you haven't formulated some theory to explain this. Not you. Not Mr. Topology."

A laugh. "I admit it occurred to me that the internal shape of the skull limits the growth of the brain. When the mind was gathering in these jars, the physical aspect of the skull was missing so part of the reorganisation of the mind built ghost walls to guide the mind's reorganisation, and these walls are still visible. This is why they are visible to all of us."

"It's scaffolding."

"It does not explain why we are drawn to them, however."

"And you *are* drawn to them."

"More than curiosity would seem to suggest."

I leaned forward. "Explain how that works. How it manifests itself. The pull."

"I cannot. It happens without my doing anything. It is tidal, or the urge that pulls you into a circle when walking in the woods or the desert. It happens in the fugue states. When I am mindless. I feel I would drift to the centre of the markers if I could keep that mindlessness to my thoughts, but I cannot. Partly because I am afraid, but also because the mind, the will, seems to create a force that repels the drift and then I have to fight to progress further. The urge to move forward, within, creates resistance to what was happening anyway. Like reverse quicksand."

"Are you thinking about the structure more?"

A pause. "Remember everything we say is heard."

I began to speak, then stopped myself. Hoskin might view this as dangerous ground, I realised. Instead, I raised a topic I couldn't – wouldn't – raise with Anwen for fear of exposure.

I told Moonfeld how emotional I felt I'd become in the house. In truth, I understood the larger part of this was coming to terms with the news about the precariousness of my heart, but I'd made the decision not to mention this. I said I found my increased emotional lability understandable – we were all in a fraught situation after all – yet there was more to it than that. There was a lurch to my feelings now. Like an unlashed cannon on board ship, my mood tore here and there without me being able to get a handle on it, each wow on plank threatening to breach the gunnels. My shouting fit at Len, the laughter, the tickle of intellectual delight making me want to giggle, the severity of my spooking in the pool the night before. It wasn't that the highs and the lows were particularly high or particularly low; it was the distance between and the shortness of the interval.

"I feel drunk some of the time," I said, "and a part of my mind hears me laughing and it sounds manic, unlike me."

"It sounds like depression," Moonfeld said. "And why wouldn't you be depressed? You're mortal."

"Yes, well—." I stopped. The word *mortal* brought to mind what Anwen had said. "Maybe you're right."

I told the mind there was energy to my mood state that did not seem to come from inside myself. To my perception, this was not just me. It was everyone in the farmhouse. Even – although I did not say this out loud – Hoskin, her bully front bravado writ large.

"You do not know them well enough to tell," Moonfeld said. "And *everyone*? Did Hoskin give you a mighty hug?"

I smiled. "Okay, not everyone." I paused. "But who knows? Her and Tom are clearly an item."

"Bless your cotton head. And it is tactless to mention sex to a man with no wherewithal."

The thought stopped me. I decided to ask the question. "What's that like? No corporeal pleasure. A hot buttered crumpet." The laugh. "I didn't mean that rudely, but *literally* a hot buttered crumpet. Ale. A deep, dark pint of bitter. A pint of Titfinger or The Blood of the Horseman. Whisky *deoch an doris*."

I was afraid I'd offended my friend as the silence lingered until the hum of computers and the chittering of the plinth was all I could hear. I said his name a few times, quietly prompting him. *Moonfeld. Moonfeld.* Minutes passed. I was formulating an apology when the mind replied—

"It is fading. The physical is fading. Whether that is a scab forming over memories that cause pain, or retreating, I do not know. I cannot tell you, Jude."

"Retreating?" A pause. "I don't understand *retreating.*"

"As in a phantom limb. I have a phantom body. I'm all stump now. Stump without substance, like Euclid's definition of a point. Everything's been amputated."

The air between us had become unnavigable, and I found nothing to say to this. I took another tack—

"What's it made of? The structure?"

"Old stone. Amongst the trees, the standing stones look the more alive of the two. You asked about the pull. The pull is the pull of the tide retreating in the sea. There is something more than physical forces pulling at me. The sea has a hand and it can yank you to your doom."

"Poetic."

"Merely pandering to your idiom, Jude."

I paused. "How would we get closer?"

"I like that *we,*" said the mind. "It is like a scientist saying to a lab mouse, *How would we test this medicine?*" Silence. "I said I do not sleep, but I have fugue states. It is in the fugue state that I drift most naturally to the structure. The path there is long and constantly changes. I seem to approach and then I am distant again. I go back on myself time and again. I eventually get near the structure but only if I allow the drift. If I concentrate on getting there, I never reach the place. My mind, the *presence* of my mind inhibits me. Like trying to focus on falling to sleep. The effort curdles the goal." The mind paused. "If we were to progress, it would be better if I did not try to talk to you while I am there. That would require too much awareness. It would be better to recall."

"How would I do that?"

"You devise a routine for me, a script. The script will need to be read through twice. On the first reading I will not answer. On the second I will answer from my memory of the first reading. Think of it as one of those foreign language exams. *Listen the first time and perform the second.*"

"But still it might not work."

"No," Moonfeld said, "but it will be interesting to see if spoken prompts guide my progress." He paused. "And I am sure you have not cleared this with Hoskin."

"No." I smiled, aware again of the need to speak for the feed. "I will need to do that, of course."

6.4 Len had mentioned the feed recordings, and the next day I arranged to have him explain how they worked. It was the only way I could gather information from Pike and Ichika, both of whom had passed within. I was apprehensive at hearing these voices for the first time.

Len told me how to access the feeds, access files, manipulate icons to drag the moment markers back and forth to where I wanted them.

"You're like a spy," he said. "You can search for words like *terrorist*, *incendiary*. If a word's been spoken in that room, the record comes up. *Device*, *cell*, whatever police look for." He grinned. "It's like a dictionary when you're a kid, though. You tend to look up *wank* and *cock*."

"Can I delete anything?"

Samuel said, sharp, "Why would you want to delete anything?"

"I wouldn't. I meant is it possible? Through ineptitude?"

Len reassured me it wasn't. "Just remember to close feeds down when you've done with them."

He scribbled numbers down, showed the filing system. Feeds went from midnight. If a recording ended abruptly, it meant it continued into the next day's feed for that particular mind. Feed codes started with a letter to identify the mind, then six digits for the date, DDMMYY.

"Stupid, really. What happens when we run out of letters?"

I looked at the display on the giant monitor, thinking of what a thousand illuminated jars would look like, each turned out of shape by the mind within. Derek Mahon's mushrooms in the Wexford shed came to mind again.

Len explained that *P* stood for Moonfeld, *J* was Elephant Baby, Pike was *L*. "Sam, what's Ichika again?"

"*G*."

"Thanks, Sam."

"Samuel."

The system was simple. Len stayed while I did a trial search. "Try *wank*," he suggested. "Don't think I tried *wank*." I typed into the search field. Nil returns. "No one said *wank* in that room, Jude. That, in itself, is of great significance." He patted me on the shoulder. "Have fun."

I set about searching for words that denoted the unknown places. *Structure, ruin, labyrinth.* There were few. As I listened to the feed recordings, I understood this was as much disinterest in the interrogators as reticence from the mind. Not only were the minds unclear when they spoke of the structures, the Tom and Hoskin I heard on the recordings were resolute in not pressing for details.

I found this astonishing. The idea the minds were seeing unknown structures in their minds was eerie, fascinating, important, but the impression I got from the recorded voices of Tom and Hoskin was of two humans with their fingers in their ears saying, *Lala lala LA la.*

Listening in on their responses – their initial evasions of the subject, the forced interest then the frustration and anger – was too intimate for me. I felt secret, furtive. I wasn't listening; I was eavesdropping, privy to conversations I was not present for. Len was right, I was a spy.

Anwen had said the minds feared the structures, and it was this tension – between being drawn to them but also afraid – that came through most clearly. Even Moonfeld sounded reluctant on the feeds. No, not *reluctant.* He sounded slow, vague. If anything, he sounded more like the Moonfeld of the pubs: bluster and fuss and spit on his whiskers. The precision of his normal speech had given way to digressions, woolliness and verbiage. I was taking copious notes, and I had my copies of Len's drawing to adapt and alter, but after an hour or so I realised I'd been writing words that did not connect or hold any sense. It was a trek narrated in scraps.

The bear went over the mountain—

Part of the frustration was the lack of specificity in the search. I'd made a list of the words that I might search for – *door,** *structure, circle,*

---

* *Pike (L020313):* At the <u>door</u>, steps lead down. Not regular. Worn. Cellar steps. Edges smooth. Rounded like a sanded banister.

Elephant Baby (J110214): Across the <u>door</u>way is a concertina gate like a metal accordion, but when the gate is pulled across the station gets wider and when it's opened the station gets narrower.

labyrinth, stone, bone, ruin, path – but some of these terms brought up far too many to listen to, and I groaned inwardly when a list of potential hits drowned the left hand side of the monitor. As she was the chattiest, and as there was no drive to get her to talk on point, most of these hits belonged to Elephant Baby, who was the most fearful and least detailed of the minds, if my initial impression was correct.

Equally frustrating was the fact two or more terms might exist in one section of conversation, so they came up again and again, and they were usually the most innocuous of the feeds. Similarly, every hit was returned, and an exchange where the word *stone*[†] was featured (a word I abandoned early on) would record a hit against every single time the word was used.

I got a jolt with *grave*. Moonfeld and I had discussed the funeral, and my voice returned to me altered, strangely high-pitched now not subject to the acoustics of my skull.

I learnt to be harsh. I spent hours filtering, rejecting, scribbling, but mostly getting lost in feeds with no relevance but plenty of fascination, mainly Ichika and Pike as I'd never heard them when they were functioning, and there were countless times I realised I'd been listening to

---

Ichika (G160713): I walk the inside of a well, steps sticking out of the sides. The steps are shallower as I approach bottom. They vanish into the stonework. The stone is worn. The bottom of the well has a trap<u>door</u>, but it is a round <u>door</u> into the earth. A round stone <u>door</u> into the earth.

Pike (L160113): No <u>door</u>s into the cells. The window is not large enough for a body. It's no <u>door</u>.

† *Ichika (G200913):* I am a sound drawn into a <u>stone</u> ear.

Ichika (G011113): I looked behind me descending the well and I saw the print of a guiding hand evaporating from the <u>stone</u>. It was not a person following me. It was *my* hand. In the well, I can make a mark on the <u>stone</u> even if it lifts in a moment. A mark of my own.

Elephant Baby (J110414): The <u>stone</u> will come down on me if I go deeper, filling in like one of those miners trapped. It'll be all around me and I'll be unable to move. I'll be trapped in a <u>stone</u> womb with no exit, no canal out, just burial alive and no way to end it, no end to it, no end, no end—

them for a good half an hour – off-topic but hooked as an eavesdropper – before dragging myself back on task.

The minds were alive, and vital, and their memories were close to them. Ichika spoke to Anwen of a time in her marriage – it was always Anwen who drew out these human moments – her husband being evenly and kindly berated by Ichika for his lack of input into domestic heavy lifting. He'd turned the tables on her in the bedroom one night. She'd given a long-understood signal, and he'd said, *I do the heavy lifting here. Say it.* And she did, telling Anwen it was the hardest thing to pronounce, far more transgression than the desired intimacy, but she did it. Pink as a rose and open as a <u>door</u>, Ichika said, *I want to go to bed. With you.*

The team at the farmhouse spoke of Pike as geriatric nurses might speak of a patient with dementia. He was dismissed as a being, and everything he might contribute was worthless, like the gateway the old pass when they cease to be thought capable of stupidity, criminality or malice and sink into a twinkly state of innocence. Pike was the same. They didn't seem to dislike him exactly, but neither did they seem to feel anything about him at all. He was simply a laconic *nothing* to them. When Pike spoke of the structures it was simple. *A stone house, a white path.*

The fascination was Ichika. She spoke of the structure in detail. This irritated her interrogators as she was all they had at the time – Baby was a long way from returning – so she occupied their thoughts and efforts, and the disturbing ruins she spoke of thwarted them, confused them, but above all unsettled them as they did not know what they were. Ichika spoke of the labyrinth‡ – *meiro* – as a circular ruin, open, but with

---

‡ *Moonfeld (P120514):* The <u>labyrinth</u> is marked by stones amongst the trees. If they are standing, they act as fingerposts to the centre, but I can pass each many times and on one pass it stands and on the next it is underfoot, flush to the earth. A clicked switch.

Moonfeld (P090514): The centre can always been seen through the trees. The <u>labyrinth</u> is less a puzzle than a pattern to be learned.

Ichika (G061013): I think the <u>labyrinth</u> was formed by the collapse of walls in a round mansion. It was not so to begin with. The halls were ordered, the rooms were closed. A collapse formed the <u>labyrinth</u>.

no possibility of seeing inside it. Time and again when listening to her feeds, I had to remind myself that what she spoke of was not a real thing but a presence in the visual field of the mind. The structure and the path to the structure had no external reality, which was hard to understand as she talked of it in such detail. The worn and lichen-dashed stones, the white grit of the winding path she interpreted as salt. The path[§] was not a wandering one through trees as it was with Moonfeld, or a warren of London streets as it was with Baby. The path was a definite, unambiguous spiral that led ever-inwards to the ruin but never reached a destination. She jumped the track somehow, and ended up as far away as before.

The way forward along the spiral was an absence of mind, Ichika said. The mind drifted there without thought, but an impetus destroyed it. It was like catching smoke, the attempt at capture was the means by which the smoke was dispersed. This was part of the reason for her vagueness. To add a commentary required a presence of mind that curdled the attempt. It was the reason why the closer the minds got to the structures, the more disconnected and vague they were. Yet it didn't explain why they never returned, unless there was something at the heart of the structures that erased them, which was not possible.

Again, I had to remind myself that all of this was happening within a chemical and organic construct beneath my feet. There was no mysticism to it. Everything was known and understood from a scientific point of view. There wasn't a dark castle floating in the chain-fluid Hoskin had somehow overlooked. The structures were part of the mind's understanding of itself.

§ *Moonfeld (P230414):* The winding path is angular, like a square spiral, because the markers form a junction sending the path at right angles. The path overlaps and intersects with other spirals, moving me away from the central structure and then back.

Ichika (G210913): The path is laid with salt to stop anything growing over it. The salt path has permanence. It is important that it remain. I feel the way it takes is always changing, different, but the path remains. It is sewn [sown?] into the earth and yet the path remains while the earth changes around it.

Ichika was the clearest. Her path was a mathematic spiral leading inwards – her *salt path* – and it led to a central circular ruin. Within the ruin was a dome of opaque air *the colour of smoke* preventing the centre being seen. *It revolves,* she said. It was her own pull towards it that caused her to explore. Within the smoke bulb, there was a hole leading into the ground, narrow steps around the outside. Ichika saw it as a dry well, and at the bottom was a stone door.

Hoskin had intimated she'd sent Ichika further in, but it was clear from the feeds this was not true. Ichika had gone in of her own accord. Once she'd made the first break into the smoke, future journeys were easier, and she went there daily (to the audible frustration of Hoskin on the recording). At first she walked down the inside of the well. She opened the stone door. Beyond was an unlit circle¶ that seemed to open into a bottomless pit. She smelt salt** again and assumed the hole was above a vast underground water source, waveless and still. Ichika stayed looking into that darkness. She reached into it, hoping to feel the coolness of the expected water on her hands, but it was beyond reach. It was completely tranquil and hypnotic.

¶ *Ichika (G221113):* It is all a <u>circle</u>. <u>Circle</u> after <u>circle</u>. This is not a well, but a secret. Wells are not secret. They are the life of the village. The <u>circle</u> is the grave of the bone.

Moonfeld (P010514): The pull is not physical, but a yearning. At first I thought it was a natural force. Centripetal, perhaps, from the turning of the chain-fluid. Now it seems more the unconscious, uncorrectable tug that makes a man in a desert walk in a <u>circle</u>.

Pike (L100213): The road is a series of loops. A scruffy doodle of a spring. Back over itself it goes, over and again. Like one of those motorways seen from the air. But from above, from the outside, the greater road is a <u>circle</u> about the stone house.

** *Ichika (G131013):* I understand I have no senses. I understand what I say is impossible. But I smell <u>salt</u>, Anwen. I smell it very closely the closer I get to the ruins.

Moonfeld (P090514): The texture on the standing stones has the look of arctic ice. Like frozen <u>salt</u>.

I checked the dates on the feeds here and found Ichika was silent for days after having been to the water, Hoskin's voice on the recording tight with frustration at the mind's truancy.

On her knees, Ichika looked into the hole, the unlit circle, no stone or pebble to drop into the gap to see if it would splash, and how long it might take for the splash to return to her. She spoke of imagining she saw a ripple across the surface, or the ghost of a reflection.

Yet there was no water there—

"As I watched," Ichika said, "the dark lifted, and a small light crossed the entrance of the hole, like a candle carried through a room many metres below."

I did a search for *and*. I reasoned that *and* was so common a word it would bring up every feed. It did, and the last time Ichika had spoken the word *and* had the same feed code, and when I listened to it the same sentence – *As I watched, the dark lifted* – played then the feed ended.

This was the last time Ichika spoke. After this, she'd gone within.

6.5 I wrote up my notes from that first day. Simplicity was a feature, it appeared, and I worked my descriptions until I felt I'd got the details of the structures down to their nubs.

I annotated the scans of Len's drawings, putting figures in to identify the common features between them for each of the minds. They were not all the same, but it did not take much to hear a similarity. If I'd won anything from this day, it was that I was convinced – as convinced as the others – that the places described were similar more than they were different, and that this couldn't be coincidence. I needed to sort my thoughts and spend more time with Pike's feeds. I also needed to talk to Baby again, as she was the only other mind who could talk.

When done, I headed a clean sheet with the words *state* and *action*, then listed similarities down the page.

Under *state* I listed the spiral, the markers, the paths, the structure, the *inwards-and-down-ness*, again a spiral, or labyrinth. *Stone. Door. Circle.*

Under *action* I listed the pull the minds felt, but also the resistance. They couldn't approach without an element of absence. Will alone could not force them. It followed therefore they couldn't narrate as they went, and as absence was a necessity, so their memories on returning were necessarily vague. And they returned quickly. I recalled Baby's rocket back home as if on elastic.

Under *state* I added bareness. The further in, the barer the spaces were. Ichika couldn't find a stone to drop into the hole. Pike talked of a helical prison with windows, but no doors, set into white stone walls. The mind wanted to throw something – again, a stone – through the hole to hear it clatter, but the ramp leading downwards was bare.

I stared out of the window. There was another thought that was reluctant to come to mind. I watched Tom in the courtyard throwing a ball against one of the converted barn walls. He looked child-like, but more than that he looked hot, stinking hot, brown from the sun and wringing with sweat.

Under *state* I wrote, *The structures are cold*. Frowning at the pad, I put a line through this and wrote, *No evidence, but I feel cold*. I wrote, *Stone*. For three of the four minds, *stone* was repeatedly mentioned, emphasised; even the exception, Baby, talked of *tiles* in her mental tube station. Pike used the word repeatedly to describe his prison structure, the steep helical ramp that led downwards, the walls—

I wrote, *Nautilus.*

Under *action* I wrote, *They cross a barrier of no return.*

After a further twenty minutes' thought, I put a question mark after the last word.

They cross a barrier of no return?

The room was close, and I wondered why I was there in my hot room. The late afternoon sun was glorious, and I heard the noise of the rest of the team chattering outside, too low for me to hear.

I closed my eyes. *Summer can be identified from its sounds alone*, I thought. Bottles knocking, running liquids, balls hitting walls, laughter, insects and hum. People talk differently in summer, and it's a real, physical fact, like the thickness of butter in different seasons, or the resilience of milk, or the lightening of hair colour. I wondered if there'd ever been any independent research into the effect seasonal changes had on the tone, volume and speed of speech. *Anwen would be the best person for the job*, I thought.

When I awoke, it was dark. I'd obviously napped, but it was Anwen who woke me so I felt I'd conjured her.

"Food's an hour," she said. "My night to cook."

"Rarebit again?"

"You're funny." She paused. "Sorry about this morning."

Laughing at my credulity around the minds' immortality, I recalled. Now she'd said it, I knew it had been with me all day, rubbing at me somewhere sensitive. It had annoyed me. It was, I realised, the reason why I'd been in my room and not out in the afternoon sun with my notes. It had a little ache to it still. I hoped I hadn't been thought sulking. Scratching my head, yawning, I waved off the offence—

"Groggy," she said.

I smiled. That accent. "Say, *Groggy froggy in a buggy*."

"Piss off." She grinned; we were mended. "Do you fancy having a flea cull then, me then you?" she asked. "I need a good night's sleep, don't you?"

I did.

We'd culled before, a few nights back. Officially it was me, Tom and Anwen in the stables, but because of the fleas Tom had moved in with Hoskin in the house. (*Not the only reason*, Anwen said.) Our cull never worked for long, but it was the best deterrent we had, and all the other measures we'd tried were ineffective.

The cull was an elaborate dance. We stripped the beds then put them onto a boil wash. Next, we vacuumed the skirting then body of the rooms, from the edges of the carpet into the centre, before dousing where we'd been with *R.I.Flea*. Opening the windows to air – the rooms never lost the stink of stale months of flea spray – Anwen tugged the chemically-stoned cat in for flea survivors to feast on and die. The dying was the good part, and an irrational part of my mind wanted to be a witness to a flea death, and to somehow ensure that it was painful.

The cull was a thankless task, but it bought a few nights of haunted respite, haunted because I was still aware of fleas in my dreams, and because it did not take long for the itch-wick to light on an ankle and the cycle begin again.

This time, before she put the cat in her room, she combed her in the bathroom. "We'll be able to gauge the extent of the cull if the cat is clean when she goes into battle," she said.

I watched her. She sat on the toilet, dunking the comb in the full sink every few passes through the hair.

"I'd like to talk again to Baby," I said.

"I saw your notes. Any time. But not without me."

The cat was purring with the attention, sometimes uttering the odd strangled sob of dismay when the comb found a knot.

"James Joyce realised cat's mews have the letter *g* in them."

"I was wondering if it was him."

I smiled. "Just saying. It's not *miaow*. It's *mngaow*."

"I read they don't miaow in the wild," she said. "They hiss and growl, but the mewling they developed to talk to humans. I think that's sweet." She gave me an intent stare as if daring me to challenge her. "Have a look."

I put my head over the sink. She'd drowned the fleas in the water. They'd sunk to the bottom, and the blood had fled from around and within their bodies, but it looked as if they'd turned to blood, as if blood was all they were.

"That's horrible," I said.

Anwen grunted. "It is, but I can't tell you how satisfying it is. Like squeezing spots. It's so grim, but so satisfying."

The cat turned her baked eyes on me and mooed like a cow on fast forward. "Poor thing," I said.

6.6 In the kitchen after dinner, I told them I'd worked alongside Sam for most of the day, antipathy coming off the man like heat, and he'd not said a single word.

"Nothing works without Sam," said Tom.

"I told him that," Len put in.

"Doesn't he have interests?"

"I'm sure he does. I'm not sure what." Anwen thought for a moment. "I'm not sure I'd care to know either."

"There's maybe a cache on the servers only he can get into. Filled with pictures of stiff wizards."

"It's odd," I said, "that all this can be happening and he's not curious. Or is he curious? I can't tell."

"He does his job," said Len. "He maintains the site on his tod and doesn't need any more work. If you look at how complex this is, you'd be amazed. But you don't care about diurnal temperature variations, magnetic drift, bulk partitioning in the chain fluid, thermal weight. I know he looks like he's building his fat backside, but he knows everything. And he's busy. Too busy to be curious."

I nodded. "But still—."

"He's been here a lot longer than you."

"Yes, but you all have. You all seem driven still."

Tom said, "If you look at the data he's building on thermal weight, it's beautiful. There's a pattern to how the minds use the different parts of their brain matter, and on the thermal images you can see the pattern pulse through the jar. It looks like a jellyfish from the deep ocean. Those bioluminescent flashes. It's beautiful. The human brain doesn't do anything like it, but Sam is building a tracked record of the pattern of the activity to try to understand why it does that. Is it integral to function, or a minor feature of how heat is dispersed through the chain-fluid? These are all fascinating questions, Jude, but you're not interested because they're sciencey." He paused. "Ask Sam to show you. I'm sure he'll tell you if you ask."

"Will he be excited?"

The others laughed. Tom pursed his lips in irritation. "No. But it's how and who he is. You want him to be interested in what you're interested in, but he's not. He's interested in the things that are scientifically pertinent and verifiable. He's the polar opposite of you. If there was a Venn diagram you'd be in one circle and we'd be in the other circle and no one would be in the intersection. Apart from Anwen—."

"Hey."

"You can't cross over. Think of it this way. We're writing a history of policing and you're suggesting Sherlock Holmes should be included. He doesn't fit."

I wasn't convinced such an inclusion was as silly as Tom thought, but I decided not to pursue it. Tom had been sharp with me for a day or so now, and I didn't want to rouse him. Moonfeld was frustrating Tom by losing focus mid-flow, and I'd the impression that, since my arrival, Tom blamed me for the mind's absences.

Anwen touched my arm and said, "Sam won't be excited by much regardless. He's an extreme male brain."

I turned to her. "That's a point. What about sex?" Len hooted. "No, I mean gender," I said, feeling myself going red. "Does it feature without the body? Was Ichika different in some essential way from Pike? Or him from Baby?"

She shook her head. "All sex markers drop away," she said. "There's nothing to show they think particularly differently. No hormones. No endocrine system. No biology. Difference is the perception and expectation your knowledge of a person as man or woman brings to the table. It unsettles me, and I don't know why, because I've a feeling it shouldn't bother me. I've a feeling I should be glad."

"There's power in there being a difference. For all genders."

"Yes."

There was a smirk in the air, poisonous as an unowned fart.

"If either of you two says Elephant Baby talks too much—." She pointed her finger at Len and Tom in turn. "Okay, so she does talk too much but—. Piss off the both of you."

Len and Tom were laughing now, an old antagonism.

"She's frightened," Anwen insisted. "She didn't ask for any of this. She was twenty-three years old and the last thing she expected was to die, and then to wake up and find she was herself. She's still twenty-three, Len. She's still twenty-three, and she's trying to think of something to say, trying to keep normality to her life. You *bastard* if you can't see how cruel that is. She's nothing to do, and the least slip will send her nuts, and then you'll put her in the room of the silent minds. She talks to keep herself sane." She took a breath, a valve to bleed her fury, but also to get wind for the last shout. "You piece of shit, Lenford. You piece of shit. All of you are pieces of shit. You're shit pieces, that's what you are."

When she'd left, out into the courtyard through the glass doors, I made to go after her. Len caught my arm—

"No." I settled back into my seat. Hoskin came in and asked what the row was. Len said, "Anwen."

"Oh," she replied. The sound had the same inflection Moonfeld had when he'd said, *Oh, a poem*. She eyed me. "I forgot to ask—. Tick tock, tick tock."

I laid out my thoughts. I was careful not to be too provocative to Hoskin, and I didn't talk about my growing certainty the minds were seeing a part of the human psyche buried deep for millennia and now sitting atop the grave mud like a daisy—

"The structures are important to all of them," I said. "If what has returned is a feature of the unconscious brain that is now visible, there are surely uncounted features. Why didn't they all come back? Why did this one feature return, the same for each of them?" I paused. "You've thought of this."

"Yes."

I was nervous, alive to the possibility of mockery, or hearing that my ideas had all been tested and found bust before I'd arrived.

"I've been listening to the feeds. The closer they get, the more the structures become similar. There's a spiral motif, and a central point that leads inwards and down—."

"Like a plughole."

"Yes." I waited out the laughter. "Tom said John's less focused. He drifts." Tom nodded his agreement. "I thought if we allow him his reins for a time, it might satisfy him, leave him more focused for Tom."

Hoskin gave me a look as if to say, *Come on*. "Out of the question," she said. "We'll lose him."

I pushed on. "I was thinking a guided tour. Strict, with an end goal. This far and no farther." I swallowed. "John said something. He said because he drifted there, talking him to the structure wouldn't work.

He suggested having a script to run through twice, once for the mind to follow as suggestions for how to proceed, then a second time for the returned mind to report back." I shrugged. "It might work, and give control, and by satisfying his urge to drift it might make him more useful to Tom. To you." No one spoke so I added, weakly, "Don't you think?"

"We can try it."

"What kind of questions?" Tom asked.

I ran through some sample questions. I'd scribbled them on a piece of paper. *What can you see? Move forward. Is there a light? Where is it coming from?* The idea was for the questions to be repeated so the mind was conditioned to take note of everything seen in all directions, but also general enough for them to be interpreted by the mind no matter the situation found. When I'd written the guide script, I'd thought myself clever, but reading it to the group embarrassed me horribly. I heard it in my oomphless voice, and eventually I faded out—

"Like that," I said.

On looking up, I saw Anwen had returned and was leaning on the door jamb. My embarrassment grew.

"It could work," Hoskin said after a moment. She took an apple and bit into it. "Use Baby as a control."

"Wait—."

"Not a request, Anwen."

"Why would you use her? She's terrified."

Hoskin bit into her apple, refusing to engage. I stepped in. "This could help, Anwen. The mind when it goes there isn't frightened. It's the conscious mind that tells of the trip that's afraid. You said that yourself."

She shifted to face me. "That's not what I said."

"I think we can talk her further, and with less harm, this way. We can talk to her. We can lead them both through. It'll be like one of those guided meditations she was talking about. Once she's relaxed—."

I'd turned to face Anwen, so I didn't see the half-eaten apple coming. It hit me with a wet *whap* left of centre forehead, flung by Hoskin with a good wind up, before bouncing into the sink. My look of hurt was obviously so pronounced that Tom and Len howled at my expression.

"Jesus," I said.

"Okay," said Hoskin, laughing herself, "I admit, that was a little more than I intended."

"*Jesus.*"

"But I'm serious. There will be no new age knobbage here. No talk of meditations and navel-gazing and I-don't-know-what."

"Jesus, Hoskin."

"Okay, I apologise for clocking you with the apple, satisfying as it was. But let me be clear, if I hear anything about astral planes or higher mind or—. I don't know. Ear candles. If I hear anything new agey, it won't be an apple. Whatever is drawing Moonfeld away from the task at hand is the important thing, and we need to either know what it is, or remove it. That's the only goal."

"Jesus," I said, quiet now.

The woundedness of my complaint didn't help. I rubbed my head, forlorn as a puppy. When I looked to the doorway, Anwen was gone.

6.7 Before bed, I lost myself in thinking of phantom limbs. I recalled Moonfeld had mentioned the term. I remembered about the site of the pain in such cases, the realignment of task in areas of the brain, changes to sensory and motor maps. This last fascinated me. The minds had no motor functions now, so what then happened to such maps? And the sense of retreating that Moonfeld mentioned, *telescoping*, where the phantom retracted into the remaining limb and gradually disappeared, the pain leaving with it—

I couldn't follow my own thinking, or parse the concept of a pain that was all phantom, for it led me to a single conclusion. Moonfeld was his *own* phantom body pain, and the idea he was gradually retreating into his residual non-existent limb bent my head.

Haunted water.

I did not sleep. I couldn't recall if I'd taken my *quinidine*, which fed into my disturbance. Every time I got close to nodding off, I'd hear my alarm clock, but my falling mind interpreted the tick as a flea's feet on my bed sheet. I wore socks to bed now, lathered from the ankles down in Tiger Balm, duvet tucked beneath me everywhere despite the despicable heat of the night, and yet the fleas remained and always found clean skin to nip.

I was up many times, lights on, spray in hand, eyes poring over my uncovered sheet for the miserable, misery-sowing sesame seed. It was never there, but when I'd again covered myself in the hot covers, my ankles began to itch again, and *things* zipped from my skin.

My thoughts turned to despair, utter furious despair. My last thought was of someone – I knew it was a woman but couldn't remember who – saying that in the midst of her insomnia she'd always hear one tick in the clock that sounded wet, and that's when she knew to give up, to wake and start her day no matter the hour. My careful consideration of the wetness in each tick was the only thing that enabled me to finally drop off.

7.1 The next day I went through more of the feed results, taking my place next to Samuel again, who retreated like a rat into the cave of monitors. I stared at the side of Sam's head for a good minute, waiting to see if he'd turn and say something. *I'll talk to him if he turns*, I thought, but the man stared resolutely at his monitor. I shut him out with headphones.

I concentrated on Pike for the morning. The mind was laconic, spare, but he'd been almost as far as Ichika, returning to tell the tale. His central structure was much taller than the others. He called it *the stone house*, and it was again circular, with one window high on the outside wall and no doors. In the peculiarity of how the minds experienced their internal terrain, Pike had to walk up the wall to the one window, yet when he was inside, all that was within was a narrow helical ramp hugging the outside wall and leading steeply down and around the wall into the depths. Into the walls were sunk dozens of window holes. *You might push a human head through*, Pike had said to describe their size.

Pike never commented on this strange arrangement of a wall that was windowless from the outside but full of cell windows when on the inside. It was a white prison, too white to be examined. Pike looked into the cells, but he saw nothing beyond the glare. He wanted to throw a stone in to see if there were indeed, as he suspected, dozens of white stone cells hanging in space. *Walls of salt.*

Pike fitted into the table I'd made the day before, and I was struck again by the image of the nautilus shell, the spiral in the centre giving onto the great white cells of the shell. For a giddy moment, I wondered whether anyone had queried the size of the minds in their internal landscape. The strangeness of the structures might be because they were small and exploring large objects, as in some B-movie, but the theory didn't hold water as the minds were human-sized in all other respects.

Throughout, I'd been making a list of other words that had come up in the other feeds, suggestive words that might have an echo in another mind's experience. Most led nowhere fruitful – no hits, or only trivial mentions – and I abandoned the listening early on. Yet one of the words, towards the end of the second day, gave a considerable shock—

One of the minds had mentioned *scarlet.* A few hits came up from Baby, which I tapped through as irrelevant. The feeds automatically started for a short time before the use of the word in order to give time to gauge context and relevance, and one began with silence, then a series of electric hiccups sounded, like a car choking to a halt on its last petrol. I was about to tap onto the next when a deep, pure-computer-generated voice rasped out, *Scaaarlet.*

The voice sent my testicles scurrying for their inguinal flue. It gave me such a fright I laughed. "Bloody hell," I said.

Samuel gave me a look.

I looked at the feed code. I'd not questioned it before, but all the feeds had come in from feeds *G, J, L,* and *P.*

This search had picked up a feed from a silent mind, *D.*

7.2 "It picks up words from anywhere. It searches for patterns, and the patterns it searches for are English words. Ichika's disappearances into Japanese didn't come through, or came through as phonetic. *May he row* for *meiro.* That's all." Anwen touched my hand. "Are you all right?"

"My heart's still going."

"Your heart's still going, or your heart's still *going*?"

I looked at her. "The second. Both."

"It was an accident of sound that sounded like a word."

"Where did the sound come from?"

"Just abrasions against the tongue unit."

This didn't make me feel any better.

7.3 Elephant Baby was having more difficulty finding the tube station in her internal field. She blamed that area of London, oblivious to the fact it was a Camden she'd invented from memory. The back streets, the side streets, the dark streets: it had never existed. Anwen suggested this was false, that Baby knew exactly where it was but was refusing to go there. "Even I know where it is better than she does," she said, "and I can picture the route. But I can't see where she makes the wrong turn, or even *if* she does."

Anwen smoothed the way by talking to her, sometimes for hours, before leading her to the station. The patience she had was remarkable, for much of the preamble was the same memories and repetitions of past conversations. Speech that referred to previous times and events again and again – they revisited the *x*-marked twin – as if they were responses in a ritual. Because I was present, they included me. *Boy Jude, who was handsome from the side only.* It calmed her, and as we led her to the structure, she began to be more confident. The process was slow, however, and took ages of a little progress and then abandonment, and then the process repeated itself.

The picture that grew was inflected with Baby's terror of the place. In truth, what she described was recognisable from my time in London as a student, apart from the fact it existed where and when it should not. The tiles from another era of design, the soot-blackened walls, the crampedness of the stairwells, the smell of long-burned dust and hair.

The centre of Baby's fear, as with the other minds, was the spiral staircase leading down to the trains. She'd never approached it, but by increments Anwen got her closer to it, then on the steps, and then some way down the steps. Baby described the staircase as a steel helix down through a dimly-lit shaft. I recalled getting the white shits from a narrow staircase in Hampstead tube years before.

She spoke of a flickering in the light. When she was on the stairs and walking down, the source of the light was from below, and the light came from beyond an irregularly turning fan at the bottom of the shaft.

"Or a candle," she said, "guttering and wide as the stairs."

Ichika, I thought. *A candle carried below the skylight in the lower room.*

Other features came clear to her. The metal steps with a rectangular motif cut into them allowing her to look through to the steps and the drop below. There was a gap between the outside curve of the banister and the sheer wall, as irresistible to look at as a car accident or a nude. A set of tiles were lettered with the name of the station. *The Lock.*

I frowned at this. *Was there such a station?* I thought. I made a note in my book to check, but later in the same session Baby said she saw the tube line in full on a rusted sign. Anwen asked her to read out some more of the stations. *Camden Lock*, she said. *Burlington Arcade. Albany. Horseferry.* They weren't actual tube stations, but the names sounded plausible, possible, and I made a note to check whether they were once real stations, but I knew they were not. Later, I enthused about this to Anwen, the wonder of the human brain that fills in gaps so perfectly even the falsehoods fit the patterns—

"When she's talking, I'm there with her. As soon as she says what she's seeing, I can see it too. And strangely, I'm building my own mental tube station, but it's constructed of parts of Hampstead and Bank in the past. It's like you could take them apart like Lego bricks and swap parts from one to another to make a whole new one."

Anwen agreed, but she'd none of my excitement. The further she pushed Baby, the unhappier she became with what she was doing. "If she disappears on me, Jude—."

She was in two minds about pushing Baby. She vacillated between being convinced the mind was immune because Baby wasn't curious and the other minds were. Baby was drawn to the structures as the others were, but there was no corresponding push from her side. This, however, made the constant persuasions to return to her tube station seem

cruel and bring about a disappearance of another kind, a disappearance into insanity, or however insanity might look when a mind existed
on organic matter locked into chain-fluid. What made this harder was
that Hoskin had intimated such an eventuality was okay with her. She'd
lose Baby in a heartbeat if it gave her more of an understanding and a
chance to save Moonfeld from the same fate.

We got her halfway down the stairs when Baby began to talk of an
echo in her steps. Anwen persuaded her to look around, for changes in
the structure of the shaft or the material of the stairs. There was nothing, but in looking around her internal space, the mind looked down,
and through the black metal of the steps saw a figure ahead of her on
the spiral staircase.

A figure in shadow. The figure of a man.

For the first time in my life, I saw hairs on my arm rise up in alarm.
I was delighted, but the mind went into the panic response of repetition
– *A man on the steps* – nothing else. Anwen pulled her out.

"Come home. Come home now."

It was an hour before Elephant Baby could be persuaded to talk
again. What she said then was innocuous, but it sounded sane and it
afforded Anwen great relief. Anwen didn't, however, say another word
to me.

7.4 It was another of those hot afternoons where I could do nothing
but sweat. Before dinner, I decided to try for a nap, but rather than lie
in the sheets and let them adhere to my skin, I pulled the chair before
the open window and let myself sweat into the upholstery. There was
something relaxing about not fighting the heat, not wiping at myself
constantly to get the sweat off, but to let it dirty the body, each bead
finding its way over the skin just as rivers find their way over the land,
pulled towards the floor and avoiding everything in its way to find the
easiest path to the great sea, the ground.

I could not find rest. My mind was ticking over too fast. I was becoming invested, I knew, as invested as the others. But the others were
motivated by concern, and the real possibility of the sudden death of a

scientific project they'd been involved in for many years; I was excited by the mystery at the heart of what the minds were telling us, and the more we were allowed to push the minds towards the mystery, the more delighted I grew, which put me emotionally at odds with the rest of the team. I'd need to temper this, I knew.

Anwen's annoyance was the perfect example. She saw this new wrinkle, the man on the stairs, from Baby's standpoint, but for me it was a positive development. I instinctively thought of the figure as a guide.

The mystery of it gave me delight but also a yearning so acute I felt it as pain. I didn't know what the appearance of the guide meant. I didn't know if it signified anything. I didn't know anything at all, but I believed wholly the minds were going through something important, and this strange process of keeping consciousness alive beyond the death of the body had enabled something hitherto invisible in the human brain to come to light, to be seen and explored. To be a part of that – even to be a witness to that – was more than I'd ever hoped for or expected in my life. And even though rationally I knew there would be no answer, no blinding flash of light, I didn't mind.

There was another seduction beneath the intellectual delight of the mystery, of the unravelling, and it was the thought that the structures were a feature of all human minds after death, and that this approach to the stone ruin was a journey that would await me when I died. It was fantastic, brain-bending, but it occupied my thoughts. What if death let the higher mind functions dissolve into rot – some last-in-first-out policy of decay – leaving the older mind to fall in on itself?

As I slowly faded out of consciousness, to an unusually uncomfortable hour asleep on the chair, I saw a human brain dismantled like an exploded diagram, death turning the key of a small meat lock in the prehistoric brain, to reveal a belief, a place, an existence so old it had fused into the flesh and become one with it.

7.5 Hoskin asked for an after-dinner meeting to discuss progress. That day, Tom had experienced more moments with Moonfeld that had been worrying. The mind was unfocused, he said, and the descents into talking about the unknown place were becoming more frequent. The mind was talking about the mathematics of the spiral—

"Hardly cutting edge stuff," said Tom.

Groggy from my nap, I presented my list of similarities: the *state* and *action* list. I'd brought the grapes from the fridge and put them in a small bowl in front of Hoskin deliberately. Understanding my reason for this, she growled in anticipation of what I might have to say—

I told them it was hard to ignore the pattern that long before their mechanic mortality would become an actuality in fused chain-fluid, the minds' thinking would become seized into strings of unconnected thought and process, becoming more absent.

"It happens to them all," I said. "You can hear it in them when they return. Part of the pull towards the structures is the need for them to be mentally absent, and this absence lasts longer each time. The mind will eventually go," I told them. "Moonfeld will eventually go."

"Tell us something we don't know."

I paused. "Okay. When Anwen is pushing her, Baby seems exasperated, or helpless, or put upon, but on the feeds, it's often her who brings the structures up. There's a delicacy when they do it, as if they're parents asking a teenage child about a relationship, wary of seeming pushy, but casting lures a child might bite at before thinking."

A grape hit me on the head. The laughter was prolonged. I pursed my lips, ran my tongue over my teeth, grinned.

"Len showed me his pictures," I continued. "He's right. The minds' experiences are all the same. Walls, steps leading inward and down. You can't approach any of them directly, and if you try – if you *will* yourself there – you find yourself at a distance again." I cleared my throat. "The possibilities I've thought of are that there is a machine in that room whose resonance they all interpret the same way." I looked at my notes. "A reaction in the chain-fluid to something in the room, again sensed in the same way by all. Or that this feature is tiny and they're interpreting it as huge."

A grape came my way again.

"We've thought of everything," said Len. "All this and more."

"The problem is we can't see," said Tom. "If we could just process image as well as sound."

"That assumes the structure exists and it isn't just some barking—." Hoskin faltered. "—ness. Barkingness."

She threw another grape at me. Anwen put her whole hand over her face to cover her laughter. I looked at each face in turn, feeling isolated from the tribe, and in my view their animation was unnatural, joyous but overso. They were too manic, the speed of their speech too fast, like the slickness of speech cocaine or m/m gives. It was the end of the day, yet it felt like we were in a party's sweet spot, everyone heated to the perfect temperature for a rolling boil before the mood splintered apart.

Hoskin loved the grapes, I realised. Unwittingly – I'd intended it as a visual joke, not a practical one – I'd unlocked a part of her nature I'd not yet seen. She was playful with me, the source of the humour rather than the witness. Chucking grapes at me allowed her to be playful without damage to her sense of self.

Even Anwen seemed to be more herself. She was telling the group of the last session with Baby. Yet when she mentioned the figure on the steps, all humour vanished. They were concerned, and Hoskin was quiet. Again, I didn't know why and gave an enquiring look at Anwen. She looked back at me as if I were an idiot, as if I'd missed something essential that should not have needed explaining, which of course I had. I'd been told from the first that the minds were alone in their internal landscape. They could interact with other minds and the human team, but inside there was no one. No loved ones, no people at all. They'd memories, but no person populated their internal landscapes—

"There shouldn't be anyone there," I said.

Tom made a critical sound, like a blown sigh. *Stupid Jude.*

"Not even themselves," Anwen said. "*They* don't even have a physical presence in there. When you walk down the street, are you aware of how your legs move, your muscles and mechanics and orientation? You're not. If you catch sight of yourself in a shop window, it's a shock. That initial lack of recognition. It's because you are eyes and a mind primarily. You're awareness in motion. I always feel like a cloud."

I was barely listening. The aloneness of the minds I'd forgotten. I was soused in sorrow at once. Gut sorrow, sorrow of the flesh, lungs beleaguered with water and throat stopped with grief. Moonfeld looked the more fortunate of the minds now. I had regretted him his barren landscape, but before death his life and thought had existed in a place designed to be unpeopled. Mathematics was an abstract, barren field. Baby was meant for the throng, the hundreds, the mob; for her world to be empty was miserable, miserable.

I felt keenly the minds' loneliness, the impossibility of ameliorating the situation apart from a few brief hours of chat and normality, which was exactly what Anwen did with her friend. Unbidden, a memory came to mind of visiting a colleague whose son had been in a house fire when he was a little boy, losing his fingers, his feet, scarred over much of his body. The father had forewarned me with the brisk callousness that's sometimes the only scab that will form over such a wound. *They're like little fat candles when they're babies*, he'd said blithely. I had been pre-pared for the scars and the difference, but not for the way the boy had looked at me. Apologetic, eyes filled with liquid bravery, willing me with everything in him to take him just as he was, thirteen and never to pass unremarked in the world.

An aspect of how I'd felt then was with me now. I'd been told over and over there was no physicality to the minds – there was no *there* there – but not to touch, to feel, to be in another's presence, even in their moments of greatest panic, was the worst of fears. For all contact to be at one emotional remove, and in the quiet times no people—. No *one* person. No children. Not even a cat. Just aloneness, and loneliness, and hours of silence while the meat-people slept. And to think I'd lain awake for an hour worrying about how Moonfeld felt about not having a cock anymore. Sparing a thought for that at all was obscene.

Tom was talking—

"He's been fading for weeks, and once he goes his attention is mush. We can be deep into something and then—. I can almost pinpoint the time it happens. Like he's hearing music in the distance. A persistent exotic tune that we can't hear."

"You can hear it on the feeds," I said. "He's a moth and somewhere a candle is lit."

"Jesus, Gandhi and Joseph," muttered Hoskin, fingering out a grape from the bowl.

"The minds have come back with something attached, or open when it should be closed. An insight, an artefact, a glitch. It doesn't matter. What matters is that this is common to them all, and the end – the retreat into silence – will happen to them all. And while that won't matter for Elephant Baby, it matters for Moonfeld. It matters for you. He'll fade, and sooner than you expected him to." I paused. "He needs to be led there, and led back. You need to take them further, or they'll take themselves further, and they'll pass a point of no return within and you'll lose them."

"You're the best person for this, I suppose?" Tom said.

I paused. "That's not my decision."

Hoskin turned to Anwen. "Sanity, please. Tell me the man Baby sees on the stairs isn't the Pied Piper."

Anwen was glaring at me, a look so cold it surprised me. She said, "I've these records of a woman called Meredith Monk. Vocal choirs and—. God, I don't know how to describe it. People hate it, but as soon as I heard it, it was something I understood before thought. I could feel it in the pit of my stomach. It was linked to my hair follicles. With Baby, who *doesn't matter*—." She glared at me again. "With Baby, I feel she's telling us she knows the song. It's a lullaby sung to her as a child, and she can't help thinking about it, trying to place it, but it's frightening to her. That's the pull they feel. So yes, it is a bit Pied Pipery. I know it's not what you want to hear but I agree. A tune is playing and all the little children will follow."

Hoskin threw a grape at Anwen. The grape hit her on the forehead. It was an attempt to lighten the mood, but it failed hard. Instead of laughing, Anwen started to cry, a helpless, silent weeping, tears running down her face uncaught. Her face grew bright red and her lips turned inside out, her mouth open at the ends like the rubber band of a clown's dismay. I tried to take her hand on the table, but she pulled it away. "Sod off," she said softly, needing to take a shuddering breath between the two words.

After a moment, I continued—

"The room of silent minds. I know they're non-existent, but some started the process. Could they have faded before they communicated with you? Perhaps they left before they ever arrived, heading for the ruins. The tune in the distance."

"No, there's nothing." Hoskin was back to her old, hard self. "I hate this," she said. "Something concrete, please. Now. Something that moves us forward, not spiralling up our own arseholes."

There was a long moment of awkward silence.

"It must be hard to have this happen to you," I said.

I meant it kindly. She looked flat-eyed for a second. "Yes."

"Moonfeld's going anyway. It's only a matter of time. He'll do what Ichika did. But we have a chance to structure the exploration. To learn something."

Silence, again, but at the end of it, Hoskin said, "Yes."

The team argued. I was immediately obsolete. They argued about *whether*, *how* and *why*; if to record and how to record the exploration; who was to talk to Moonfeld and who would be to blame if he never returned. After a time they worked out contingencies, stories – lies – to cover them if it all went wrong and they ended up with a bowl that howled.

Anwen wept on, hands between her thighs palm outwards. It was a hard weep, and the silence of it was disconcerting. Her wind came in short pants as if she was carrying her breath up a steep flight of steps. I watched her, barely registering the eventual decision of the team that the exploration of Moonfeld would be done by me. I could do it without reprisal. They'd even confected a lie to clothe their decision to let a stranger question their prize jar. If Moonfeld did not return, they'd say the mind had refused to speak to everyone except me.

The team left, Len putting a hand on Anwen's shoulder. When they'd gone, I said, "I'm so sorry. I didn't mean to say she didn't matter. That's not what I meant."

"I know. I know you didn't." She looked at me, a window wet with rain. "It's the fact she *doesn't* matter. We don't even use her name."

7.6 That night I lay awake, thinking of Anwen and what she'd said about Meredith Monk, music strange but known, like hearing as an adult a lullaby sung to her as a child. She'd broken open my memory of a piece of music equally other, one personal to me – a tune sewn into a seam of collective memory, never before heard but always known – which I'd first heard years before. Lying in bed, I couldn't get it out of my head.

The tune was one of Gurdjieff's dances, *Duduki*, and it stayed with me, winding about me like a snake, until I slept and it entered my ear. I dreamed the song was playing in the white cave of my empty skull on a record player positioned at the base of my brain where the spinal column entered. The record player was on fire, and each note of the tune fled upwards as motes of soot, covering the ceiling of the white cave with musical notation. Beautiful at first, over time the notes overlapped and formed patches of black, darkening the interior of my skull until the only light was from the guttering flames of the burning turntable.

8.1 Implicit in the decision to guide Moonfeld to the structures was a change in the needs of the group, so Hoskin decided myself, Anwen and Len would focus on the minds, with Tom taking a back seat, talking to Moonfeld when we were finished. Tom did not take this well.

Hoskin insisted Elephant Baby be kept as a control. "Keep pushing her," she said. "Push her as hard and as fast as you're pushing him. Keep her returning, and if she vanishes, I want to know." Anwen told her this was cruel, unnecessary. Cold, Hoskin got close to her and said, "It's in your interest to keep her to heel then, isn't it?"

This stung Anwen to immobility. Later, I asked Len in private what I'd missed between the two women.

"Nothing," Len replied. "She cried. You can't cry."

"Bloody hell."

I had written my script to lead Moonfeld in. I ran it past Len who put his head to one side then the other. He started to hum to himself.

While waiting for Anwen, and engaged in desultory chat with Moonfeld, I noticed the odd formation in the jar, which Anwen had pointed out the first time we'd been in the hut. She was right, the sac-shape did look scrotal despite the shape being loops of matter and containing nothing. I'd understood the shape to be twists in the chain-fluid, a herniation of the line. *Another mystery*, I thought, *another unknown*. I'd only examined Moonfeld's, and then only in passing on that first, terrifying – *loosening* – day.

Now, waiting for Anwen, I examined the others, going from jar to jar, viewing them like display cases in a museum. I felt squeamish, ashamed, as if I were covertly and minutely examining a stranger's vulva or testicles. Baby's sac was elongated, a twist in the lower loop turning it into a figure eight. Ichika rode high, and the tendril was longer, cupping the lower loop tightly in a near-parallel arc. Pike—

Pike didn't seem to have one. I searched the jar, and then searched again from the top, my eyes tracking across in bands. There was nothing there, but I recalled Anwen saying each of the four fully-delivered minds had it. Yet Pike's was not there, and its absence gave the jar the appearance of being empty. I was about to ask Len about this when I saw a glisten at the bottom of the jar.

"Look," I said.

Len came over. "It's weeping," he replied. "I'll tell her."

8.2 For the sessions with Moonfeld, Len was to be the cartographer of the internal space. Making a three-dimensional theatre of the terrain where the walls were his sketches photocopied onto card, he said he'd fashion models to physically represent what Moonfeld was describing. Scale was a problem – the mind had no legs with which to measure out a stride – but the assumption was the mind's view of himself in the space was the same as it was in life, so Len went with that as the measure. He was excited.

Anwen was not. She was to monitor the feeds and push Baby in the off times. In her preparations for this latter, loathed, task, she'd come up with an idea for regulating time while the minds were absent. She'd found a bronze singing bowl in a shop in the local village. She rang it with its padded mallet every ten minutes. To the human ears, it was a soft sound, but to the minds the sound could be heard and felt throughout the chain-fluid, not hurtful, but the resonance of the rung bowl lingered enough for the minds to be aware of it no matter how distant they were. Hoskin thought she was trying to antagonise her by bringing the bowl into play. I privately agreed as it was too perfectly the kind of object that would anger her.

I asked Hoskin about it during a hiatus. I'd intended to try to speak to Pike, less in hope of an answer than to show that I'd tried, but this plan had to be aborted after spotting the damage to his jar. While she was repairing the damage, I asked her about the bowl—

"It's like a temple," she said, quietly, intent on her work.

"That's a problem?"

She shrugged. "I go to a temple or a church, I see lazy men. Lazy people who've chosen a life of giving because it inoculates them against criticism. They always want to be thanked. Virtue signalling. Like those women you see who have babies because working's hard. It's not that the way of life they've chosen is easier, but it's more self-centred. That's why they bleat on about their altruism so much. It's to disguise how selfish they are. How self-centred their focus on themselves and their belief and their needs are. Every time she rings that bowl, it's like some self-satisfied guru saying, *Thank me, thank meee.*"

I recalled Moonfeld had said a similar thing about her.

I watched her work. No one had paid any mind to Pike for months. Hoskin had checked his jar and found a small bump the size of a thumb tip had pushed out at the base. This was unusual, for once a mind had returned a jar didn't further change, and like the chain-fluid itself, the surface increased in brittleness as it aged. This change in the jar had caused a split in the tip of the new bump and chain-fluid was slowly weeping.

"The jar's herniated," Hoskin said.

It took an age to fix, but she worked carefully, kindly. This was her area, I realised, her skill and her art. I was watching the genius-of-the-jars, business-like as a vet, at the work she did best. She fashioned a cap from the same substance as the jar, filing it until it covered the area of the split exactly. Using a gel that melted when she heated it, she tested the cap for fit, re-filing where the hot gel seeped out until the seal was hermetic. When she was satisfied, she glued the cap on and put more glue around the join, neatening the edge with her thumb.

"Your face," she said.

"What about my face?"

"You look disgusted. You look like I'm lancing a boil."

I knew she was right. The bump in the jar, weeping a thick fluid that clotted rather than flowed, repulsed me, and it was exactly as she'd said: like the crust of pus on a boil. Organic. Animal. Human. It had been in my thoughts since I'd first seen the damage in the jar.

When I was alone with Anwen and Len, I mentioned the fix on Pike's jar. "She cares for those minds."

"Pike always needs maintaining," Len replied.

"They've a worth to her," Anwen said, quiet. "They're part of her audit trail."

"Easy," muttered Len.

"Shut up, Len. Moonfeld's to keep churning out the work, without pleasure or cease. And the grave robbers expect him to keep going. What happens when the reality hits so hard there's no way out? They can't even commit suicide in there. Silence is all the protest allowed."

"Grave robbing?"

She glared. "It's his mind Tom's mining, but do you think anything they get from this will have Moonfeld's name on it? He died last year as far as the world is concerned."

I thought about this. She was right to glare – it hadn't occurred to me, another in a long line of things that should have been obvious – but ultimately I didn't think Moonfeld would care and told her so.

"Tom gets the glory," she said, savage. "Mediocre Tom will seem like a brain, as if life hasn't dealt him enough goodies with his tits and teeth." Len began to laugh. "Don't laugh, Len," she added as she walked to the door. "You know what I mean. Nobody earns anything nowadays."

"She's right there," Len said, quiet.

Anwen had changed. A measure of her equilibrium had not returned after the night of the grapes. She and Hoskin, normally – naturally – a little antagonistic, but mostly friendly, became hard towards each other, as if offence had been caused but both sides claimed innocence. Len blamed Hoskin, but I wondered whether this wasn't simply an instinctual siding with the more bothered.

Anwen's antipathy towards Hoskin was marked now, and I sensed Hoskin was far more upset by this than she had the tools – or the status – to express. She had to be herself, and she had to be the boss. I felt for her, because things were slipping from her control and I suspected that allowing minions an ever-lengthening leash was the torment she could endure the least.

I said this to Len—

"You're right," he replied, closing the door through which Anwen had passed. "She's a great synthesiser. What she put together here beggars belief but she'll need others, experts like Tom, to pull the fruit out of her creation. Part of her wants to stand alone on the mountain, but she can't. It's not that she doesn't understand it's impossible. No one can be an expert in maths and physics and blah and blah, and no one expects her to. Apart from her." Len looked at me. "Have you thought about the minds they want to come through here? Because you'd know some of their names. That still blows my mind. Not just the fact of rooms of geniuses, but if there will be a list of names to be approached, sign their names up, proposed or seconded. I don't know." He shook his head to fling the thought out. "And what if it's all public knowledge one day, and you're not asked? Anwen was snippy about Tom, but she's right. He's not a genius. He's in on this from the start, but at the end of his life, he won't be asked."

And he knows it, I realised. "Conspiracy theory."

Len grunted. "Looks like the process is screwed anyway."

8.3 I ignored the antagonism. I focused on the routine of Moonfeld going out to his structure.

The remit for the minds was simple. To go a little further, return and report. Use the bowl's ring to find the way back to the hut and the world outside the mind. I liked the pendulum nature of this, and the call of the singing bowl. Moonfeld felt it was like rattling the house keys to call a cat.

In the absence of any other mind to work on, Anwen had been working solely on Moonfeld's voice for weeks now, and his voice had gradually been smoothed. The blunt laugh had been tempered, replaced with a reverberant hum that was not too far from accurate. It didn't sound anything like the man I'd known in life, but the voice was sanded into a human shape. It wasn't as mutable as Elephant Baby's, but I read this as Anwen's differing attitudes towards the minds. Baby's voice was a labour of love, Moonfeld's a testament to her professional skill.

On exploring, the two minds spent a lot of time on the approach, which was difficult with Moonfeld as the central structure was set amongst trees. In tracking Baby, it was obvious when the mind jumped between streets, because they could see it happen in Len's mapping of the description pictorially, but with John the presence of trees confused the issue. On the first pass, Len ended up with what looked like a bent spiral formed of box-zigzags, question marks where he was unsure of the route as Moonfeld had avoided the tree.

Taking it slowly revealed details even the mind had not been aware of. The winding path through Moonfeld's woods had to be taken a set number of times before the approach to the building could be made. I had assumed the minds jumped the track, like a needle in a record's groove, as they spoke of walking the same path twice, three times, four times, but the path was not the same in all particulars.

I kept being reminded of an old Durutti Column song titled *Favourite Descending Intervals* where each cycle of the melody entered through the same door of the octave above. The notes were the same but in a different place; here, the path was the same, but on a different level. Moonfeld allowed that this was not *Idiocy in Extremis*.

"A dance," I said. "The necessary passes in a dance before the next part. Ritual."

"Everything is ritual, Jude. Humans are ritual in meat form."

Len was frustrated with the detail, but I felt it was needed. I asked about the trees and the stones underfoot. The trees were low, just as they were in the Fallen Woods (where Moonfeld had guessed the place to be) but the stones were long and flat, like grave markers, and covered in lichen. I had him get close to the surface of one of these half-buried slabs and feel it. I expected the mind to swear and tell me not to be so stupid, but instead he answered, as if the request was possible to obey – as if he had fingers with which to feel – and told me of the feel of lichen. Moonfeld described it as feeling another person's fingerprint. Again, I could not compute the detail the mind could pull from the internal landscape, but I understood it was as real to the mind as the world had once been.

Shortly before we ended this second iteration of the script – I was sensing the copper bong behind me – I asked Moonfeld to turn around. It was the first note of concern we heard in his voice, because what he expected to see, the home that was his entire existence now, was not visible. All that was there in his visual field were the trees.

"The path is gone," he said.

Anwen hit the copper bowl. "Come home," she said, as she had with Baby. It worked. Moonfeld was immediately back in the room.

"Does this interest you?" I asked the mind before we left for the day.

"It does," Moonfeld replied. "Not in the way you think. Not in the sense of discovery. I'm interested to know what will happen if I don't come back, like Ichika. I might not return because my mind becomes extinct. Or trapped. Or I will not want to return because there is a cake shop there." I smiled. "The thought the others did not return because they were damaged concerns me. I tell myself if that happens I would not know, but still the idea disturbs me."

I again felt the absence of touch, the pull in me great to lay a hand or pat a back.

"It's important to me that you return. If you can," I said. "I'm not saying that to make you feel guilty but so you know." I swallowed, hard. "Obviously if there's a cake shop there, I'll understand."

9.1 After each pass, the three of us got together to talk about what had come back. Tom was waiting thundersome on the steps, reduced to second dibs.

Len drew, humming *Stuck in the Middle with You*, which was jammed in his head. *Earworm*, he'd said. What I thought of as dance, he'd drawn as the sections of a helix. He cut a ring from a piece of card, snipped it and pulled it out of shape.

"He said he was on the same path but different. This ring's a circle but it joins to the next ring. Climbing," he said. "*The bear went over the mountain to see what he could see.*" He drew a shape on the paper, a spiral going up a cylinder, a screw without a point. "The shapes are pre-cut and then assembled. That's how they build multi-storey car parks."

"A ziggurat," I said.

Len gave me a look. "Did you ever hear the expression about hearing hooves and thinking it's zebras?"

"I'm offering a theory."

"I know. But if you jump straight for the zebras, you close off the horses. You know what I mean?"

"I don't think I'm closing anything off."

"I agree with Len," said Anwen.

I nodded, said I understood, but beneath the surface I'd the sense I'd been discussed beforehand and in private. *Keep the new boy from weaving fancies.* Being exposed as the outsider was a familiar feeling. Moonfeld had often made me feel credulous as a child when we were out drinking, and I'd left many encounters holding piss-wet fireworks, secretly bruised.

"So it's like the sections in a multi-storey car park," I said.

They laughed, and the tight moment passed, but that night I sat outside with the others in the heat of the evening mentally absent. The thought they'd discussed me, discussed how to rein me in, itched at me, but intellectually I knew they were right. I did have a vein of romantic credulity that needed to be tempered. I convinced myself that was why I was there in the first place. The team had scientific knowledge, but not artistic knowledge. What I needed to do was display it with rigour and not be beaten down by the weight of scientific scorn. I was convinced the meaning to the structures was not measurable by science. *There is austerity to the structures, purity, but also wisdom*, I thought.

Stone. Doors. Circles. Stairs. The circle is the grave of the bone.

9.2 Moonfeld said, "The entrance to the hallway is rectangular. There is a bar across the top. Professor Negri had something similar in his office doorway for pull-ups. His ickle muscles like tangerines in a garden hose. A second lintel.

"Above the doorway is a saucer without a cup. Long. The stone is granite. Everything is stone. The stone hallway to the core of the ruin is formed by huge standing stones. Huge. Seven feet wide and twice that tall. The light is changing. I hear the sound of a bell.

"At the end of the hallway there's an open space and a figure passes the doorway. It's running in a circle around the room inside the ruin. Its body is larger than mine. There's something missing about his hands. His hands hang too low. His arms are too long. It's too dark to see his face. He doesn't seem to have any hair at all. He's running in a circle past the doorway, but the light vanishes just as he passes. It's as if I am blinking and I am not. There should be a smell. A smell of animals. The sourness of a tramp.

"I don't know where the light is coming from. There's a bell ringing.

"I saw a zoetrope in a film. It span and had rectangular slits in it, and inside a strip of paper had images drawn on it. As the cage span, the images moved. I've remembered this. But the running man is not between the slits. The arms are so long. It must be a feature of how I'm seeing things, but it seems the stones are moving like the slits in the zoetrope, but the man is not. He won't stop running. He has no more substance than the card in the zoetrope.

"In the centre of the room there's a hole in the floor, stairs going down in a spiral. The steps are the same as the wall stones. There's that bell again. The steps are the size of these stones laid flat. Great stones. Great old stones."

9.3 "It took three calls to get him back," Anwen said.

"The features are the same," Len said, full of gloom. "The path, the walls. It's the same pattern as the others. They've read the same place differently. What is for Baby the tiles in the tube, for Moonfeld is the standing stones in a hallway. And now the flickering is the same. This bloody man. This man unnerves me."

"If it's a man."

"The rectangles of Baby's steps match the slits in the stone zoetrope. The figure is seen through alternating blocks of light and dark." Len shook his head. "A zoetrope creates the illusion of movement. And the spiral. Again the spiral. Or helix." He looked up. "He sounded absent to me. He sounded like he was going."

"It took three calls to get him back."

"In ancient art," I said, "the spiral can represent the passage between two worlds."

Len laughed. "From the earth to Debenhams. It's a multi-storey car park, Jude."

"That's what I meant."

"You know," said Anwen, quiet, "Indigenous Australians believe a human has three minds. A gut mind, a heart mind, a head mind. When people go out into the outback alone, they warn them not to spend too much time in the head mind. The brain. They say *that* mind is chaos. It's too young to handle too much solitude and very quickly goes insane."

10.1 I regretted my careless comment about Baby, and I was anxious to show I was treating her with as much attention as Moonfeld. Whenever Anwen talked to her mind, I was there. Often we never left, just asked Moonfeld to allow us the privacy to *change our mind* and we'd re-orientate ourselves in the room to face the glow of Baby's jar.

I agreed with Anwen. Hoskin's use of the mind as a control was cruel. There was a growing time-lag between the travel and the return. It was Anwen's idea to get the minds to narrate in the present tense what they were seeing – she believed it put them more in the moment than past tense narration – and this was adopted by Moonfeld immediately, but for Baby this seemed to turn up the distress on her experience, and she began to withhold her compliance. There was a note of distrust when she spoke to Anwen, never there before, and I sensed her descriptions of the tiles, the line, the staircase and the entrance onto the station was seen from the corner of an eye or behind a hiding hand.

"I feel like I'm getting her progressively more drunk for a man I know will do her harm," Anwen confessed on the next flea cull, herself at the vacuum while I sprayed the carpet from the edges to the centre.

Anwen had got Baby onto the tube station platform now, the line empty and the platform very short. The figure had gone, but there was an open door to a utility room (*Or worse*, the mind had added, making me laugh). She would not look at the door without the most concerted yet gentle persuasions, and when she did, she described a four-fingered hand gripping the edge of the door. The third finger was the stump, and the hand was dirty. "A dirty hand," she said, then fell into the repetition that denoted machine panic.

Moonfeld on the other hand was more drawn to the room in the centre of the building, his *stone zoetrope*, beyond which we did not ask him to go, even though we'd no power to stop him. According to Hoskin, this accelerated the mind's decline, and she clearly regretted her decision. That she'd no choice upset her control, and there was an air of impatience in the house when she was around, but also of futility. I hadn't paid attention to the centrality of Moonfeld to the house. Now that he was becoming vaguer, and his thinking was no longer clear on his reason for existence – the continuing of his work on the cruciate ridge – everyone's status slipped into a passive, maintenance role. Only Anwen, and the ever-functionless me, were now busy and motivated, and Len had joined in with us, but Hoskin and Tom were at a loose end, and dealing with it badly.

Tom took to his bed when he was not sweating at the obstacles to the work. "Chocked aeroplane," he said one day, referring to Moonfeld's mind. "Props turning but no flight."

Hoskin was grumpy as a child with a toy that had lost its batteries, or wound down. She found herself work to do, but it was make-work, with make-work's inbuilt frustration at not being the real thing. She asked for updates and complained about the speed of the progress—

"What is it with the stones?" she asked me. "Why are you asking him about every stone in the shop?"

I told her it was to help him remember his way back, in case the minds were lost rather than missing or broken. "The stones don't change," I told her. "He can remember the way back, if he chooses to."

Hoskin accepted this. "It's driving me mad," she muttered.

It didn't help that I was in my element. I'd gone beyond Len's caution now and was convinced a part of a deep human past had been unlocked in the delivery of the minds. I had Moonfeld walk around the central henge looking for objects on the floor – plants, stones, pebbles – but the room was as bare as Ichika's well and Pike's nautilus prison. I asked the mind to describe every stone in the circle, not wanting to admit how much I yearned for a symbol or writing. Len was bored. Anwen was bored. I could tell sometimes in the way she hit the copper bowl.

Even Moonfeld was bored. "I saw the number forty-two once," he said, "does that help?"

I experienced a wild second of joy before I understood his joke.

In the moment, however, Moonfeld was hypnotised, methodical, describing the stones as minutely as I'd asked him to. I read this as reverence. Len thought the mind was stoned—

"I'm serious. That's what people on LSD are like. Hours spent on tiny details. Perhaps that's all this is. Progressively more stoned bowls of mind. Like that bastard cat."

Len was so smitten with this LSD theory he took it to Hoskin, who took long, cold pleasure in demonstrating how stupid it was.

11.1 Something happened to severely test the equilibrium of the facility.

In an effort to keep herself busy, Hoskin was with the silent minds fiddling with a new patch for Pike's jar, using an unwarped glass cylinder to experiment with the seal. Anwen was in the hut working on the speaker for Moonfeld's plinth, the door open so she had a clear view of Hoskin. "We didn't say a word to each other," Anwen said later.

Like Len, Hoskin drew to centre her thoughts, but her drawings were lined with figures and symbols, millimetric dimensions for the glass, materials. Using a recorder, she liked to talk herself through her thoughts, as bewildering to the lay person as a pathologist narrating steps in an autopsy.

Hoskin was dictating into her recorder when Tom came down the ladder. He had a roll of paper under his arm for his maths flipchart, and with the perfection of a clown with a plank, he turned and the end of the paper roll knocked the recorder out of Hoskin's hand and into the next jar, one of the minds half-formed, with the twist in the glass that signified a minor form of cerebral clenching had turned the glass. Before Anwen realised what Hoskin was doing, and perhaps before Hoskin herself realised what she was doing, Hoskin had reached her hand in past the wrist, grabbed the recorder where it was slowing in the fluid, and pulled it out. Elbow high, she let the arm drip into the jar, smoothing off the lube-like chain-fluid.

"Her dictaphone thing, her hand, her wrist were all wet. The hairs on her wrist. It was fluid, and in that fluid was all that had come through of a human mind. It appalled me," Anwen told me.

"Would it have made a difference if the recorder had ended up in an unwarped jar?"

"Yes," she said. "Maybe." She looked down at her hands on her lap. I'd heard that minute examination of the hands was a marker for despair but couldn't recall if the person who'd told me was an expert or a man in a pub. "I don't know," she said finally. "I don't know how I'd have reacted."

I'd heard from Len how Anwen *had* reacted. She'd lost all restraint on her temper, shrieking at Hoskin, swearing at her. There was even suggestion Anwen had hit Hoskin, but this was more that her arms, in her complete unhingement, were pointing in emphasis, opening out to include the hut, the pool, the world, and Hoskin, her hand and wrist still above the jar letting the chain-fluid drip, couldn't move out of the way.

I smiled. "Len said you called her the bad word."

"Please," Anwen replied, "I *started* with the bad word."

Her voice was colourless, unlike her. It was dispirited, or de-spirited, the essentials of human speech remaining but the kicks and the jumps gone, like a spring lamb swaddled. It occurred to me she sounded like one of the minds.

"What did she say?" Anwen asked.

"Nothing." I shrugged. "I think she's still in shock. I expect she'll get over it. With her charm and charisma, it can't be the first time someone's lost their chips with her."

This got a smile at least. Anwen looked up, drained. "I felt she'd the top of a skull off and she'd pushed her hand into a brain. A bowl of porridge. Two fingers into silly putty. It was that violating."

I nodded. My reaction would have been muted, but I also saw the chain-fluid as a more-than-organic substance. I knew it was a chemical construct like oil or glue, but emotionally it felt of human origin. I told Anwen that when Hoskin came out of the pool to wash her hands, she'd put the recorder in front of me. She'd scraped most of the fluid off with card, but it was still wet. I'd made a fold of paper for it and packaged it within, as careful not to touch the machine as if it were a turd.

I told her I'd caught up with Hoskin at the outside sink, washing her hands. She hadn't mentioned Anwen at all. Instead she went for me—

"Len's told me what you're thinking. It's shit, Jude. It's mystical shit. If a car got a rattle or started pulling to the left, you wouldn't posit a strange attractor or a black hole. It's like a cat mewing at the ceiling or a cupboard. *Oh it's a ghost*, you'll say. Nonsense."

"I'm not a scientist. Those are the only answers I can give you," I said, then added, knowing it was cutting, "The people who can give you the answers you'll accept have failed."

Hoskin shook her hands, wiped them on her trousers. "Thanks for pointing that out." She looked directly at me. "Push on with it. Get it done."

"She's angry because she doesn't understand," I told Anwen. "That will surely pass."

Anwen looked neither comforted nor convinced.

12.1 Although there was a rapprochement of sorts, brokered by Len, the house splintered after the argument. The team, once upbeat, settled into various negative states.

Hoskin finally reached a place of resignation, waiting for the process to end one way or the other. Anwen remained on edge, and I thought she was becoming paranoid there was an unspoken agenda where the minds – Elephant Baby – were concerned. Len agreed.

Tom was dismayed that the speed of Moonfeld's decline was increasing. It wasn't that the mind didn't talk to him; he did, but the mathematics was disjointed, and his attention would vanish in the middle of a thought. "Like a dog hearing a whistle," he said.

Len was engaged but suspicious of my intentions, and what he felt was my slipping into loose thinking. *Culpable Idiocy.* I did not intuit this. His opinion was written all over him, and occasionally spoken. In part, this was because I was in my element, my mind turning and turning the possibilities of the ruins, of the structures. I was still cautioning myself against going overboard, but it did not work. I was becoming lulled by the siren song of the structures and what they might mean.

Len's mockery was in truth the only thing that kept me anchored. I'd told him of a dream I'd had of Stonehenge rising out of the earth to reveal it as the circle on top of an immense *cong*, dirt falling in house-sized clods from the indentations up the sides.

"Do you know what the *cong* reminds me of?" Len said. "It reminds me of a multi-storey car park."

13.1 "We won't ever ask you to do this again," Anwen said.

I looked at her in the light of Baby's jar. This had not been agreed, but Anwen's expression was fixed and I knew I would comply.

We led Baby to the underground station in her internal landscape. As with Moonfeld, the further we penetrated the station, the faster the earlier steps progressed. It took half an hour to narrate the mind to the base of the staircase and onto the platform, which was short, room enough for one ordinary tube carriage. Anwen had her pace in the direction away from the utility room door, trying to get her used to the station platform, and to calm her before she turned her and forced her to face the mutilated hand around the door.

"There's a flickering," said Baby when at last she turned. "The hand is gone."

The utility door remained open. As she approached, the flickering grew more random. It emanated from the open space in the tube station wall but seemed connected to the overall ambient light of the station, for all lights went dark when the light in the wall was off.

"It's like I'm inside someone else's eyes when they're blinking with their eyes," she said.

In her voice, I heard the speed and repetition that denoted panic.

The mind reached the door into the wall. Rounding the edge, she looked inside towards the flickering light.

"It's long. The man is there up above. Up above in the tunnel, the long tunnel."

As she described it, the tunnel was stone, like a utility tunnel under motorways and within dams, bridges. The mind could see no source for the light. When Anwen began to ask about the figure in the tunnel, Baby's panic ratcheted up a click until she was barely coherent. She spoke of a man with long hands, waking sideways as the great apes do, hunched into the tunnel. In the narration, which Anwen intoned like a guided meditation, Anwen asked her to step into the tunnel.

One step—

"Are you stepping into the tunnel?"

"He's turned. He's turned when I went in. He turned in the tunnel. I'm in the tunnel. A man there in the tunnel. A man with long hands. He's looking at me. Checking to see if I'll follow. His eyes are white."

She span into full panic then, repeating *white* over and again. Anwen looked at me and very slowly drew a finger across her throat. I nodded.

"Come home," said Anwen.

I took her narration pad. As usual, she'd checked off the steps as she'd led her through. We'd only missed one thing on the guide narrative: the investigation into the tunnel itself. I was about to mention it when Anwen gripped my arm hard. I turned, listened—

The mind was singing, very low. We listened, both rapt and spooked at the same time. It was the rhyme Anwen had written down when Baby was first returning – the rhyme the mind had denied all knowledge of when fully returned – and was now singing again. The song was complete, including the parts Anwen had not managed to scribble down at the time—

> Needle teeth, needle teeth,
> sleep in the boat you'll bleed beneath.
> Open your mouth for a scream's relief.
> Needle teeth, watch for the bone's glow.
>
> Needle teeth, needle teeth,
> eat to the fill for your greed's release.
> Open the wooden door underneath.
> Needle teeth, watch for the bone's glow.
>
> Needle teeth, needle teeth,
> listen for darkness's endless peace
> dancing attendance on light's decease.
> Needle teeth, watch for the bone's glow.

14.1 Moonfeld never met the figure in the zoetrope. The guide. The flicker that gave the impression of the revolving stones in the first place never left the central henge-like space.

The pattern was well-established now. I would talk the mind through the narrative. Anwen would mark time and the route. Len would draw, occasionally reminding me to ask about scale. If the mind's internal body shape held true to life, the diameter of the zoetrope was about thirty feet, which meant the guide was in the distance, but still sufficiently large for detail of the figure to be seen.

I had Moonfeld describe the figure from top down and bottom up. I asked him to tell me about the hands and felt a thrill when Moonfeld replied, "There was something odd about the length of the arms and the shape of the hands. The hands are not complete. The fingers are not complete."

"That detail again," Anwen whispered.

We spent a long time on the stance of the figure as facial and physical detail was always in shadow. Again, the lack of human proportion struck Moonfeld, but the idea I'd leaped to – that the figure was ape-like – was scotched from the start. The figure ran upright like a man; the silhouette of the skull was the same as a human's. It was the arms that were wrong, together with the stance on the few occasions Moonfeld saw it at rest between two of the standing stones. The figure stood on the front of its feet, the long arms loosely bent at the joint, elbows out, a nod in the wrists.

"A fighter at rest," he said. "Those long, waiting arms they have."

The man leant forwards, which with the weight on the balls of his feet gave the impression of readiness for flight.

"He's started to fall," Moonfeld said. "The gravity of a fall begun is as much a part of flight as the ability to run. To have started and held that fall will buy it precious milliseconds."

Abruptly, the figure was gone.

15.1 Len worked on the stones. For all he said he was bored by the pace of the sessions, he was as obsessed by the minutiae of what Moonfeld was describing as I was.

He showed his art one night, taking me to his room. It was a haven of gear, worse than it had been the first time I'd seen it, full of books and plates and the droopy mats of his linocuts.

"I feel you're watching from the corner of your eye," I said as I looked at his drawings and prints. "Like you're suspicious of me."

Len looked towards the window. "No. Not that."

I nodded, attention still with the art. "Not that then. But something."

Len took a moment. "I'm waiting for you to embarrass us," he replied at last. "To me, what's happening is very simple. He's losing his mind. They're all losing their minds and, god love her, it's killing Hoskin because it's killing the project. I don't know what's causing the problem, but I know it's something mechanical, or chemical, and I'm worried you are going to start jumping up and down saying you've found a magic caveman. Whatever. If and when we find the reason the bellies go spiralling up their own shitters, it'll be the magnets shearing the chain-fluid over time and that'll be that. They'll fix it or they won't. It's as simple as that. Hoskin needs to look to that more than anything else. You being here at all is a failure of nerve and initiative on her part."

I nodded, hurt but relieved Len's itch was out in the open. "I don't think he's losing his mind," I said.

"Listen to him. Weird rhymes in his speech. *That long, waiting arm. A nod in the wrist.* What does that mean?"

"I know what that means. It's an image. I see a boxer. The balance. The readiness of a fighter. A hunter."

Len made a face. "I don't think poetry has any place here. You're buying into it because that's your bag."

"The same's true in reverse, Len," I replied, heated now. "You want it to be—. Whatever it was you just said. Metal fatigue? That's *your* bag. But there's discovery here. It's not your discovery, or the discovery Hoskin expected, or even in any special way *my* discovery, but it *is* discovery."

Len nodded to himself. "It's not," he said, quiet. "There's nothing but the mechanic or chemical failure of a wildly ambitious project at the earliest stages of its implementation. And Moonfeld's going. Talk to Tom. The mind's being going for weeks now, if not months. Christ, he was probably going from the moment he got here." He held up his palms. "I'm not saying I'm not interested. I am. I am *stone* fascinated. But I'm not going along with the boat. As the French say." He smiled, anxious to remain friendly. "Look at me, Jude. This man is your friend. He is going to die on you again. Have you spared a thought for that?"

This shook me. The possibility of Moonfeld leaving me again had lived like a grub in the base of my skull, never faced but always moving, pulsing along its segmented length, yet I turned from it always.

To change the subject, I asked Len to see the drawings he'd made of the sacs in the delivered minds. I'd asked Anwen about the absence of the sac in Pike's jar, but she'd told me to ask Len.

The conversation had been as awkward for Len as for me, and he briskly clapped his hands and found the notebook with them in. I flipped through. They weren't like the appearance in the real jars – it would have been hard to achieve in pencil what was translucent in actuality – but I recognised the shapes. I knew them from past perusal, so I didn't need to examine them further. I was looking for Pike's and found it. Again, it was similar in the structure of the sac, but different in the innards. What was surprising was that I'd not seen anything like it in Pike's jar.

15.2 I told Anwen I'd looked again and not seen Pike's sac. "It's there," she said. "I've seen it. I'll show you."

"If his wound is healed, perhaps you could."

"Okay."

Again, she had the colourlessness in her speech. She was absent, withdrawing into her own world. Everyone was: Len into his artwork, Anwen into talking to Elephant Baby or her work on Moonfeld's voice. If the mind was retreating from the world, so too were we humans. Tom, eaten alive by frustration, was spending more time at a pub he'd found, poring over calculations that seemed to go nowhere. Hoskin walked long and alone on the land around the facility, gone most of the day sometimes. Len was right: she'd lost her nerve and initiative. I dreaded her returning one evening and yanking every plug in the pool in fury. Their efforts had been rendered futile, and the perceived inevitability of Moonfeld's decline had tugged the rug from under all of their moods. Only I had the hope that they were wrong.

"How's Elephant Baby?"

"I'm not taking her there again."

"That wasn't what I was asking."

She looked up at me. "She's come back. She's stopped singing. She seems flatter than before."

I paused. "So do you."

She sighed, heavily. "It's nothing. I've spent so long on this now. So much time on their voices, evening them out, making them human. The hours I've spent—."

"Moonfeld's improved so much."

"I'm not asking for whoops, Jude. I'm just saying. If it all goes the same way for the minds, the work I've done on Ichika and Pike and Moonfeld dies with them. I'm not being snippy, but it'll be bloody ironic if after all the work it ends up in silence. And it makes me miserable."

Moonfeld had noticed this withdrawal. "My afflictions have not been around." He meant Tom and Hoskin.

"You're not much use to them."

"That is cruel."

"Apparently Tom is beating his head against a wall."

"Perhaps that will help."

I breathed for a few moments. "They're concerned that you're not focused. Do you feel it in yourself? You said before the physical was fading for you, gradually sinking into memory. Your field, your work, is that fading?"

The mind was a long time in replying. "Mathematics was the world. That was why I did it. What you and I are doing now is equally absorbing." Another long pause. "It is odd, but it was not until you asked that I realised it was interesting in the same way. The shape of a space must have meaning."

"I don't know what that means, John."

"A space doesn't have the properties it has by accident."

I massaged my temples. "Thanks. That's much clearer."

I knew I should ask the logical follow-up – *Have you abandoned work on the cruciate ridge?* – but feared the answer. I feared more the answer being recorded for Tom and Hoskin to hear. If the answer was *Yes*, the mind's worth vanished – my own worth vanished – in one syllable.

I closed my eyes. I'd been doing this more and more while talking to the mind now. It centred me, and I felt more in tune with the mind when only the voice in the dead air of the room was reaching my senses.

"What draws you there?"

"I don't know," said the mind. A pause. "You used the word *seduction* once. That sounded like the right word."

"You know that the concern is that you won't return."

"Like Ichika."

"Like Ichika," I echoed, thinking, *Why not like Pike?*

"It makes you sad."

This caught me off guard. "Yes," I said, too late.

"Definite pause there." I laughed. "This fascinates you, doesn't it?"

"Doesn't it you?"

"Of course. Perhaps that is the key to it. I cannot wait to see what happens. Because it is unknown to me, and it should not be unknown. Nothing has been unknown to me since I returned." Silence. "I spend more time in my memories now. I cannot tell you how remarkable it is that I still have them. I have no idea where they live now, and I have no independent knowledge of if they are the same memories I had when meat, or even if they are real in the first place, but part of my memory is telling it to you, so you are my corroboration.

"You said the word *seduction* the other day, and I thought of something that happened when I was sixteen. After the children's home we were pampered, and the foster families joined forces to take us away on holiday. We went to Germany on a school trip. We were in these huts in a circle by the side of a lake. Chalet arrangement. I got up to go to the toilet in the night, and when I was returning from the block that housed them, one of the girls was there. Rebecca. Rebecca Guest. She seemed sleepy, but she said later she had been waiting for me. She said she had been sunburned. She pulled one side of her knickers down to reveal the tan line her bikini bottoms had left at the top of her thigh. The crease of her hip. The edge of her pubic hair. I was sixteen, mind. Then she said, *Feel the difference in the heat*, so I put the back of my hand over the tan line to feel the cool in the unburnt skin and the heat in the burnt skin. I cannot and never could remember if there actually was a difference between the two because the tips of my fingers were touching her hair there. I was a sixteen-year-old hetty, Jude. All of my mind, my awareness, was in that hand—. I cannot tell you.

"Nothing happened. I think we kissed. That fragile kiss you have when you are that young." He paused. "You asked if the room of the stones fascinated me. It is not fascination. I am nervous. I am nervous for myself. There is danger. There is danger for myself. I know there is change afoot, and like sex I might walk through a door that turns into a wall when I close it behind me. And it is the same as it was with that girl. I am in danger of changing and I am not sure I want to. But there is no way I am moving that hand."

"I remember you telling me about Rebecca."

"Strange that your memory is all I have to guarantee the accuracy of mine," said Moonfeld.

"Is there anything I can do to stop you from leaving?"

The mind was silent for a long time. "I cannot answer that question," he said at last, "because I do not have the intention to leave. A son does not mean to leave his parents for the world of sex. He just goes. It happens without mind, and failure to do so is an unnatural thing, an aberration. But Jude, you need to bear one thing in mind. *I have already left*. It happened in a hospital in Cubton months if not years ago and my body was placed in the ground. And anyway, what would it matter if I did not return from one of our jollies? All this continued existence is just gravy, Jude. What would it matter?"

I opened my eyes. The glow of the jar was always much brighter when I did so, a massed bag of transparent cankers dimpled all over with dips and bumps. It had a personality, and its shape in the world had come to be as much to me as Moonfeld's face had once been: a recognised object in a crowd, a harbour. This construct, this glowing sack surrounded by the exploded cloak of the magnetic blades and scoops, tubed and patched and leached and bled, this strange thing, the strangest thing I'd ever seen scant weeks before but now a beloved object, this *man* was vital.

"It would matter to me, John," I said.

15.3 On coming up from the pool, I felt desolate. For some reason, I read through my journals from my time here. They were jumbled and unclear, full of half-formed thoughts. The idea of pulling together a narrative came to me.

That night was when I began to write this testament.

16.1 Days passed.

One evening, the farmhouse was deserted and the kitchen was dark, as it ever was at that time of the evening. Normally, the team put a note under a fridge magnet to explain where they were, but the notes there were old. I'd not been to the pub myself. I knew roughly where it was and contemplated going for a drink, but the thought of my likely reception stopped me. I pictured faces at the bar failing to hide their disappointment. It was paranoid, unwarranted, the rational brain in me knew. I made myself a tea instead and sat staring at the wall, not really thinking of anything at all. I'd been there for twenty minutes when a stranger walked into the kitchen and opened the fridge.

The adrenalin roared through me. I pushed back from the table. The stranger was huge, about six two, and he carried his weight in his buttocks. I started to rise, thinking of weapons, but also – unhelpfully – of the word *steatopygian*.

I got to my feet. "Hey," I said.

The fridge door closed. "They belong to everyone," said the stranger, and only then did I recognise him. Samuel, the socially-neutered IT geek, three cans of pop in his hand.

"You scared me."

This had no meaning or effect for the man. He was already leaving.

I waited for my heart to return to rest. My relief gave way to annoyance, and in my lack of company I stoked this into an outrage the man hadn't apologised.

"Wanker," I muttered, winding myself up for a show-down. When sufficiently angered, I went to find the feed room. I took my tea.

Samuel wasn't there. Anwen was in front of the monitors, headphones on. Even from her back and spine, I could tell she was upset. Her elbows were out, and I assumed she was looking at her hands again. I didn't want to frighten her as I had just been terrified so I turned the lights quickly on and off, and as she turned, I caught a glimpse of what she was listening to. Feed *L*, Pike's feed. She took off her headphones.

"I was looking for Sam," I said. "He scared the life out of me."

"I told him to go," she said.

"I was going to tell him the same thing in the vernacular." I pointed at the monitor with my tea. "Is Pike talking?"

Anwen didn't answer. Her face was drawn, white. That she was weary was obvious, but there was more to it than that. I could tell by the way her eyes moved about the room. She was normally a direct person. She looked at you, or she didn't. Something had disturbed her.

"Who's here?" she asked.

"Samuel. Me. Mary Celeste's in the lav."

"You were right about the sac in Pike," she said. "It's not there anymore." She turned to the desk to pick up her tablet. "I took this. Look." She opened a picture on the screen, zooming in until it was translucent white, an extreme close-up of one of the jars. "It's Pike," she told me. "I was ages looking into his jar. The sac hasn't travelled. It's gone. This is where it was. Look."

I looked. The screen was filled with a featureless white, exactly as the other jars were, with only the imperfections and warpings of the glass visible as shadows. There were motes within, as always, and with the zoom I noticed the suspicion of a line through the fluid, as though the contents had separated into liquids of two different specific gravities about the midline.

"What am I looking at? The line?"

"Yes, the line." She cleared her throat. "I think she took the sac out. I think she put her man hands into the mind and cut that ganglion, or whatever it was, out." Her mouth turned savage. "Pike's always in maintenance," she whispered.

I zoomed in again. The view got more smudgy. I said, "It doesn't mean it's her."

"Come on," she muttered. She picked a tongue unit from the desk behind her, pulling a wire from the back of it. "Look at this. This is Pike's tongue. The connection to the feed's been cut. We know Pike went silent, and I'm ninety-nine percent certain his silence is real and that this – whatever this is – happened after, but at a certain point someone snipped the feed line, ensuring he remained silent. So I replaced it this evening with a fresh one."

I searched her face. "He's not silent?" Anwen began to speak, failed. "What are you saying?"

"I'm saying she fiddled with him. I'm saying he went silent, and he was expendable so she cut out the sac as an experiment. She'd have monitored him to see if there was a change, and I think there was so she tore out the tongue unit."

I saw where she was going. "And?"

She turned to the monitor and unplugged her headphones so the feed played through the room speakers. She turned it up loud. What came through was noise, but noise that felt like distorted speech, some so clear it was like hearing a profoundly deaf person speak.

The more I listened, the more the long sounds took on the form of words, but words in a lost language: a language of a people who practised mouth mutilation as some rite, or cut the tongue for some religious purpose. I stood for a moment in shock.

"Turn it off," I said. She stared at me for a moment. "Turn it all off," I said again.

"I can't," she said.

My ear interpreted the voice in the feed as screaming. It wasn't screaming. I'd no idea what the sound was, but it was screaming to me. The scream someone might produce when terror had eaten through any shackle on sanity until only the mechanics of a scream were left functioning.

"Please turn that off, Anwen."

She plugged her headphones back on, cutting off the room speakers, and turned back to the console. She resumed staring at her hands. "There's something else," she said, her back to me. "How many minds are there?"

"Thirteen."

"Thirteen."

"Spooky," I said. "Do you think that's significant?"

"No, it's not the number I'm thinking about, Jude. What letter's been assigned to Moonfeld on the feeds?"

"P."

"P. The sixteenth letter of the alphabet."

I saw what she meant. I'd never questioned it before, but now she had it struck me as odd. "Maybe there's a reason they missed letters out. Like car registrations. Or postcodes."

It felt like a stupid thing to say, and Anwen didn't deign to answer. She clicked play on the feed, drowning me out.

16.2 I couldn't sleep. The fleas were out again, so I did my stations of the cross with the spray. While the stink was clearing, I hung my head out of the window staring at the night. There was no breeze in the air, and the summer had kept at its relentless ratchet on heat. I didn't think I'd ever been so uncomfortable in summer in my life.

I was miserable, I knew, and it wasn't just the heat. In truth, the jolt the sudden appearance of Sam had given me could still be felt in my heartbeat. I didn't feel ill, and I took my medicine like a good boy, but a sense of offness was in my chest. I'd managed to ignore the truth of my illness – it only surfaced as monumental dread at the thought I might drop dead without knowing – but the fluttery sensation would not shift.

Equally, the noise in the feed Anwen played had shocked me profoundly, and irrationally I blamed her for poisoning my evening. The more I thought about it, the more I believed everything was being poisoned. Hoskin driven to take the nail clippers to one of her own minds, Anwen forced to guide Baby deeper into fear, Tom corrupted into falsehood. Anwen was right. There was grubbiness to the question of attribution, but less in the fact Moonfeld wouldn't be credited with the work than in the fact it was Tom would need to publish any results, to fudge origins, to claim work as his own that belonged to a secret other. I felt for him, and turned my thoughts to how Len and Sam were poisoned by events, but that didn't fit the pattern. They both seemed as content as always. Len even looked happier, given licence to please himself. The fact they didn't fit the pattern made me angrier.

"You're being ridiculous," I muttered to myself.

There was a bright spot. My relationship with a friend had been renewed. Beyond all expectation, it was not the same as we'd had before. It had deepened through the strangeness of our lives now into something closer and more fine-knit than we'd had before. If anything, I liked John more now. What Len had said the other day was true, and it was foolish of me not to have thought of it. I would miss Moonfeld desperately if and when he went, and the nature of the loss would be different than the loss suffered over a year beforehand. It was a new Moonfeld, shorn by technology of the froth-speeched buffoon-manqué into a clean voice, a human voice—

I winced, thinking again of Anwen playing the warped feed from Pike's jar. It was the thought I'd been trying to close off. I tried to persuade myself I'd heard nothing – no words, no mutilation of voice – and what came through was computers trying to interpret sounds and, being programmed to find them, played what it thought was a voice. It was (perhaps literally) just chains in barrels rattling, and believing the noise was speech was as foolish as hearing a ghost in the pipes of an old house. And yet I couldn't quite sell myself on this as a part of me believed I'd heard the strangled articulation of a *self* in the ruin of a mind, as upsetting as seeing a lung still taking in breath in a butcher's offal bucket.

I understood this was the source of Anwen's distress. Hoskin's hand in the silent mind had curdled her completely, yet this howl in the feed was worse. Pike had once been a consciousness that could communicate, and now he was lost to words. To believe he'd become subsumed into a visual construct was one thing – there was hope there – but to think he'd been subject to a guesswork snip and left to shriek was too awful to think about.

What if this disappearance into the internal ruins was the same? I wondered. The assumption was that the mind would go onward and inward to find a place of peace, of rest, of understanding, but this was naïve, rose-scented rubbish.

In the distance, I saw a torch moving in the lane. Soon I heard the voices of those returning. They were singing. The sound made me feel desperately alone and hurt they'd gone off without me, without even asking me. I didn't know why the thought caused me such lonely, lonely pain, and it is only now that I am writing this that I realise how worry about my heart dictated the track of my mood and thoughts.

No wonder everything looked like death—

I couldn't blame the team. I was a stranger to their group after all. I was the stranger, yet their hopes of rescue lay in me. I should have pitied them.

17.1 "I've a dream for you," Anwen said the next morning. She seemed more herself. "Nice shorts."

"You seem chipper. I thought I'd be cleaning blood off the floor."

"Don't you want to hear my dream?"

I nodded, and she told me she'd dreamt of seeing a window high in the farmhouse with no corresponding space within. She'd searched the interior where the room should have been and found a wallpapered door, beyond which was a room, empty but for a man cuffed moaning to a dentist's chair, his eyes, nose and mouth stitched shut. Periodically, his head gave an exaggerated nod as though indicating something on the floor in front of him. This nod was sickening as his skull had been opened and the top pulled off, and a jar filled with chain-fluid was jammed into the hole made. The nod caused the fluid to slosh. Wires ran from the side of the jar down into the brain stem, trapped at the lip of the cut skull by the force of the jamming. Grotesquely – for the jar reached high above where a skull usually rounded – an attempt had been made to pull the scalp over the top of the jar to hold it in, but the skin had torn, and the best that had been achieved was like the tying of a too-full binbag.

"—or the hanky that holds Dick Whittington's belongings on the end of a stick," she finished, cheerily, and went back to her cornflakes.

I turned. I'd already figured out the dream was not for me, and I found what I expected to find. Hoskin was behind me, staring levelly at Anwen. She took a sip of her coffee and went back into the farmhouse.

"That's a little antagonistic."

"You're the dream man," said Anwen.

"We all dream now," I replied. "Have you noticed how vivid?"

Anwen wasn't biting. "I went to see Baby last night. She's slipping away, Jude. We're not guiding her there, but she's being pulled anyway." Her voice slipped. "She's scared. It's horrible to know she's afraid. And for her, if she's afraid and doesn't come back, what will that mean?"

"Anwen, I don't know what you want from me."

"Pick a side," she said. "I want you to pick a side."

"*My* side," I snapped. "I'm the only fucker *on* my side."

This wasn't what she meant. "I'm not talking about some philosophical division between science and art, you dick," she said, "I'm talking about whether you look on the minds as tools for you to use, or as human beings."

"Humans. Of course, as humans. What the hell, Anwen? That's not fair. I'm doing what I can to keep them returning. To keep them here with us. If I don't do that, I'm complicit in his disappearance, in his death, surely?"

"What?" she replied, loud now. "*No.* You are not complicit in his death, Jude. You're complicit in his *life.*"

17.2 "She had a good last line, I thought," said Len as I was coming down the ladder into the pool.

"There's no privacy here."

"Don't worry. She'll come around. She's invested in Baby, and sometimes it's convenient for her to forget she's as complicit as the rest of us."

I wasn't so sure she would come round. "She called me a dick," I said. It came out more wounded than intended.

Len had made a model of the stone zoetrope for his little theatre. It was fixed to the card by a pin and he had to reach his hand underneath to set it spinning. He'd also cut out a picture of his approximation of the guide-figure from black card, and we both viewed it through the spinning slits in the zoetrope. It didn't quite work, but the flicker was there.

Len flattened the sides of the theatre – the parts where he'd drawn the winding path to the labyrinth – and asked me to look down on it from above. I did so and saw the familiar pattern of paths approaching, then the circular ruin, the stone zoetrope, the spiral steps leading down in the centre. Laid out like that, the whole pattern showed a spiralling into a single point.

"What's your point?"

"They're circling the drain." Len touched my arm. "I'm kidding. My point is that we should take him further in."

"You mean you *don't* think it's the magnets."

"I know it's not the magnets. Do you think Hoskin didn't check the magnets?"

Anwen did not come. I didn't expect her to. I took charge of the singing bowl. I narrated the path to the labyrinth. I had Moonfeld step through a gap in the henge and approach the spiral steps leading down. I asked the guide questions—

What can you see? What's to the left of you? What's to the right? Move forwards. Look up. Look down. Where is the light coming from? Touch the stone. What can you see up ahead?

17.3 Moonfeld did not return after the first reading of the script. The routine was that we'd wait until he returned before talking him through the same route, this time relying on his memory of where he'd been.

He didn't return.

To his credit, Len seemed as upset as me at this, and not just for the fear of Hoskin's reaction. We both stayed in the hut, reluctant to leave and as shame-faced as two wet dogs caught on a couch. "I'm not telling her," he said at one point. "This was your crazy idea."

I kept ringing the copper bowl. The deep note was out-of-place in a room filled with computer hum. The sound seemed to swallow all the brown noise of IT until the tone faded and the hum returned, a form of silence in the room because it was nothing at all, a sound only detectable by its absence.

"I'm not telling her," said Len. "I'm just saying."

We waited, we paced as far as the wires would let us, we watched. The great white jar appeared to grow in the room, so closely were we focused on it, and I wanted it to grow, to glow, to change colour, to move, to do anything at all to signify there was activity in the mind. Unwisely, I got close to the surface of the jar with my earphones in. I wanted to see the tongue in the base, to see if it was as still as the silence suggested, but I put my head past the barrier of the magnetic guide blades, which sucked the earphones from my head. When I'd retrieved them, I hit the singing bowl and my hand was shaking so much the mallet connected twice.

"Please come back," I whispered. I recalled Anwen's imperative tone with Baby. "Come home," I said, louder.

Two hours passed before we heard the first sounds from the speaker in the plinth. As a joke, Len got on his knees and bowed to the floor of the hut three times.

I laughed in relief. "Where have you been?"

Moonfeld said, "I did not hear the bell."

"It's good to hear your voice."

"I can tell."

The relief took a while to disperse, but when we were calm, I took the mind through the questions again, this time with Moonfeld offering answers where he could, and extrapolating when he was able.

He'd approached the hole in the centre of the henge and descended the stone slabs. It was not comfortable, he told us, as the slabs were so wide he needed a step and a half to get to the next so he had no rhythm to his walk. *Like a child.*

"There's a behind me flicker," he said, "and the deep of the stones grows."

I asked the usual questions about each of the slabs, but now Moonfeld was not biting (and Len was audibly annoyed on his stool). He said they were simply *in dark* and unable to be seen. This was corroborated by step seven, when the mind reported there was no light at all. What remained was a lightless stairwell Moonfeld travelled by touch alone.

There were few steps, far fewer than in Baby's internal underground station, and the end step led onto an uneven rock surface. "A tunnel pulled through the stone," Moonfeld said. "No scree. It is brushed clean."

I talked him forward, through the wide winding rock tunnel, Len beside me noting where the tunnel narrowed or shrank. The mind had no sense of direction now. He could tell when the tunnel moved left or right, but not down or up. The walls were wet. The walls were wet with a white substance.

"Doorways," he said. "I have the impression I passed through stone doorways."

The tunnel continued on, but that was as far as he'd gone.

Len showed his pad to me. The tunnel on it curved ever to the left in a new spiral, now wide, now narrow. It looked like a section of intestine. Len clearly thought the same way as he mouthed, "Up his own backside."

We unplugged ourselves from the plinth. At the door of the hut, I stopped and returned. "Explain something to me, John," I said. "You said the steps weren't comfortable to walk. You said it needed a step and half to get to the end of each one so you couldn't just walk them one step at a time. *Like a child*, you said."

"I did."

I didn't know how to make my point both clear and tactful. I decided to dispense with the tact. "You've got no legs," I said.

"I have a greater physical presence the further I go in," the mind said. "Did I not tell you? I have far greater physical presence the further I go in. It is quite seductive." There was a pause. "Could you call Tom? I need to talk to Tom."

17.4 It was still early in the day. Len and I had lunch outside. In contrast to the recent heat, it was windy and chill but Len insisted. In houses with a lot of computers, he believed, there was a flattening quality to the air, dryness plating the lungs like cheap jewellery with zinc or silicone.

My elation at Moonfeld's eventual return had trodden a brown road from joy to dismay, for the mind brought nothing truly new or exciting back. We talked for a time about the oddness of some of John's phrasing. *A behind me flicker. No scree. The deep of the stones grows.* Whether it meant something or nothing, we'd no way of knowing.

I found myself talking of my young fascination with the roots of my idea. I talked myself back into happiness with the talk of tunnels and their significance. The earliest art, I told him, was created in the guts of tunnel systems, images burned or painted or hewn into the rock deep below the earth. It fascinated Len. I described how I'd found echoes in Len's drawings. The spirals and the mazes, the long lines of the winding paths and the sequence of the stones in the ruins, the prison, the labyrinth, the tube. Spirit houses and *churingas*. I persuaded him to search for a picture of the Hypogeum at Hal Saflieni, and Len was rapt by the image, so close were the stones and black exits of the shrine to the drawings he'd made of the outward-facing structure of Ichika's ruins; the windows in Pike's prison; the innards of Moonfeld's stone zoetrope.

Lastly, I showed Len a drawing of the emergence of ancestors into the spirit world. Placing it by Len's sketch of Ichika's travels within, he traced the lines with his little finger.

"The lines and the match are remarkable," he said.

I paused. "Moonfeld said something at the start. Trite, but—. He said he would always think like himself because he was the one that was thinking. These theories that Hoskin hates so much? They're seductive because they come from a part of human existence common to everyone. We cannot view our own minds with our own minds. No one can know the mind of another. But so much of mind is unconscious." I pointed to the convoluted shape on the page. "It's thought this shape represents the emergence of the ancestors into the light, into the living world. Another way of viewing it could be the emergence of the ancient brain into the conscious mind."

I felt the temperature of Len's interest drop precipitously.

"Go with me," I continued. "When delivery of the minds happens, something comes through in clear and they can see a little of the whole, the structure of the mind. When Moonfeld said he only knew his own mind, he actually knew a little more than his own mind. Whether it's dreams, motivations, emotions. They belong to the darkness, but we need to make sense of them in the light, using only the tools laid out in the light." I took a deep breath. "But the brain has tools it once used in the darkness. They're crude, but they still work. You can still knock a nail in with a Neolithic hammer. And they're the tools for understanding the world that artists reach for. Symbols, tales, templates, myth. The winding path they talk of is just a story, the same story. A friend leaves on a journey, endures trials, returns changed. The symbols resonate with things very old in the brain. Art is how the hand thinks, the ear thinks, the eye thinks." I paused. "I can't tell if you're quiet because you think I might have a point, albeit garbledly expressed, or because you're about to hit me."

"Garbledly?" said Len, nothing more.

"What John said about the tunnels, it reminded me of a detail. When Neolithic humans entered the tunnels, they'd no light at all. This is below the earth, the darkest dark you can get, and their only light was burning moss carried on a bowl of fat to keep it lit." I was fired, the image had always enchanted me. "Can't you see it? Walking through absolute darkness, not knowing whether a cave bear will be waiting in a lair above you, or your feet will find a mess of snakes. And at the end a picture of a buffalo, or a tiger, or a pregnant woman? But it was *everything* to them. It was their source of life and ultimate worship. It was their food. It was the god. The first churches. The tunnel was long and hard and dangerous because to *see* that image had to be earned—."

"D'you know that's how John Lennon met Yoko?" said Len. "There was a ladder against a wall, and at the top a spy-glass attached to the ceiling. You had to climb this rickety ladder until you were at the top and look through to see what she'd written near the ceiling in tiny letters. It was the word, *Yes.*" I was silent. "Lennon had an epiphany. Everything else around him at the time was negative, but to make that effort to find a *Yes* at the end—." He shrugged. "I'm just saying. It was a positive word, and he had to earn it. For your cave brother, it's a buffalo on a wall. *See the magic tasty food.* Imagine going all that way and it was a cave painting of a head of lettuce. Or kale."

I think he expected me to agree, and I can't now know why this detour caused me such offence. I stared at him for a long time, blinkless, not hostile but with measure and attention.

"Maybe you're right," I said and got up to leave.

"Hey, don't get narked. I'm just saying. I'm trying to give a little grounding here, Jude. You're a romantic. Moonfeld's in his own head. There's no answer there. He's not going to give you an answer." Len was talking loudly now as I was walking away. "We're going to lose him. We're going to lose him and he won't come back because this is probably what happens. He's not crawling down a tunnel to enlightenment. He's interpreting some physical event we don't yet understand according to best fit. *Jude*. The answer will be an unsuspected property of the chain-fluid, or the hut's too hot, or too much sugar in his pop. Some bloody thing. Hoskin will find it and fix it or she won't."

I stopped. "Then why do you draw it? Why've you got page after page of shapes and symbols? Why've you put that much effort into understanding this if the answer you expect is so mundane?"

Len was standing now, arms wide, looking helpless. "It's just how I think. It's how my hand thinks. It's how I visualise things."

"Shite."

"Come on, Jude," he called, but I was head down and barefoot on the coast road. "Jude," shouted Len, "come on."

17.5 I returned in the evening to elation.

Tom had spent hours with Moonfeld, and the mind had been so forthcoming, so clear. "I could hear it," he said. "It all just made sense."

Hoskin told me I was stood down for the next day. I nodded acceptance of this, sensing Hoskin's need for battle. Anwen was not there.

In a bid to make myself more indispensable, I told everyone I'd take a turn at the cooking, which I'd not yet done. It put me in the kitchen with Tom's excitement.

"He's given me everything," he said, "everything."

Tom explained the theory of gravid numbers and their relationship to the cruciate ridge. I remembered it from before, something about a kidney-shaped tent. The weights of these gravid numbers were different, and this was what Moonfeld had given him. He put a finger on the pad where he'd made his notes and frowned.

"What's wrong?" Hoskin asked.

"Probably nothing. He keeps calling it by an odd name. I can't be sure, but I'm sure he's saying *Khrushchev ridge*."

Hoskin laughed. "Not likely."

Len caught my eye.

Tom foundered a bit, and there were backtrackings in his explanation of the theory, specifically Moonfeld's concept of the *robustness* of a number and how this feature – which pertained unusually to the *gravid* but not the *buoyant* – could be interpreted positionally, visually. As balloons in varying stages of helium loss sit lower in the air, or the sealed capsules in a glass barometer float according to how they react to atmospheric pressure, so the robustness of the gravid number would have a position—

"—except it's fixed," Tom said. "The property is fixed so you can plot them. God, I could do it now." He looked up at the faces watching him, suddenly tearful. "I forgot the main thing," he said, voice failing, tears falling. "The points are all on line. *They're all on a line.*"

Everyone laughed. We'd so little followed the explanation his emotion was ridiculous. Tom didn't mind. He looked wet-eyed and pleased – boy-pleased, blushing, his grin not under his control – but with the uncertainty beneath his pleasure that marks praise for an outcome that was largely luck.

18.1 Come the next afternoon, Tom was devastated.

He'd spent the day with Moonfeld plotting his points. The mind was as alive as ever, he reported, but as he checked the calculations, he got the suspicion there was an error, and by the time he'd performed the manipulation to plot these points in a visualisable form, the points – which I thought were the ones that were all on a line – could be viewed from a number of aspects, and on rotation, formed a perfect circle.

"He drew me a circle," Tom said. "It's a circle."

He was bitterly dejected, although no one understood why. Even Hoskin was bemused.

"Why can't it be a circle?" I asked.

"Because it can't. It'd be like finding a square tree. It's too ordered. It doesn't work like that."

"I thought that was the point," I said. "There was order to be found in the chaos and that's why you search."

"Yes, but it's not—. That's not what it means. That's not what *order* means. The answer is not going to be a polka dot pattern. There might not be any order in the chaos at all. It might be chaos all the way down."

I smiled. "Like William James with the old woman who believed the world rested on an infinite number of turtles. *It's turtles all the way down.*"

"Yes, I know," replied Tom with deliberate patience. "That was the joke I was making. You can be a patronising bastard, you know that? And it was Bertrand Russell."

Len said, sharp, "Don't wail at him 'cause you dropped your lolly."

Tom puffed and dropped his head. Hoskin asked if the circle might be the cross-section of a solid. Tom gave a look of fleeting exasperation. I felt for her. She'd revealed her lack of understanding, which was the same as ours but was more painful because she cared.

"No," he said, deflated now.

I cooked again. Tom grew maudlin, drank a bottle of wine, grew thoughtful. By the time I was serving the meal – Basque chicken – he was sketching interlocking circles on a piece of paper. The others watched him in silence.

Everyone was driveless now, and this inertia had spread from Hoskin. In her frustration, she'd retreated from control, and once she'd stopped being a leader it wasn't the case we were leaderless, but that everyone was a leader. Now it was Tom, and we watched him filling the pad with calculations, attempts at understanding, numbers and symbols so devoid of significance to us the whole might have been a pencil rubbing or a collagraph, textural effect rather than symbols that held meaning.

"There's something," he muttered. "Something—."

Lenford washed up. He stared out at the night "Hot again," he said and added, to a chorus of complaint, "I'm sweating into the washing-up water."

18.2 I read for an hour before bed, yearning for a little wind – the least gust of air – to come through the window and cool my skin. I felt again the sense I was being slowly run through a laminator in an envelope made of my own plastic sweat.

Just as I was about to go to sleep, a flea tapped onto the page. I slammed the book shut, instantly all itch from toes to scalp, but I had the flea in the book. Forcing the pages together all over the cover, I cursed the flea with a bad death, swearing as lavishly as I knew how, creating verbs out of the dirtiest nouns and nouns from the more active verbs, tasting the meat in each word. I'd tried a similar murder when I'd got one between my fingers before, but no pressure I could bring to bear killed it. It struggled free no matter how hard I pressed, surviving I'd assumed in the whorls of a fingerprint, but between two flat surfaces this evil pip would die.

When I peeled the pages open, the flea was still leaping from place to place, a truant letter on the page. I managed to shut the book again with it still between the pages, keeping it shut with all my strength. Putting the book on the bedside table, I again pressed down on every section of the surface, pushing down with the heels of my hands like a paramedic doing CPR.

Finding the page again, I opened the book. Now I could see a tear in the page towards the spine, a hole where the flea had either been forced through or it had eaten a lair. I wondered how fast it could eat. I smoothed the page down until I could see into the hole, and the flea, hiding just below the shade of the page, leapt out again, this time clearing the book.

"No," I said.

I couldn't believe it had gone. I'd lost it, somewhere in the folds of my bed. I heard myself make the most abject noises – *No. Oh, no. Please, no. Please, no* – desolation taking me so completely my legs gave out and I sat down hard on the floor.

The desolation flattened me, burying me alive under despair for the presence of the flea. I lay on my back, legs still crossed. It had been years since I'd wept, but I could feel a storm of weeping in me at the top of my lungs and no strength to dam it there. I wept there on the floor, silently, getting my breath when I could in shuddering sucks, every now and then squeaking like a rusted screw giving grudging way to a spanner. With the night's heat and the sweat I was already wearing, my face was baked with dirt, but still I wept on, helpless for it, so much liquid coming out me it stopped up one of my ears.

And then in an instant, the despair was gone, lifted. The flea would bite, and in the morning I would lather myself with Tiger Balm, tugging on my pair of imaginary menthol socks, and be on my way. Although I'm hot with embarrassment at recalling this now, once that thought had come, I vanished into sleep.

19.1 Somewhere in the night, I accepted my time with Moonfeld was at an end, at least until the progress Tom was making was either resolved or abandoned. Hoskin would not risk the possibility of the mind going the way of Ichika whilst there was an unwrung drop in the rag.

I woke with the resolve not to let that happen. To steal my time with the mind.

I found one of my old handwritten notes under the fridge magnet – *Gone for a walk* – and moved it to the front so it was showing, then descended to the pool and hid in the disused steam room with my notebook from the sessions. Tom had gone in early – foolish o'clock early – and left in a rush three hours later, meaning I only had a short time to wait. As he left, Tom passed the entrance to the steam room, muttering, "Not circles. Not circles at all."

19.2 Moonfeld asked, "You believe I have old knowledge?"

I paused. "I believe you are having an experience no one before you has had. I don't believe, like the others, that the pull to your labyrinth is your interpretation of some routine glitch as yet understood. I think it is a real thing, not something you've clothed in romantic garb. I believe that whatever that is, it's an insight we as humans haven't had before. Just for that novelty, it must have worth."

"You choose your words with care. Was I ever romantic?"

I smiled. "No."

"But you were, Jude, and you sound like you've got a little lipsticky religion on your shirt collar."

"I've not been unfaithful to you, John. You know me. I am not a religious man but I know man is a religious creature. To have an insight to where that lives in the brain would be an insight worth knowing. Worth sharing."

"Does it matter my objective opinion is that, all things considered, Hoskin's view is the more likely?"

Yes, it mattered.

"You said you were drawn there, and the pull was as elemental, as irresistible, as sex. A human yearning. Is it likely to be a moody supplement patch, or a kink in a magnet? And for all of you, for every one of the minds to be drawn there, to that place, regardless of your levels of fear or personal curiosity—." I glanced at Baby's jar. "There's something. There has to be something."

"I think the human yearning is in you, Jude."

I rubbed my eyes. I couldn't think of anything further to say. Having the earphones in plugged me directly into the sound of the mind's voice from the speaker, which made me deaf to anyone approaching the hut, setting me on edge.

"There is a hall there," Moonfeld told me then. "I've been there many times since last we spoke. I can think myself there now.

"The hall is deep below the earth. Below what I interpret as the earth. The walls are uneven. The floor is uneven. The hall is narrow. If I put out my hands, I can feel them on either side and I do not have to stretch. The hall reaches straight onwards into the darkness."

I dared not breathe, willing Moonfeld to talk on, but the mind remained silent. I kept my tone even. "It must have such a pull. To have lost two minds to it—. What's the nature of the pull?"

"I can touch the walls."

I wanted to scream. "John."

"You're not listening. I am a human figure. Perhaps I am even the human figure I saw on the surface. The guide. A body. I am a body. The farther I go into the labyrinth, the more I am human in my mind. I haven't felt human for so long, Jude. This is the seduction, the pull. To be a body again. To do what a body does."

I heard an off-note in the mind's voice, an absence in the tone I couldn't define.

"The hall leads downward," the mind continued, "and I still want to walk down the hall to see how much more of a body I will feel. Yes, it is frightening. It's like standing on the edge of a cliff and wanting to leap off. But I have to walk down the hall to the end, and if it ends, to peek over and see the drop."

"The abyss."

"No, Jude. You load my words with concepts they are too weak to carry. Like attaching a kettle bell to a sparrow. The word *abyss* has connotations that aren't what I meant. What I am describing is my best interpretation of an unknown in my consciousness. I don't know if it exists. I don't know, in all truth, if *I* exist. For all any of us know, I'm endlessly searching a loop of chain-fluid a bit of my consciousness is trapped in." A pause. "Sorry if I've offended you."

"You can't offend me, John."

We agreed to continue. I went through my questions, talking into the earphone-muted silence with my eyes closed. *What can you see? What's further along the hall? Are there markings on the walls? Is anything written? Is the way underfoot smooth, or are there stones? Is there light? Where is the light coming from?*

When I returned to the threefold ring of the singing bowl, Moonfeld described his route again. The winding path, the stone zoetrope, the figure and the descent of the spiral steps. He described the tunnel again, and I followed it on a pad, trusting Moonfeld's count of the number of steps he was taking, the angle of the turns underground. I thought again of Len's smart comment about going down the plughole. The path taken was a convoluted loop, random, but within the uneven circle formed by the first path, and on a slight decline so the tunnel occasionally passed under itself. Aside from the fact the trail was inside the line made by the first wide shape, the route didn't resemble a spiral. It was too random, a thread dropped on a swatch of cloth.

Moonfeld entered the hall. A section of the tunnel dropped then went straight, and the mind was travelling – walking now, physically able to feel legs beneath him – along it, his hands against the walls. There was no light, nothing on the walls to suggest a line or a marking.

The hall went on in a straight line, and still there was no feature to the walls or floor, just an endless journey. Yet for Moonfeld, he spoke of a change. He became aware of a smell, not a pleasant one, which he saw as belonging to himself. *Salt*, he called it, *Burnt salt and meat*. At intervals he heard the sound of breathing, not magnified from himself but inhuman breathing, like a bull winding itself up for a charge, from around and within the rock.

There was light.

Moonfeld couldn't tell where it was from, but in his sight he saw discs moving against the walls, which he thought of as quartz in the rock until he realised they were his fingernails illuminated by the faintest of light. The light grew, and the hallway grew, the right-hand wall opening out like the widening of a country lane to provide a passing place. The gap was not long, about ten feet, and on the floor was a flat stone—

"Like a tabletop flush to the rock's surface. You enter at this end."

At either end of the stone there was a gap leading within, and it was from here that the light shone, flickering. The hall stretched on into darkness, a dark deeper now after the sight-ruining effect of the light in the hole.

"Can you see into the hole?" I asked.

"It's just a flame under a flat stone."

"Look into the hole."

"The hall continues on," said the mind.

"Don't go," I whispered. "We can go there later. Stay a while with the stone."

"It's safe, Jude."

Something in the voice, I thought. I was gripped with panic as vice-like as a stomach cramp. "It's not safe," I said.

"Someone has gone before."

I could not breathe. "Ichika?"

"Not Ichika."

The mind said nothing more.

19.3 An hour passed. I tried our methods of communication, but a man can tap a singing bowl only so often. Repeating Moonfeld's name felt futile, and I could think of nothing else to try. A human I might yell at, or poke, hunt eye contact, chase for attention, but the mute jar was untouchable.

My worry grew to the point of feeling sick. I'd come here without exactly being denied – my excuse, formed in the early hours of the morning when I'd picked myself off the weeping floor and got into bed – was that I was following the normal protocol for my time with the mind. *I've done nothing wrong.* Yet now I was in the mitts of it, I knew it wouldn't wash. It wasn't normal procedure. Len wasn't there. My truancy was as apparent as a child's.

It was afternoon when I gave up. By chance, Len was passing the top of the steps. *All or nothing*, I thought. "Where were you?" I called.

Len frowned, looked at the notes I was carrying, swore.

"No, you didn't."

In the face of my obvious transparency, I bottled it. I shrugged, said, "She wouldn't have let me if I'd asked."

Len was furious. "Not just her," he hissed. "Don't put it all on her. This is all of our work. All of our lives." He glared down the stairs. "You'd better pray she doesn't find out, Jude."

"She's going to," I said. "She has to." The guilt was like heartburn. "I think I might have lost him."

Len closed his eyes, centring himself. "Okay, let me listen."

Once in the monitoring room, Len found the latest P feed. Samuel was there, his presence again a shock. The man was less a human than a pet, a virtual cat kept to maintain levels of computer vermin. Len asked him – told him – to leave.

Len played the last of the exchange twice. "That's all? The last thing he said?"

"Yes. Nearly two hours ago."

"Two hours is nothing," Len said. "We don't need to be worried about this. Yet. Nothing about it sounds final to me." He turned, hands on headphones. "I can't believe you did this. To be that selfish—."

"What about the last words he says?" I asked.

Len played the feed again—

Jude: Can you see into the hole?
John: It's just a flame under a flat stone.
Jude: Look into the hole.
John: The hall continues on.
Jude: Don't go. We can go there later. Stay a while with the stone.
John: It's safe, Jude.
Jude: It's not safe.
John: Someone has gone before.
Jude: Ichika?
John: Not Ichika.

—and said, "So what? He's seen a figure there before."

"What about the way he says, *Not Ichika?*"

Len played the last bit again. "I'm not hearing it."

I had been running the last words in my head for an hour now. To me, they'd had a meaning subtly other from the assumed one, and I'd convinced myself Moonfeld's last two words were not a denial but a *definition* of Ichika.

"I can hear it," I said. "Can't you hear it? He's not saying, *Not Ichika.* He's saying, *Not-Ichika.*"

Len didn't bother listening again. He took the headphones off, hung them on their hook, folded his arms.

"I love you, Jude," he said, soft. "I really do. You're the most hopeful bugger I've ever met. I can't pin you down. It's like trying to get one of them fleas. You always wriggle out." He held out a palm. "I'm not saying anything. I think it's great you believe so hard. But me—. No."

He walked towards the door. I said, "So do we need to tell her about this?"

Len turned back. "I love that *we*, too. I really do. I *love* that *we*. There is no *we*, Jude, just as there's no Neolithic Christ at the tunnel's end." He left, turned, came back, angry now. "Whose side d'you think I'm on? I'm not on your side. You tell her, you tell her now, and if she kicks you in the nuts then throws you out, you take your licks and nick off."

19.4 Tom and Hoskin were angry but less so than anticipated. At one time or another, all the minds had gone for days on end before, so a matter of a few hours was nothing.

When Moonfeld hadn't returned at the end of the following day, Hoskin asked to see me in her room. I'd never been to Hoskin's room before. It was laughable, like being in the headmaster's office, Tom and Hoskin sat at her desk while I sat on her bed. In the interim, they'd listened to the feed in its entirety, conceding I hadn't done anything untoward. The substance of Moonfeld's words they didn't comment on at all, not even when I asked. She was adamant I not do anything like that again, and seeing the seed of forgiveness in the word *again*, I was craven in my acceptance of the terms. Tom said nothing.

"I can get him back," I said.

"You have to," she said, cold.

"All through, I've stressed how important it is to return."

"Important to us, not to him," Tom said.

I nodded, anxious not to antagonise. "Did the circles mean anything?" I said, an attempt to pacify.

Tom looked blank for a moment. "I've questions," he said at last. "Questions I may never get an answer to, thanks to you. You fucker."

"Tom," said Hoskin.

Tom wasn't done, but he moved his anger. "It was wrong to bring Jude here. You were wrong, Claire. He's too close and his priorities are not ours. His priorities are personal."

He left. Once the thunder on the stairs had gone, Hoskin said, "He's angry. He was angry anyway, but now he can be angry at you."

"You're not? You seem disturbingly calm."

"I've been doing a lot of walking."

"Cryptic."

"Maybe. But you put your finger on it. He was going to go. He was always going to go. I accept that reality now, and if I have to start all over again, I will." She smiled. Her eyes glittered. "You fucker."

20.1 Moonfeld remained silent.

I went down the ladder on the hour during daylight, ran through the questions, called his name, bonged the bowl, all as if I'd made a promise to always be there.

There was no response.

I expected grief, a returned and renewed grief, for Moonfeld, but I was waiting too hard. Perhaps there was no capacity for that in the human mind and my grief, spent once months before, was like a match, not to be relit.

Instead, there was an ache where an answer should be, an answer that lived in the man's words. When not in the hut, I returned to the words over and over, listening to the feeds so much I managed to engage even Samuel's concern. He brought me a sandwich.

I concentrated on writing this testament and my hours of vigil. It is hard to recall how flat and calm this time of waiting was.

When I slept, I dreamt of the flame under a flat stone. My sleeping mind crawled over that tabletop in the ground, open at the ends. *You enter by this end*, Moonfeld had said.

The alcove where the flat stone was sunk was ten feet long. The hole was a reasonable length for a body. In my sleeping head the stone was a rectangular slab on the floor of a church, the seal too tight for my fingers to get a hold.

Hoskin resumed her walking. Tom worked on what he had. (*Nothing*, according to Len.) A week passed. No one talked to me, which I understood, but this was because there was no one around. I even thought of following up on the sandwich and trying to spark a conversation with Samuel just to have someone to talk to.

There was always Lenford. He'd got his affability back, but I sensed I was being humoured.

Mindful of Anwen's criticism, I made sure to talk to Baby when I was in the hut. I couldn't hit the note of easy chat Anwen had with the mind, and our conversations were marked by hitches and silences. I wanted to ask about aspects of her life that I knew she would natter about for hours, but I couldn't. My knowledge of them came from eavesdropping. Talk of the structure was forbidden by Anwen—

Out of boredom, I asked Elephant Baby where she thought Moonfeld had gone. I didn't know if mention of this would upset her, but technically I wasn't breaking the pact made with Anwen. As expected, she said she didn't know then added—

"He is still there though. I can hear him. When all of you are gone and it's quiet, I can hear him."

My heart clenched and held. "He talks to you."

"No. Noises in his jar. It sounds like he's opening creaking doors on a floor above where I am. I don't think he's awake. It's involuntary. Like a dog chasing rabbits in his sleep."

I pursued this for a while, but Baby had nothing more to add, and the noises were so ill-defined I didn't know if there was enough there for hope or not.

I tried a different approach and asked her where she thought Ichika had gone. There was a long pause before Baby said, "I think she dropped into the hole above her stone hall. She didn't know she'd have weight inside the room and couldn't get back up."

Ichika's room beneath the stone door, I recalled. She'd thought the door opened onto underground water, but then a figure had walked across the floor far below, carrying a candle across the gap.

I thought for a moment. "She has weight?"

"We all do. The further in we go. That's what *further in* means."

This made no sense. "What's in her lower room, do you think?"

"I don't know," she said, and I heard the familiar note of strain in her voice. "She didn't talk to me."

I pushed. "A figure was in her room. A guide. In the room beneath the stone door. My friend saw a figure too. Someone ahead of him in the dark. You saw one as well. Who's the figure, do you think?"

"I don't know. I don't know but they shouldn't be there."

I pushed on. "Do you think Ichika met the figure?"

"Yes. Yes, she met the figure. She met her and she did her harm. The figure hurt her. She had bad hands and she hurt her. She hurt her because she has no mind. The room has no mind—."

She was getting increasingly frantic, but I couldn't leave it.

I said, "She has no mind? Like an animal?"

"Yes. No. Yes, like an animal but not. Less than. More than."

The panic was setting in, the voice now coming in fits, as if she were (impossibly) panting, or her speech had been torn between words.

I stopped it. "Come home," I said.

She was slow to return. I spent the time considering whether what I'd heard was significant. It wasn't, I decided. All I'd done was access Baby's panic through a side door.

"Sorry," I said when she was back. "I didn't mean to upset you back there. I won't ask you any more."

There was a long silence, so long the hum of the machines became a physical weight in the room. I couldn't think of anything to say, or perhaps I mean I couldn't think of any way Baby could help me further in my unendurable need to know more.

Baby broke the silence. "You're lonely, aren't you?"

I looked up. Her jar glowed like a knot of keloids lit from within. I didn't know how to answer; how to admit such a thing to a mind living in loneliness greater than anything any human had ever known.

"Yes," I said. "I wish I wasn't, but I am." This admission exposed me, exposed me doubly as it would be on the feed recording. I didn't care. "I missed John more than I thought. More than I remembered."

"You sound lovely."

I tried to smile. "Thank you. Thank you, but I don't think I am."

"Your friend doesn't have any answers for you."

I knew, but facing that would take more strength than I had. It was too important for there to be no ending ahead. It didn't have to be faith, salvation; it just had to be certain. It had to be *known*, and if I could know it ahead of time, through Moonfeld, there would be comfort—

I found myself telling her of my experience of Brugada syndrome, and the doctors' decision not to fit an implantable cardioverter defibrillator because of the risks the fitting itself would kill me. I explained I'd an abnormality on gene SCN5A, encoder of the cardiac sodium channel, that there is no cure, and even were I within reach of medical personnel who would be able to treat me, I could still easily die of fatal cardiac arrest.

Elephant Baby was upbeat. She said, "Lucky you're in a hospital."

I couldn't make out the meaning until I realised that she must think a hospital was where she was.

"Yes," I replied. "Lucky."

I sat there thinking how tired I was of ageing, of hearing that limp wet tick of one year turning to the next. I was tired of the weakness and greyness of my life, and the sickening realisation every change or action I'd ever made to try and break this weakness and greyness was thwarted by my presence in the attempt. I took myself with me every step of the way, when what I wanted most was to be erased, burnt back to the element and then sharpened anew. That would never now happen—

"What's your name?" I asked.

"Annabel Perkins."

"Annabel. A nice name." I couldn't think of anything to add until inspiration hit. "Knock knock," I said.

"Who's there?"

"Annabel."

"Annabel who?"

"Annabel—." I stopped. *Shit*, I thought, *I'm thinking of Isabel.* "I'm so sorry," I said. "I messed that up."

The error didn't matter. I could tell by the sound from the speaker she knew what I'd been going for. *Isabel necessary on a bike.* God, I was such a fool.

I listened to her laugh, thinking how purely human the moment was, how close the relationship between us as speaking beings.

And the laugh. *Like an old lady pissing on porcelain.* The work that must have gone into that voice was otherworldly. A labour of love as intimate and involving as dressing a child, or caring for a sick spouse. The level of care Anwen had put in to craft that voice hurt my lungs.

"Do you wonder—?" I began. "Do you wish—?" Silence. "Annabel, do you think they shouldn't have brought you back?"

The mind didn't reply for a long while. I was about to rephrase the question when she said, "I don't want to seem ungrateful."

"I won't think you're ungrateful," I said. It was hard to speak. "Just tell me the truth."

Jude Golby's testament ends at this point.

Journal

Anwen has closed about an impenetrable grief. I'm too tired to want to find out. I'm exasperated by her. I talked about the conversation. She'd made that snippy remark about me not speaking to EB when I was in the inner room so I told her what we'd talked about.

I told her EB's name was Annabel.

Her: *I know her name's Annabel. Why the hell wouldn't I know that?*

Anwen: *The minds are expendable. It doesn't matter to H. what happens to them. They're not human to her. To any of them. You're the only one who can possibly see this. Sometimes I think Lenford cares but it's hard to tell——. The minds are like a ladder they'll climb up to reach a second storey of knowledge. A storey she has no right to, but she owns it entire. But they'll give it the same care as they would a ladder, and if it doesn't reach where they want it to go, or the rungs break, they'll store it for wood.*

It terrifies me, Jude. It terrifies me for Elephant Baby. It terrifies me for Moonfeld too. They're mentally alive, and we've given no thought to how we care for them. How we nourish them. We turn them on and then leave them burning away like pilot lights. What happens when they stop being of use?

I'll have no say in what happens to her. You'll have no say in what happens to him. If Hoskin ever gets the go-ahead for more minds, Elephant Baby will lose her novelty, and they won't switch her off. They'll stick her on a shelf. She'll go insane. She'll go insane and she's already partway there. Even Moonfeld will lose his charm for them. What will his life look like? Because you and I are the only ones here who see them as alive.

I'm complicit in his life.

25th of August

Dreams of caves, flames burning under stones, a figure ahead of me in the dark. A guide. The figure carries a plate with floating plant matter on it, burning. The flames light the wall. Paintings, handprints, lines.

I've decided to ration the quinidine. Half dose buys me a two-week window to repeat the prescription.

I found out Sam sleeps during the hottest part of the day centred between two fans. Clever.

26th of August

Nothing. Waiting. Tom snippy as a rat-dog. The heat on me, in me, is unbearable. There's no wind from the open window.

A flea bit me, a flea on my ankle, and I was taken over by the urge to take a sledge hammer to the room, my belongings, even hammering my own clothes before starting on the equipment and books, the walls and the door. The sheets on my bed.

27th of August

The hunt. The root leads down to the hunt. The hunt is the root of the human. Need for food begat magic, a belief in magic. Successful hunts sparked in the mind the belief the tracking of prey was itself part of the hunt's success, became ritual, became part of our *meat*.

The spiral is the soft tread of hunters through the grass, and what is at the end is the kill. Around the kill is ritual, prayer. The magic that makes the luck grow.

The root is where luck grows.

The root is the rite.

What is at the end of Moonfeld's hall?

The light, the figure. The sense of human weight and human shape the further in. Gravity, EB said. *That's what 'further in' means.*

The nature of the rite. The root of the ritual.

28th of August

I walked the whole day. The feeds are dead. I ate out.

I couldn't sleep. The coolest place in the house was the pool. I climbed down the ladder into a darkness and coldness so welcoming my sweat clenched on my skin.

Under the boards I could see nothing at all of the silent air-conditioned minds, but I sensed them out there on their horseshoe of plinths, wires like gangs of snakes pooling about their bases. I found a spot against the outside wall of the hut, and eased my back onto it. I saw a red light on the wall-mounted monitor flash every second. I watched it, willing my eyes to droop despite the hard tile.

The red light blinked off and stayed off.

I stared at the place where it had been, and into my field of vision Len's face appeared, Tom behind him. Such a shock.

Len: *Easy. Have a beer.*

They've been coming here since Hoskin had covered the deep end of the pool with boarding to give the air conditioner an edge over the increase in the external heat.

Down there with the jars of the silent minds, the gleam of the crane and truss high up on the pool edge, the thick tube that ran through the ceiling and into the monitoring rooms above, it looked like a morgue.

Len said he was thinking of leaving.

Tom: *It's done. If John doesn't come back, she'll pack everything up and then we're all done.*

He wasn't talking to me, but I knew he was talking for my benefit. I didn't engage. I was too hot to argue with him.

Len said he thought Anwen was 'fried'. I think he was quite drunk. Then he told me the real reason he was leaving.

Len: *I'm off because I'm unhappy. What we're doing here never felt wrong before. It feels wrong now. It feels wrong because of you, Jude. I don't mean your theories, but because you care for him. I never saw the minds that way before. I feel guilty now, and I never felt guilty about them before.*

Me: *Not even with Anwen? She feels the same as me.*

Len: *She never knew Elephant Baby though. She bonded over the voice. There must be something about working on the voice. It's not like with you. She sentimentalised Baby. She created a link with Baby. Or allowed a link to form. You arrived with a link to Moonfeld. Sometimes with you, when you're talking with Moonfeld, I can hear your grief. And what's worse is that I can hear his grief as well.*

I didn't know what to say. I could see his outline, the beer can and the sweat on his face. Now my eyes had adjusted, the light in the pool was alien, touched with the pale blue of the tile. Behind was the horseshoe of plinths, and the jars of the silent minds threw up shadows on the pool wall, looming over us all like standing stones.

Tom whined for a few minutes. A river of whiny whiny blame. Len told him to give it a rest.

The sodding cruciate ridge. Are there a hundred people in the world who care about that bloody ridge?

I could have taken the sledgehammer to Tom. *Mr Tits-and-Teeth.* I've felt for him, felt for the dilemma he must have faced knowing he was not the originator of the thoughts that would be attributed to him, the shame and deceit he would feel.

Perhaps Anwen is right, and maybe he doesn't feel like that at all. Perhaps Tom feels the ease of his success is merited, because he takes luck as correlating to his own qualities and confidence. There is a bitterness to him, and a greed that sounds unpleasant now all sympathy for him has fallen out of my head.

I told him John never recognised him. I told him that until I came, John thought he was someone else. Someone better. Someone brighter.

I had to explain to him who you were.

Bad Jude. But so satisfying.

29th of August

Len made an etching plate in the courtyard. It looked complicated. He used a mirror as he was scratching letters in, which needed to be reversed if they were going to print the right way round. I asked what it said. He held up the mirror to the plate. It was a surprise. He was writing out the quote from *The Odyssey* I'd mentioned ages ago, the one about the gate of sawn ivory and the gate of horn.††

I thought of what we talked about the last time we actually seemed to connect. The brain's old tools buried under millenia of evolution but unearthed on delivery. The tools that belong to the darkness, but which we need to make sense of in the light, using only the tools laid out in the light.

For Moonfeld the brain's old tools are in reach to work the nut free on the bolt that locks the truth/reality beneath symbol.

Still that image in my head, my dreams. No light in the tunnels, the caves, the deep chambers. In the deepest dark, their only light burning moss carried on a bowl of fat to keep it lit.

Waiting was a punishment today. Waiting was a bed of ink staining anything that tried to cover it. I couldn't read, and walking would have taken me too far from the house. I'd be miles away and the call would come and I wouldn't be there.

I can't sleep. I keep asking what exactly it is that I want or expect. It isn't an answer. (Or so I tell myself.) It's simply to have a bit more information, a little more light. A bead of hope like a pea under my mattress that will not let me sleep.

---

†† "Stranger, dreams verily are baffling and unclear of meaning, and in no wise do they find fulfilment in all things for men. For two are the gates of shadowy dreams, and one is fashioned of horn and one of ivory. Those dreams that pass through the gate of sawn ivory deceive men, bringing words that find no fulfilment. But those that come forth through the gate of polished horn bring true issues to pass, when any mortal sees them. But in my case it was not from thence, methinks, that my strange dream came."

30th of August

I listened to the feeds. Pike and Ichika. Nothing new.

In the afternoon, I saw feed *J* was bubbling, which meant Baby was talking. I turned the speakers up to hear. She told Anwen a heart-breaking story of an old boyfriend.⧉ I closed my eyes to better listen to the

---

⧉ *Transcript—*

Baby: He was that guy from the university. Do you remember I said? He went to his room late at night and when he turned his key it snapped in the lock. So it's eleven and he's tapping at my door, but quiet, spooky. The security guard in halls had told him he couldn't fix it until the morning so could he grab the floor in my room.

Anwen: Right-ho.

Baby: It wasn't a lie. I went with him the next morning and his key half was in the lock. He showed me the stub.

Anwen: Yeah, he did.

Baby: You are mucky. [Pause] That was later.

Anwen: I knew it. [Laughter]

Baby: If we can get back to me, he stayed the night on my floor. We talked. About anything. I can't remember what it was. But the lights were out and his voice in the darkness was weird. It didn't seem to be coming from the floor but seemed to be moving about the room, and I wondered if he was creeping around looking at my stuff, which he couldn't be because it was completely dark. It wasn't like I hadn't talked in the dark before but I hadn't done that with a boy, and it was so—. Alerting. Is that a word? I was so alert.

Anwen: Did you know him well?

Baby: No. He was little. And blocky. And cheeky-looking. He talked about space. But you're right, it was crazy of me to let him in, and I shouldn't have let him in, but I didn't even think, I just knew it would be okay.

Anwen: And it was?

Baby: It was. This is Jake I'm talking about.

Anwen: Oh, Jake.

Baby: Stop it. Shut up.

Anwen: You shut up. [Laughter] You said he talked about space.

Baby: Distances and that. Some theory about life on other planets. An equation that says there must be life somewhere but it's too far away. Boy stuff, you know. [Pause] He was exciting. We went to unusual places and things, never the bar or to clubs. We went to museums. Old films in churches or forests. I was always surprised by him. One time he took me on a tour round an old Tube station that hadn't been used since the Second World War. They make films there. It was so out of place it was scary, like it was haunted. The tunnels didn't go anywhere. The ticket hall was empty and when the tour party went in there it felt like we'd barged into a stranger's funeral. We were so out of place.

Anwen: An old Tube station.

Baby: Yes. [Pause] Oh. Do you think that's why my out-of-the-way place is a station? But no, it's different. [Long pause] Do you think I should tell Jude?

Anwen: No.

Baby: He took me to a shop-front gig. The audience were all on decorator's tables. So dodgy. So dangerous. Magical. We drove to France. Whatever we did together, it was always interesting. And then I got ill.

Anwen: Annabel.

Baby: Well, it's true. I got ill and he left. And I understand he was a kid like me, and I'd have done the same if the situation had been reversed and he'd got boy cancer. [Pause] This woman on the wards said if you're in a cage sinking into the sea there's nothing you can do to stop your own panic or your own drowning, but there's only so long someone clinging to the bars outside can hold on before the survival instinct kicks in. I understand that, but I understand it with my head. Do you know what I mean?

Anwen: Intellectually you understand it but not emotionally.

Baby: Yes. But it killed me not to see him. If anything I needed—. If there was anything I needed then, it was distraction. It was weird fun I missed, and losing that was so desolating. Is that a word? It was awful. [Pause] He saw me once after I'd shaved my head. I'd gone to see an old friend and weirdly he was in the same place at the same time. This was after university. He was shocked, you know. His mouth was running ahead of his brain and he pointed at my scalp and said, *Drastic.* Like it was a fashion choice. Then it hit him and he looked so appalled, and so tearful and so hurt. And I remember thinking, *Oh my god, he's just a kid.* And then I thought, *Oh my god, I'm just a kid.* [Pause] He put his hand on my arm and I said, *Get out.* But I women talk. It was lulling. My mind drifted in and out of their conversation, thinking of summer days as a child, in the garden and adults chattering in the distance, words not quite clear. The precise words were not important to a child, but there was meaning and comfort beyond the words and in the fact people were talking at all. It was something to return to. I got a vivid picture of mother with her friends. My mind had put the dog on the memory so it seemed more idyllic, more cliché, but the core of my childhood reality was there. Murmuring and laughter, and myself the ear floating amongst the chatter without understanding. The meaning of the words didn't matter; what mattered was that there were words.

At one point, EB made a link to the tube station. She asked Anwen if she should tell me of the link and Anwen said, *No*. Anwen's *No* bothered me. Through the headphones, no body language to give the word anchorage or ground, the *No* could denote anything. Kindness, malice, pity. I could bear the last two, but not the first.

Anwen is still engaged. She listens. She remains.

What the two women spoke of was nothing, everything. I search for something, anything.

Baby called herself *hydroponic*. The word is perfect as the body is the soil for memories, and without it the only new things are cerebral, artificial. Without the body, there is nothing.

---

didn't mean *Go away*, I meant *Escape. Flee. Get out of here. Save yourself!* And he turned and walked out the door. And too late I realised he didn't understand and he must have thought I'd told him to piss off, but I didn't mean that. I meant I was in a sewer of dying and I was saying, *Don't come down here. Don't come down here because you're clean.*

Anwen: You should stay away from these thoughts.

Baby: They're all I have. They're all I am. I'm hydroponic, Anwen. Those memories are all I have. There are no new ones. I'm a bag of thoughts. I'm a colostomy bag of thoughts with no body attached. I'm all the shit you didn't bin with my corpse.

31st August

Nothing. I pulled together more of the narrative. My testament. (Fancy.)
Otherwise, nothing. Waiting.

1st of September

No loosening of the heat. If anything it was hotter. I'm so used to the
hot stinks of them all. The off sweetness of the women, the sour reek
of the men. It's all just human air.

2nd of September

There's a sense of absence in the house. I can't tell if that's a feature I'm
reading in the atmosphere because of the actual absence of John or not.
Probably. Physically or mentally the team is absent.

The house was so oppressive I took myself off into the hinterland,
steering clear of houses when I found them. I made for a hill I thought
would look over the sea. Of all people, Hoskin was there on a bench. I
could tell her first thought was something had happened. I didn't know
whether to walk away, or sit and talk, but the chance for a breezy wave
and continuing on was past.

I sat a little way off. I looked back the way I'd come. The house was
visible, and to the left the village. The pub I've never been to. I'm only
now realising I isolated myself here. There is no reason for it. The secrecy at the start was nothing but signing a non-disclosure agreement,
yet I've behaved as if I'm sequestered. None of the others have. Is there
enjoyment there? The feel of being part of something secret with its own
language of *chain-fluids* and *oobleck* and *artefacts*. The structures feed an air
of mystery and silence, and closing a cloak of secrecy about the mystery
gives it an extra sense of delight.

I was almost at the nod off when she said, *Tell me.*

The invitation to talk felt too late, too like a trap, but I took a chance.
I told her of what excited me. The similarity of the symbols, the spiral,

the maze, the descent into the darkness. The resonance of the fact the approach to the structure was hard, winding, but the minds' compulsion to go there did not become discouraged, because there was a motor at the core of the structure pulling at a fundamental human part of the minds, a part only conscious from the delivery process.

She didn't respond. Her lack of response could have been openness or—. God. Whatever word would fit there.

Whether it was wise or not, I pushed on. I told her about Len teasing me for being religious. How much it irritates, because religious is the *last* thing I am.

She felt different. Her listening felt different. The fact she seemed to be listening at all was a major change. So I pushed on and laid out what I've been thinking about over the last few days. That delivery of the minds has unlocked the roots and spoor of *the hunt* in the human brain. It has made visible the rite that fed the first humans. The further in Moonfeld goes, the more he becomes human. He sees his hands! He is becoming visible to himself the closer he gets to the end of the structure, and the end of the structure is the revelation of the flesh.

The pattern of *the hunt* was woven into human behaviour over so many thousands of years it became part of our *meat*, and the complexity of the paths of the animals we hunted became the first symbols, the mazes were the feeding and migratory patterns of great beasts, the paths changing and becoming more frenzied as the humans neared. This is not religion. It's the *soil* of religion, the rootstock. It's where the search for meaning was born.

Strangely, I thought of the parallels I wrote about back in July. The suspicion we are still the same. Modern and ancient humans. The drive in *the hunt* is the human drive to possess, to know, to subsume. For academics the hunt is sublimated into the drive for knowledge. What drives us is similar in part to what drives colleagues, cousins in other disciplines. The search builds on the past, the history of the field, what gave the drive impetus and anchorage in the human psyche hundreds of thousands of years ago was the habit of tracking, repeated patterns of behaviour weaving themselves over repeated iterations into the brain.

Hoskin finally replied. *The perverse aspect being this habit of tracking made us prone to seeing patterns where perhaps there are none?*

I paused. I felt caught but I said I agreed.

You reason like a child, she said.

She didn't say it unkindly. She said it because she saw it as true.

I replied that in such matters we *all* reason like children.

The conversation was valuable. It's been on my mind ever since. I don't know if it was the fact we couldn't be overheard but a hitherto closed door was open in her. I asked her why she kept me around, and she told me it couldn't hurt. My emotional bond with Moonfeld had a value. *It's the one thing we didn't have with the others. Your presence gave him a reason to keep returning.*

This was hard to hear, but it made sense. I wonder now how early she accepted failure. I thought her acceptance of failure as being in the future. Now I wonder if it was in the past, probably from when she started walking. Everything since then has been data-gathering. Hoskin waits and watches to see if the knot that binds Moonfeld and I will hold while Tom milks the teat for whatever last drops he can get.

Also hard to process is the realisation this is why they never want to hear what I have to say. It's irrelevant to them. It's not why I'm here. They need me for who I am not what I can do. Len is wrong. I've been embarrassing myself all along.

Hoskin said the one thing she wanted to avoid was *this air of fancy*. She seemed to get she'd tempted it. In extending a mind beyond the death of the body, she (they) opened that door. *The kook door*, she said.

I get that the word death *puts people to thinking of what comes after. Of questions meant for priests and vicars. When I hear people insisting on religion, on spiritual answers, using all their energy on belief and denying the evidence of science or senses, what I hear is that moment on the news after some sick killer has been caught, trophies from his victims in a box under his bed and blood on all his knives and clothes, but his mum's being interviewed saying,* He didn't do it, not my boy, he's a good boy, he didn't do it. *That pitiful resistance to accepting the truth that death is the end.*

I'm not sure I don't agree, but there's perverse irony there.

She said something that's been on my mind ever since. I resisted but she's right. She said every word we've spoken in that room she's listened to. She said she dumps it onto her phone and listens to the feeds while out walking. She said in all the questions I asked, all the answers I looked for, I never paid any attention to the one John gave right at the start.

He asked you about the funeral. You asked where he'd been. He said, Nowhere special. *That was the answer. He died. There was nothing. Why didn't you hear it?*

Is she right though? I don't know. She'd a vulnerability I'd not seen before. It was welcome. Before I left her she said, *It is hard to fail. I don't do it well. All this work we've put in, we can't just end up with silence.*

I doubt she meant it to have the meaning I heard in it. *All this work we've put in, we can't just end up with silence.* So strange considering all she said, but I wonder if we are talking about the same thing but from diametrically opposite starting positions.

I'm not sure I don't agree. Needlessly complex expression.

3rd of September

A question from Hoskin that I forgot yesterday—

Why are the structures old? I've never understood that. For all of the minds. The similarities can all point to a single cause, but why are they old, *Jude?*

4th of September

Moonfeld has returned. My body and mind feel wrenched to and fro. Working a chicken leg from the carcass. The bloodiest night.

Len was changing the jars' patches when he heard noises. The sound is hard to describe. A metallic song somewhere between the whalesong language the minds spoke amongst themselves and human speech. The noise made me think of the twisted voice Anwen played me.

The hut was tense and crowded. We were stood so close I could smell their lunches on their breath.

Anwen got the singing bowl from the drawer, hit it with the padded mallet. With the bodies and clothes in the room, the sound fell dead.

Then he was there. He said my name. Ridiculous how pleased I was. Pathetic. I felt I'd won a special prize for being the bestest boy [...]§§

---

§§ *Transcript*—

John: A woman's here. At the centre. [Pause] A creature in the rock, in a cave with no entrance. Grown there until it fills the cave. They've knocked through holes the size of a fist. I can look in. [Long pause] The hole that sees the eye is prized the highest.

[Silence, 2'03"]

Jude: Are you there?

John: The creature's maddened out of mind. [Pause] The whole place stinks of a thing long-rotten. Shit, musk and rut. I don't mind the smell. I can smell myself, my meat. [Pause] I have a body here.

[Silence, 0'41"]

Jude: You have a body there.

John: I am a human creature here. I can touch my hands.

Jude: What is this place?

John: A widened place, a room. There are other rooms further on, but no mind up ahead. The woman goes there freely. [Pause] They keep their fires under stones and cook their meat on top of the stones.

Jude: Why have you come back?

[Silence, 1'19"]

Jude: John.

John: To ask you something. [Pause] A favour from an old friend.

Jude: Anything.

John: Remove the tongue.

[Sounds of activity, 0'39"]

Anwen: That's not right. There's nothing there. Literally. Not even the turning of the chain-fluid.

Lenford: We need to move some of the bodies out so the fans can catch up. It's too hot in here.

Jude: John.

[Silence, 1'47"]

Lenford: He's cooked.

Jude: John, describe the room for me. What's in the room, John? [Sounds of activity] What are you doing? *No!*

After the obscene request to remove the tongue, the jar went silent. Not the silence of not speaking, but an inanimate object's complete inability to communicate. Anwen heard it first. She pushed past me and put her hand on the jar. Her bracelet was pulled to the closest magnet so hard the inner band dug into her flesh. She put her ear to the plinth speaker.

That's not right, she said. *There's nothing there. Literally. Not even the turning of the chain-fluid.*

Len tried to move us out. He said it was too hot in the hut for the fans to cope. I kept trying. No one would help.

Hoskin stared at the singing bowl. Stared at it with enough hate to make it ring by glare alone. Then she moved forward, fast, pushing past me. She put her hand into the plinth and tore out the tongue unit. She ripped the root of the wire from the disc, letting the feed root dangle and the tongue unit rock on the floor.

We retreated to the kitchen, the atmosphere bloody. Anwen didn't come. When I left the room of minds, she was swinging herself in the crane's truss. I thought nothing of it at the time. I just left her there. She said she was sorry. She looked like a little girl on a swing.

The rain was battering down. The heat had increased. I'm sure it was shock but I clicked between wanting to laugh and wanting to kill. Sam pushed past me for supplies. Oblivious and completely uninterested in why there were so many people in the kitchen. Like a fat pet with its robotic pursuit of consumption. I'd the crystal [clear] urge to follow him back to the feed room with a hammer from the tool room and knock holes into his skull with the peen until he was bone and blood.

Alcohol came out. The stupidest decision.

Processing John's last words is likely to take me years. Len thought it was the end. *We're cooked. We've no other mind to send after him.* Tom was convinced the last words were nonsense, evidence of John's mind finally fried. Hoskin neither agreed nor disagreed with him. I've no way of knowing what was in her head. She was just not there. Not then.

Tom talked. He tried to draw Len in. I couldn't speak. Len drank beer and gave mono replies. *I just want to listen to the rain.*

Eventually Hoskin roused herself. She asked us each to say if we'd any doubt John wasn't coming back. Anwen wasn't in the room. Tom and Len had no doubt. I couldn't lie. I knew he wasn't coming back.

Suddenly everyone was ravenous. Between us we emptied the fridge of anything edible. We left nothing for Anwen.

I watched the storm. A bone-rattling storm. Rain battering down on the courtyard and windows with the sound of coal being shucked from a cart. The rain was enormous in the courtyard, raising a white line of splash a few inches off the ground that was pure visual static. It fell like lead from a shot tower. Hypnotic.

I don't think I started the argument. Not exactly. I'd tuned out watching the rain. No idea what was being said. Then I heard Tom say, *Archive*. Something like, *The archiving of the four.*

When I asked what this meant, he came for me. Why was I talking? Why was I still here? I was the reason everything went bad. Went south. *We wasted so much time on this hippy. This has nothing to do with you, Jude!*

(Have I ever been called a *hippy* before?)

I gave a defence. Half-hearted. I was so tired. I can't recall what the defence was but the last thing I said was that at least we knew John was gone. Tom went up like lighter fluid—

At least we know he's gone. At least we know he's gone. At least we know he's gone. Let me get my brain round that appraisal of our amount of knowledge. That's the least we know.

Len: *With Moonfeld gone there's no need for a third-rate mathematician, Tom, so to my mind this has nothing to do with you now either.* He left a distinct pause, then added, *Son.*

The *son* landed like a bomb. I felt the tightness in both men. The readiness they held themselves in. The squeak of their chairs as they pushed themselves backwards. For a second it really did seem there'd be an actual fist fight in the farmhouse kitchen.

It didn't happen. Hoskin hit the table top hard. *Give me a rapid increase in adulthood, now!* Maybe she was rescuing Tom. Tom's anger stood outside his skin, outside his control, doubtless overriding the reality Len would have battered him flat.

This is where we were when everything went to hell.

I saw it first. I'd pushed my chair back ready to run from the fight. I was hard by the window and could see all the way up to the hayloft. Movement at the door.

Understanding what was going to happen took no time. Events and words clicked together.

Anwen was not there, Anwen was swinging in the crane truss, Anwen had told me over and again what she knew and I'd deafened myself to it.

Just listen, she'd said.

A mind was in the truss. Clearly the truss was how she'd dragged it up there. She braced her hands on the sides of the hayloft door and used a foot to topple the mind from the third storey.

I made a conscious decision not to speak. There was no time to stop her but even so. I made a conscious decision not to warn anyone.

We heard the smash over the sound of the rain. The communicant glass of the jar shattered over the courtyard. Shards hit the glass doors of the kitchen. A smear of chain-fluid gathered on the glass and slowly peeled off.

I was first through the door. In the courtyard the chain-fluid sank away. The rain came down so hard it smashed the fluid apart, thinning it until what had moments before been a clear, thick puddle was suddenly gone, diluted away. At one with the rain.

The glass had shattered to pieces about the size of a hazelnut. Here and there a larger chunk rocked under the force of the downpour, the rain sluicing it clean. Piece after piece was indistinct. It was mostly diamond gravel, then I saw a bit with the finger-like protuberance, a feature of Baby's jar.

We were all soaked to the skin. No one heeded this. The shock silenced us all.

Len picked up the big chunks of glass, cradling them in one of his big hands like the shards of a broken pot. *It's Baby.*

I looked around. Hoskin was not there.

Anwen was framed in the hayloft door. It was a kindness she'd performed. I understood that. I nodded to her.

Slowly the word *archive* and Hoskin's absence connected in my head. I went to the corridor that led to the basement and the pool. For the first time since I'd been there it was closed, and even before I tried the handle I knew it was locked. The keyplate was thick and solid steel, the keyhole an inch deep and big to accommodate a fat farmhouse key in a fat farmhouse door.

Hoskin was at the other end of the corridor. Her hands were in her pockets. She leant slightly forward on the balls of her feet.

Me: *He's my friend.*

Her: *He's my project.*

Me: *He's my friend.*

Her: *I know.*

Hoskin took her hands from her pockets, folding them on her chest. The movement stretched the material of her shirt pocket, outlining the key there. She was still in her shorts, legs planted thigh-width apart.

Ridiculous, I thought, *What a ridiculous, ridiculous situation to be in.*

Me: *He's my friend.*

Her: *It doesn't matter.*

She stepped out of the light.

Len replaced her. I knew his look. Rueful, firm.

I think we'd all be happier if you and Anwen went back to the stables to cool down a little.

I left. Tom was at the kitchen table drying his hair on a tea-towel as I passed. He smirked at me. *Mr. Tits-and-Teeth.*

I went out into the rain. The door was locked behind me.

I saw Anwen walking out into the evening, into the rain.

I remember being filled with the urge to do something. To lob a brick through the courtyard window. Something. But as I stood there all the next steps started to slot in. What would I do after? An image of the bastard brick bouncing off the glass, Tom staring at me and laughing. What then? Climb in through the window? Would I actually punch someone? Ridiculous. The whole thing was just ridiculous.

I went out after Anwen, into the hot summer rain. It was getting late now. The sun was just about set. I could see the moon. I didn't call her.

I followed her to the lane's end, catching her up as she hesitated at the road, looking down the lane to the village and the lights of the houses and then up to the hill. She heard me behind her and turned to look but did not speak. She pointed to the left, to the hill.

As we were on the climb, the rain lifted as fast as if a hand had snatched it back to sea. The land was only intermittently lit by the moon. At the top Anwen sat in the grass shy of the woods. I joined her there. I'd spent the climb fretting she'd send me away. I kept going. I needed to be with another human. I knew a strange breed of grief was sleeping behind a closed door within me and would soon begin to roar.

The storm moved off round the headland, great fists of it turning high in the sky. In another quadrant of the sky it looked like nothing had happened. No storm had travelled through there. The moon shone hard down.

Neither of us spoke. It felt like a bet, a game of who-can-keep-quiet-the-longest an adult will play with a rackety child. There was movement at the tree line.

To break the silence I said, *My clothes are almost dry already.*

Her: *You understand why I did it.*

I said I did.

She lit a cigarette, saying she only smoked one or two a day.

Her: *It's perverse to think all that remains is to believe he's gone to another place and will not return to this one.*

Me: *Same old story.*

Her: *Yes.*

Me: *What will happen to you for doing that to Annabel?*

Her: *Nothing. Nothing will happen to me. I think that's what I've been saying all along. I didn't commit a crime. I didn't do anything wrong.*

I understood that. It was the question in my head but it wasn't quite what I'd intended by the question. I meant how would she deal with it. I didn't chase the answer. With the passing of adrenalin I had no energy left. I had nothing left.

Her: *Years in the future, we'll look back and see ourselves covered in blood for what we did here.*

I told her I was putting together a testament, writing up all I remembered. There would be a record of everything.

Her: *It won't matter. It will never be seen.*

Gradually the storm passed. She lay on her back, staring at the night sky. I was fascinated by the edge of the tree line where night animals were at fuss in the grass. I watched as wildlife came out to rootle in the undergrowth.

At first it was movement, an altered tone to the night as one darkness moved against a background of another darkness. Then I saw ears and the familiar red glow of hares' eyes. I watched them move about idly, carefully in the still damp grass. I wondered how the storm had felt to them underground.

The hares circled and paused and watched. At times, when either of us moved, they stood still and watchful then took a more circuitous route to their lair.

By this time I'd a fair idea of the likely locations of their warrens. To be creatures of instinct, no knowledge of mortality to throw panic into the mind when approaching death, yet to have hard-wired the need to fool the hunter, was remarkable. Wonderful.

To follow a path down into the warren, into the animal mind, would be an extraordinary fate. Not death, but death of the knowledge of death. Going down the rabbit hole (hare hole?) and following the root down into the animal mind and closing the way behind.

I cleared my throat. The hares scattered, not one choosing a direct line home but each darting along a random path, one side to the other, before they vanished beneath the ground.

Me: *What is it about hares?*

Her: *I know what you mean. You've a snail on your shoe.*

I looked. I did. The moon was so bright even the track's glisten had a different quality of light. The snail was heading towards me over the toe of my shoe and as the shell crested, the spiral fell into my gaze, catching the moonlight, and in an instant I was asleep.

Anwen shook me awake. I'd only been out twenty minutes or so. It was around ten. We walked back down the hill. At the turn-off for the village, Anwen put out her hand. She said she'd get a room at the pub. She wasn't going back to the farmhouse. She asked me to pack up her stuff and she'd make arrangements to have it picked up. That was it.

She held me for a long time. We held each other for a long time.

The last I saw of her she was walking into the pub. I stayed waiting to see if the owners would turn her away. I stayed for ten minutes watching. When she didn't come out, I knew she was safe.

I'll pack us both tomorrow. So tired.

2 a.m. Someone's just locked me in my room. The turning of the lock woke me. This is beyond belief. This

Jude Golby's journal ends here.

The Feed

This is still not the way to Professor Cole's rooms

rooms were a warren in the old halls true
near the attic but even so

I am certain she was off the quad up the staircase
these are Escher stairs
that picture
figures walking up stairs but remaining on one level

I do not remember the names of the other faculty

their doors are stones

Professor Cole

Martha

Martha Cole

off the quad up the eastern stairs
across the wooden walkway

the stone spiral stairs up to the attic

her room faced east over the fields

what is it with Beckett and the letter m, *Jude*
it cannot just be the fear of the thirteenth letter

a fire burning

I do not recall her door like this
it was plain oak
this door has panels

eight

it reminds me of something

I Ching

it must be the place
there is light under the door

all the other doors are stones

cong

a hole in the centre of the floor
covered by a rug

wolf trap

the design colourful spirals
circles

the village I went to
circular dwellings
stones in the grass at the top of the hill

trou de loup

Arthur Guinness sinking through the hole in the floor
when he steps onto the carpet

the film

The Horse's Mouth

Alec Guinness

quicker now

quicker now

I drift to the centre

the staircases connect as if sections
have been removed and snapped back together

Scalextric

Scalextric
the smell of the electricity always reminded me of blood
underneath the cars a little notch
to fit the groove of the track
grooming the tiny copper moustaches

a yellow Mini and a red Mini

the quad

I am not facing east

all the doors are stones

Professor Cole's door is an eight-dimpled wooden door
behind is an empty room
a crater covered by a rug
covered in red and yellow circles

a rug in the centre of the room covers a hole in the floor

I step onto this crater

I know it covers a hole
my weight carries the rug
slowly
down into the room below

I remember this room

this is Professor Cole's room

the room is dark and empty

a candle burns on the floor in the corner
another light is there

the light comes from under the hearthstone
the hearthstone is thick slate

the stone does not quite cover the gap
light comes from underneath

the light comes from underneath
removing the stone shows where the hearth
backs onto the hole
chimney below is darkness

no heat
no soot

clean spiral
darkness leading down
light came from underneath
where is the light now

a spiral chimney

nothing below
the chimney could be a well

water down there
cold like water from a mountain tarn

stone water

cool

the spiral dark is filled with water

cooled air

cool stone

cool air

stone air

far below
a figure carries a flame
across the end opening of the chimney

far far below
no candle

they spent less than a second in my sight

the light was a small nest of wood alight

I can smell it

the smell is sweet

the smell is

the smell is sweet

the small smell is metal
the smell is sweet

the light has ruined my sight
the spiral dark is even more impenetrable
the light has eaten my eyes

the chamber below the hearthstone is wide but low
I need to stoop

I need to stoop!

ahead the figure with the burning nest
held aloft in one palm
no protection
it burns there on her skin
it is woman
her arm is long

the hanging arm

the waiting arm

the waiting arm is long
its hand is holding a stone

woman is walking the stone hall

a stone hall is ahead

a shape in the centre of the chamber

taller than me
rounded but not a stone
not a boulder
clay formed about a frame
wooden lintels and raw branch ends proud
wooden frame sticking out of a shell

I cannot see past woman
and before I reach the entrance to the cave
she presses the nest of wooden light against the wall

embers fall

darkness comes

breathing

dozens
hundreds are breathing

no other sound

they face the chamber wall
I do not want to turn to see them

breathe in

the unseen presences behind

they do not turn from the wall

light flickers around me

light illuminates the cave wall
a line of stick figures

the vast clay egg in the centre
a structure on top

woman the guide approaches the clay egg
she presses an eye to a hole

dozens of holes dug into the shell of the great stone egg

a thing inhuman breathes within

I can tell from the sounds

bull-like breath

dismissive as a bold bull snort

I wish the light were not here

above the stick figures on the wall
a magnificent creature drawn in soot
coloured with brown paint

its horns are not horns but two human hand prints

the firelight grows

the breathing

the guide at the shell wall staring within
the thin figures come from the wall naked

climbing they find a stabbed hole into the great egg

I find a stab-hole into the great egg

the creature is maddened out of mind
grown into the clay trap

stench

the thin figures climb over the egg
clinging

treefrogs on a balloon

my hole
my hole sees the eye

the eye is black to the centre of the world

trapped creature
trapped young and fed through the hole
grown to the limits of its cage

oh god

the structure crowning the stone egg is a wooden boat

they want me to climb to the wooden boat

the wooden boat on the crown

the wooden boat hooked at prow and stern
a crescent

I do not want to look at the boat

I do not want to look at the lord of the stone

I do not want to look inside the boat

the boat I saw

in the boat is a louder breath

the thin people are eating

the boat is raised on stones
at the height of the stone altar

it is no boat

on the ground at the head and foot are circular pits
bones within

the bones have meat on them still
marrow sap

up the clay shell climb figures

come figures

climb figures to hang from the gunnels of the not-boat

they eat

one tosses a bone along to head or foot

to the place with the bone grave

to place into the bone grave

the breathing

the firelight

the sounds

I reach the not-boat

many figures surround the not-boat

bodies block out the firelight
my eyes fill with shadow

I see horns and the head of a creature

it is not a bull
it is not a creature I have seen

it has no length of snout and it is screaming

the tips of the horns have been forced
through two holes at the top of the not-boat

a wooden strut holds the jaw tight

wooden pegs anchor it to the not-boat so the head is fast

horns in a crescent from the tip protrude

scream

screams

the creature is eaten alive

fists of its meat torn out

the figures surrounding the not-boat
holding the edge of the not-boat
not to fall

hunger

the not-boat is filled with blood

the meat does not end
gristle worked
to free it for the feast

the creature screams

the torso is open skin
now human

a bulb of it high
great round belly dome

the meat is never ending

not-boat is a trough a blood groove a wooden dish

wooden-rough thin and tapered like a bean pod

a bull-woman eaten as she gives birth

a bull woman eaten as she gives birth

her thighs full-thick with muscles

straining to push out the child

my hands on the not-boat

man at the stone crouching

man at the stern crouching
a pilot

he is covered in ash blood

a channel in the base of the wood-dish

the channel is where the blood flows
what blood is not caught is a river down the clay egg

the ash-blood figure gazes up at the birth
the shudder in clench-flesh
as the contractions come

the bull-woman is filled with rooms
rooms smaller and smaller a spiral

the birth mouth

the birth mouth roars

needle-teeth

needle-tooth woman has her fist
in the side of the bull-woman
up to the elbow twisting
high under the rib cage twisting

open for the blood

his pilot-mouth

open for the blood

throat

swallowing

an offering

woman with needle teeth

luckless breasts gloss with blood
nipples erect
offers to join

to eat
to feast

roaring of the creature beneath

under the shell a howling

[Come home]

woman offers participation

woman offers participation in the feast

the child is born

the ash figure
the pilot

he has dominion
takes the child out
slides down the river of blood
legs of blood and ash
penis long as a length of branch

a boy

pilot places the boy in the grave of the bones
climbs back to his stern perch
opens a mouth for the blood pissed from the wood-dish

the circle is the grave of the bone

the child is silent

[Come home]

the blood-woman
the woman of the offering

the bloodneedle woman offers

this is the root
the root of mind
the root of rite

I reach out my hand

[Come home, Jude]

four nails
thumb bright in the light from the fires

I can see my hand

I have a hand!

moons
four quarters of the moon
fingernails four moons
moons
four fingers alone

I have a hand!

moons
four quarters of the moon

four fingernails for moons

moonnails

little finger cut

teethmarks at the stump

given to the ritual
given

the woman
the pilot

want me to *take*

[Come home]

I

me

a lighthouse

a flea

lighthouse

naughty lighthouse

nautilus

lighthouse

who is speaking

who

who speaks

who is it who is speaking

Hoskin

you are Hoskin

of course
I remember

no John

here I am now
I remember here I am now
I remember where I am now
the room of minds

[Welcome home]

Hoskin I had the strangest dream

Afterword

I have constructed the majority of the narrative of *Delivery Artefacts* from documents that were in the possession of Jude Golby when he died.

Jude Golby died of *catecholaminergic polymorphic ventricular tachycardia*. I anticipate the temptation will be great to assume malice was a factor in his death given the abrupt end of his journal. No malice was involved. I was there. Jude Golby was dead when we opened the room.

In the years since the events in this narrative, I've experienced great changes in both my life and my faith. It is not my place to expand upon them here. It is important to confess, however, the extent of my guilt in what happened after Jude's death. Despite reservations at the time,

a) I agreed with the decision to delay contacting a doctor;
b) I was fully complicit in the decision to deliver Jude's mind;
c) I withheld this information when the body was handed over to the family.

I also believe there is the possibility that locking Jude into his room, although an action taken to prevent any attempt on his part to enter the basement of the facility while we were asleep, might have been a trigger for the cardiac event, despite the fact, as his own words make clear, he had been under consistent high stress for many days. I therefore also carry the burden of

d) I was the person who locked his door.

None of the people at the facility had any knowledge Jude was a sufferer of *Brugada syndrome*. This only came to light on the reading of his journal and unfinished testament.

The section of the narrative I have titled *The Feed* is a record of his returning mind thirteen months after delivery. This is the only part of the text above that I, to a certain extent, constructed from the feed. I assembled *The Feed* six years ago when I was a very different man from the man I am now. I offer it without comment as to its meaning.

As time has gone on, however, and as my faith has turned into a ministry, I can no longer believe *The Feed* is a true account of a human experience. Nor can I confirm that it is the true and accurate testament of the delivered Jude Golby. (I am also mindful of the considerations of the family in this regard.) This is the reason for the unusual authorship of this book: Jude Golby and Another.

In the text, reference is made to the following works of literature—

'A Child Half-Asleep' by Tony Connor, *Jude the Obscure* by Thomas Hardy, *The Odyssey, Polar Star* by Martin Cruz Smith, *Ulysses* by James Joyce, and 'A Disused Shed in Co. Wexford' by Derek Mahon.

Finally, much of Jude's reasoning came from memories of a book he'd read when he was younger. It is clear from my own recollections of our conversations, and the texts in the narratives that make up *Delivery Artefacts*, that this book is *The Gate of Horn* by G.R. Levy.

De profundis clamavi ad te, Domine | Domine, exaudi vocem meam.

Lenford K. Smith, OFM Conv.